MURDER AT
MACHU PICCHU

MURDER AT
MACHU PICCHU

A Jamie Prescott Mystery

Mariann Tadmor

This book was printed in the United States of America.
To order additional copies of this book, contact:
Xlibris Corporation
1-888-795-4274
www.Xlibris.com
Orders@Xlibris.com
15225

For Rachel, Ethan, Zackary, Karen and Yoav.
And for Brian,
who would have been proud.

ACKNOWLEDGEMENTS

I am greatly indebted to Michael Lesparre, journalist, writer, and friend, for moral support and editorial assistance. My loving thanks go to Francine for keeping my head above water, to Karen for believing in me and for lessons in Tae Kwon Do, and to Rachel and Yoav for supporting me in all my endeavors.

CHAPTER 1

IF I could do it all over again, I wouldn't.

But I'll no doubt end up taking other tour members to far off places.

It all goes back to Bob Makowski, veteran P.I., my former boss. I can still see myself with him in a dark Washington, D.C. alley, gun fire all around, a man dead through mistaken identity, me on the ground with a slug in the shoulder, Bob leaping to cover for me and going down, too.

I've played this scenario, and several similar ones, regularly, to remind myself why three years ago I removed myself to the Maryland suburbs to give up sleuthing. At least, that was the idea.

I bought my Cape Cod style house in Bethesda when Topsy and I decided to start our travel agency. The remodeling job brought about a separate entrance to the second floor where I've lived since. Topsy worked as a travel agent before she married lawyer/lobbyist Jack Bannister, but gave it up while she produced and raised two energetic children, now energetic college students.

And I, let us say I have traveled a lot both before, during and after my marriage to a charming Frenchman whose company sent us on prolonged trips to foreign countries. Topsy and I felt that our combined wisdom, and a small inheritance I fell into, were sufficient grounds to set ourselves up in business. We hired a seasoned travel agent, who quickly brought us up to snuff on the mechanics of computerized airline reservations. And we engaged a gofer who doesn't do coffee.

On this particular morning Topsy and I were at our desks early. I was preparing for the tour I was taking to Lima, Cuzco and Machu Picchu. Ten people had signed up, three of whom were traveling with me from Washington while the rest had been booked in Lima through Mundotours, a collaborating agency. The new guide I was checking out for the fall schedule would be conducting the tour.

"Jamie Prescott!"

"What?" I swivelled around to face Topsy. I consider it my great good luck that we both ended up in the Washington area which, of course, also happens to be where we both grew up. We have only one bone of contention: my single status.

"Jamie," she said, "I'm taking you out for lunch!"

"Well!"

"Yes, I want you to meet a colleague of Jack's, just moved to town, not had a chance to meet any gorgeous women yet. And don't shake your golden locks like that, Jamie. It's only lunch, for God's sakes!"

"Just make sure you're not setting me up with another fugitive from justice!"

"It was only tax evasion!" Topsy protested.

"Yeah, right!"

"Otherwise he was very respectable. What do you want me to do, have the FBI investigate my guests before I introduce you? And he was good-looking *and* spoke four languages."

"Okay, okay."

We laughed. As usual, she was winning.

"I sometimes wonder if you and Bob are in on this together. He suggested I call up the legatt at the embassy in Lima. James Quentin Brown!"

"That settles it," Topsy said firmly. "You'll meet Archibald Brewster. You don't want a long-distance relationship with someone south of the equator!"

"I'm leaving," I said and scooped up my briefcase. But I was smiling all the way up the stairs.

CHAPTER 2

Sara and Stanley Robinson were on the edge of the back seat of the limousine peering at me with a mixture of curiosity and excitement.

"Are we late?" they said with one voice.

"Not at all," I said and climbed into the seat opposite them. The Robinsons eyed my single carry-on bag with apprehension. I knew from experience that they would have two voluminous totes and two just as voluminous suitcases in the back of the limo notwithstanding my admonition to pack small.

Stan Robinson was a large, fleshy man with white combed-over hair, yellow at the tips, set with hairspray. A piece of polished skull with large liver spots showed through the stiff strands at the highest point of his dome.

His wife, Sara, looked rather more tired than he. Her eyes were ringed by mournful bags and her pink hair glowed in a halo around her full face. She had her pudgy hand on top of her husband's.

They looked at me with the kind of trust and utter dependence which makes me feel a twinge of impatience at my self-imposed role of guide and mother figure. Topsy is so much better at this than I am.

The limo took the back roads parallel to Wisconsin Avenue to avoid the interminable traffic lights and morning rush hour. We emerged at the entrance to Georgetown and coasted slowly along R Street past Dumbarton Oaks.

My third passenger, Ms. Elsa Bronski, was at the basement door of an imposing Victorian house set high on the grounds in a well-manicured garden. The Robinsons and I watched as Ms. Bronski locked, double and triple-locked the door, put her shoulder to it, rattled the knob one last time, picked up a newspaper from the ground, threw it in the trash can, and finally gathered up her bags.

I noted that Ms. Bronski belonged to my minimalist movement: a medium size brown tweed Hartman suitcase with leather binding, and the smallest of totes.

Until now my only communication with Ms. Bronski had been by phone when she booked the tour to Machu Picchu. Unlike the Robinsons she had arranged for her own accommodations in Lima but had accepted my offer of a lift to the airport. She looked more or less the way I had imagined. She was dressed in sensible shoes and a light suit over a not so sensible frilly organdy blouse. As she settled into the seat next to me, my overactive mind, admittedly one of my minor flaws and, as Bob often points out, sometimes a hindrance to investigations, caused the scenario of Ms. Bronski's life to flash before my eyes. Her minor administrative position at a minor government agency, her barely affordable basement apartment at a prestigious address in Georgetown, now spending her savings on expensive luggage and the trip of a lifetime.

This type of flight-of-fancy was often the only background I got on tour members until we were well into the middle of a trip.

Ms. Bronski pressed the lever to roll down her window as a small boy came bounding down the sidewalk waving both arms.

"Toby!" Ms. Bronski's features came to life miraculously as she cupped the boy's face in both hands and placed a quick kiss on his cheek.

"Can I come?" he said and twisted free of her hands, not unkindly, just in the way of a six-year old.

"No, my dear, I'm on my way to the airport. You go home to your mother now and I'll be sure to bring you a souvenir from Peru."

"Bring me an elephant! But a real one!"

Toby bounced back the way he had come. He entered a garden several houses down, flung himself onto the back of the gate and swung violently back and forth.

Ms. Bronski, her face flushed, waved.

"An elephant!" she exclaimed. "That's my neighbor's son. I sometimes babysit for him."

Aha, I thought, the woman adds to her meager pension by babysitting neighborhood children, and I suddenly felt overwhelmed by compassion. I looked at Ms. Bronski's thinning gray hair, her faded blue eyes, listened to her slight accent, and was about to conjure up the sad background of her childhood. Instead I introduced her to the Robinsons.

That done I let them get acquainted in preparation for the camaraderie of their mutual trip.

I tuned out in favor of recalling yesterday's lunch with Topsy and Archibald Brewster. We went to an Italian restaurant on Cordell Street. Brewster arrived late just as we were finishing a second serving of garlic bread and about to order more white wine. There had been no uncomfortable silences, he just slid into his chair looking at home.

What's the matter with Topsy, I thought at first, the man looked fresh out of law school. But on closer inspection I noticed the fine sprinklings of gray in his hair and a few wrinkles around the eyes. This was the kind of olive-skinned look which would never crease deeply or hang in folds around the chin. Everything about him was lean, just the way I like it. His nose, his cheekbones, his hands, his wrists and what I had managed to see of his body.

I had become conscious of the need to say something intelligent when Topsy decided to disappear towards the restrooms. And I said:

"So, you went to Harvard?"

He had laughed.

"Why would you think that? Do I look like a Harvard man, assuming anyone can tell?"

I had looked at him, this time more frankly, and almost said, let's see if your heels are scuffed, when he crossed his legs and dangled a well-polished shoe just visible under the folds of the heavy white tablecloth. If not Harvard there had still been an unmistakable New England intonation.

"Boston U." I said firmly.

"Bingo!"

"Really, you're from Boston?"

"Born and bred."

"When?"

"When?" He laughed again. "You mean, how old am I? Thirty-eight." He folded his legs back under the table. "And you?"

"Born and bred right here."

"I mean, how old?"

"Forty-two!" Kind of a surprising comeback but I didn't mind. Then he told me his life story which wasn't that long. His father sounded like old money, his mother, now dead, third generation Italian, two brothers, three sisters. Catholic. Joined the Peace Corps straight out of college, law school at twenty-eight, legislative assistant on the Hill, and now at a Washington law firm. So, he wasn't strictly the new man in town Topsy had indicated.

When Topsy returned she immediately picked up on our relaxed mood and beamed at me. We ordered Lasagna and more wine and Brewster told about his participation in a human rights fact-finding mission to Peru. I liked the way he looked upset when recounting how a group of prisoners had obviously been deloused and bathed before being presented to the members of the mission.

I woke up from my reverie when Sara Robinson put her hand

on my knee and squeezed gently. People don't usually get that familiar with me. I'm told I'm somewhat reserved, but as I would learn, nothing could hold back Sara Robinson.

"Is it going to be safe?" she said. "My husband says not to worry but I can't help it."

I looked into her trusting eyes and told the literal truth: "I travel to Peru on a regular basis and have never been in any trouble. We'll just take the normal precautions and we'll be fine."

Sara and Stan Robinson sank back in their seats looking satisfied and intent on preserving their vacation mood. I felt a certain pang of conscience thinking of various incidents reported in newspapers.

And, suddenly, there was Reagan National Airport, its silver and sunshine-yellow departure hall gleaming in reflection of daffodils and pansies in the ample flower beds. The flight to Miami was uneventful and in relatively short order we settled down for a cup of coffee in the transit hall before boarding the plane to Lima.

Ms. Bronski sat next to me on the flight but we didn't strike up a conversation until lunch was served. I looked at the lackluster tray and picked at a wilted salad. Ms. Bronski did likewise.

"So," I said, "where will you be staying in Lima?"

"With my sister. She's married to the French ambassador. This is actually my second visit," said the surprising Ms. Bronski.

Aha, I thought, her sister sends her the tickets. But aloud I said: "And do you enjoy the diplomatic life? Dinners, receptions, beautifully furnished homes, butlers, waiters, cooks, housemaids, gardeners, chauffeurs . . . ."

Ms. Bronski let out a strangled laugh.

"Not really," she said. "My sister spends her time on frivolous activities. You see, she's a pediatrician. But as a diplomat's wife she's not allowed to do her own work."

"I know what you mean," I said and eyed Ms. Bronski with more respect. "They haven't come as far as the rest of us."

The flight attendant came around with coffee and after that Ms. Bronski began rooting around in her handbag. She pulled out her passport, leafing through it nervously, then did the same to her ticket. In the end she pulled out a pair of shiny knitting needles and proceeded to knit away on an indeterminate garment from a ball of bright red wool.

Thankful for the respite I decided to read the Spanish language daily I had picked up at a bookstore on Connecticut Avenue. On page 3, I found a headline which did not exactly inspire confidence: "Terrorists trying to regroup in provinces . . . ."

Let them stay in the provinces, I thought.

CHAPTER 3

ONE man looked decidedly Indian, the other more Spanish. The Indian had a heavy, dour face with high cheekbones and straight black hair pulled back in a long braid. His massive torso was encased in a half-open shirt of homespun, striped wool which showed off his burnished chest.

"Boris Ivanovich Garcia," he said and took back the clammy hand he had offered me. "Tour guide, Mundotours."

The second man looked greasy, his hair too long around his shirt collar, dressed in a shabby brown suit. He looked around the lobby as if uncomfortable in the opulent surroundings.

We had arrived at the Jorge Chavez International Airport a few hours ago. While Ms. Bronski was whisked painlessly through passport control and customs by a uniformed driver from the French Embassy, the rest of us had our luggage subjected to a thorough search.

The Cesar Miraflores hotel had sent along an aged black Dodge, polished to a dignified shine, its original chrome parts still spotless. It took the Robinsons and me slowly through a rush of traffic which rattled by in noxious puffs of black smoke. Everything looked so gray. Gray people, gray pavements, gray sky. Even the trees were gray. It was almost eight in the evening when we got to the hotel.

The Robinsons had gone to their room on the fourth floor and I to mine on the fifth. I have always liked the decor—Colonial with touches of indigenous art—even if they do nail the paintings to the wall.

I was ready in jeans and a t-shirt after a refreshing shower when the phone rang from downstairs announcing two visitors. I had only been expecting one.

The Indian stood immobile like a tiger watching its prey, his eyelids half closed. He pointed to his companion.

"Pablo Alvarez."

When no further explanation was forthcoming I nodded to Alvarez but addressed the Indian.

"Boris Ivanovich!" I said, trying to catch his eye and said undiplomatically, "You don't look very Russian!"

He wasn't capable of a real smile but, of course, here I was, a prospective employer, and he parted his lips just enough to reveal some gold and black fillings. He now looked straight at me.

"My father, Andrei Ivanovich, the Revolutionary, came here from Leningrad," he said in heavily accented English. "My mother, Domitilia Garcia of Ayacucho is a master weaver."

He looked as if this was more than he had been prepared to reveal and I broke the uneasy tension by inviting them to the bar. But Pablo Alvarez excused himself, shook my hand vigorously and bowed himself out of the revolving doors with a look of relief. I got no explanation of why he was there in the first place.

Ivanovich and I sat in the bar and pored over the schedules to and from Machu Picchu and the hotel accommodations in Cuzco. After tossing down several shots of whisky he mellowed somewhat. We moved to a small table near the wall, carrying our drinks, and Ivanovich brought out a list of tour members.

I nodded at the sight of the names of Sara and Stanley Robinson and Elsa Bronski.

I pointed to the next name.

"Pablo Alvarez?" I exclaimed. "You didn't tell me he would be on the tour. Is he a tourist, then?"

Ivanovich pulled himself up, his face bland, his tone dismissive.

"He is not a tourist, he is an antique dealer. He enjoys traveling in his own country."

"And the rest of the group?" I looked at the names. "Vicky Anderson. Says here she lives in Lima. Another local tourist?"

I realized I sounded out of sorts. Ivanovich had that immediate effect on me.

I moved my finger down the list in silence. José and Elena Hernandez, Lima. Charles Lupesco, New York City. Padre Orion and Padre Octavio, Ecuador. With Sara and Stanley Robinson, Elsa Bronski, Pablo Alvarez and Vicky Anderson, that made ten as I'd expected.

"Do you know any of the other members?"

By now Ivanovich had put away four straight whiskies and his eyelids were drooping. He bent over the list and studied it closely.

"Dr. Hernandez," he said finally. "Chief surgeon at the Miraflores General Hospital."

"And Charles Lupesco?"

Ivanovich shook his head and looked as if he was about to slide under the table.

"The gentleman booked yesterday at the Mundotour branch at the Sheraton Hotel. That is all I know."

"And we have two Catholic fathers . . ."

Ivanovich, looking more dour by the minute, said: "I do not know them also." And with this he got up holding on to the edge of the table and excused himself.

I followed his stiff walk towards the restrooms but he stopped, instead, at the public phone which sat on the barroom counter. In the stillness of the empty room I heard him dial carefully and watched his impressive profile in the dim light.

When he spoke he did so in a loud voice and I realized he didn't know I understand Spanish.

"She is here," he said. "A very overbearing *gringa*. I am not sure I want to work for her but I need the money and she'll be leaving soon." Then he lowered his voice and I couldn't hear the rest. Overbearing, indeed.

When he returned I was standing next to the table having signed the tab. No more whiskisitos for him.

I reminded him to make sure the group was at the airport the day after next at least an hour before the 10 a.m. flight to Cuzco. The group would tour Cuzco with him during the afternoon and I would catch the late afternoon flight and join them the following morning on the train to Machu Picchu. I needed the time in Lima to talk to the people at Mundotours.

I watched Ivanovich walk rigidly across the lobby floor, battle with the revolving door, and disappear down the busy street.

And this was the guy I'd have to spend several days with?

CHAPTER 4

IT was 5 a.m. and the San Pedro train station in Cuzco was pitch dark.

I stepped onto the platform and took a firm grip on my small backpack and the strap of my camera bag. The heavy iron doors slammed shut behind me and the echo rolled towards the Machu Picchu train. The domed wagons loomed out of the mist some hundred feet away.

Shrill sounds of a whistle and suddenly the shadows under the half-roof to my right became a shuffling mass of bodies swelling in a stampede towards the train.

I fell in line behind a squat Indian woman in a white stove-top hat garnished with a blue satin band. The woman trundled away five steps ahead of me and entered a third-class wagon. She climbed up the steep iron steps with surprising agility. I continued briskly towards wagon no. 5, first class, where seats had been reserved for my group.

Ivanovich stood in the middle of the aisle. He turned around when I entered and spread his arms across the backs of two seats as if to say, this is my territory, I'm in control here. I suppose he found it overbearing of me to be staying at the posher Regina Inca hotel instead of with the group at Las Cruces but I wasn't about to apologize: I was checking out the Regina Inca for future groups.

"Here's our leader," Stanley Robinson boomed, and Ivanovich turned his back on him. Stan and Sara were seated opposite Elsa Bronski who already had her knitting out. I settled into a window seat on the other side of the aisle on an unyielding wooden bench. A drawn-out whistle sounded and the train jerked to a start. The dusty-green eucalyptus trees and truncated mountain tops soon became a blur outside the non-too-clean window panes. It was suddenly almost daylight.

I took stock of the tour members before getting up to greet them. First a man facing away from me. His clean profile fairly shouted Romantic Actor. No doubt about it (and I could hear Bob Makowski's warning voice): George Clooney in person. His eyes were fixed at a point above the reddish head of the woman opposite him. Susan Sarandon.

I continued my fantasy until the woman turned her head and her profile rather dispelled the notion. I walked over and introduced myself to Charles Lupesco and Vicky Anderson.

Although presumably they had only met the previous day they seemed more than friendly. Vicky Anderson, who looked quite a bit younger than he, bubbled over in a breathless voice and put her hand lightly on Charles Lupesco's arm.

"We're so glad to meet you," she said.

"Yes, indeed," said Lupesco. On closer inspection his perfect profile changed into a rather crafty face with pale, close-set eyes and taut lips. But the hair still curled nicely around his small perfectly shaped ears. He spoke with a slight British accent.

"We are, indeed, very pleased to meet you. We are honored that the owner of the travel agency herself is gracing our tour!"

"Yes, well, it's *my* pleasure," I said. "You live in New York, I believe?"

"Yes, indeed, but only as a visitor, you might say. I'm a translator with the United Nations."

"Isn't that fascinating," Vicky Anderson bubbled. She then

told me in many words that she had only been in Lima a few months as a drama coach at the American High School. This was her first venture in local tourism.

As I retreated, Vicky and Charles Lupesco bent their heads close to look out the window.

I continued to the next tour members. One priest was tall and skinny, the other short and rotund. They wore black cassocks and had bad skin and yellow teeth. But their smiles exuded good will.

"You speak Spanish, Señora, what a relief," said Father Orion, the tall skinny one. "And very well, too," he added gallantly without having heard more than a few words from my lips. Father Octavio, the rotund one, seconded all Father Orion said with nods and smiles. It appeared they were Jesuits from Quito on a mission to Peru whose purpose was not made clear.

The fathers had been conversing with what could only be Dr. Hernandez, the chief surgeon, and his wife. Dr. Hernandez, sporting a pencil-thin mustache and rimless glasses, was dressed, incongruously, in a dark three-piece business suit and tie, and would have looked more comfortable in the boardroom than he did on the rickety train to Machu Picchu.

Señora Elena de Hernandez, his obviously younger wife, was in a summer dress more appropriate for a garden party, her face obscured by large sunglasses. All I saw was opulent red lips. Her coiffure was elaborate and stiff from hair spray.

"I love to travel," she said and flashed a bejeweled hand. The kind of jewels I, owing to my tourist mentality, would have left at home in the strongbox. "We spend a lot of time in our condominium in Miami, my brother lives there, he's the Consul General, and . . ."

She would have continued if not for her husband who tapped her knee and pointed out the window. There seemed to be nothing of particular tourist interest out there but I took the hint and moved back to my seat.

The last member of the group, Pablo Alvarez, the antique dealer, sat in a far window seat, asleep, his mouth gaping. He looked completely out of shape, wide in the middle. His brown jacket was slung over his knees and swept the floor around his large, flat feet. Greetings would have to wait until later.

I pulled up my knees to steady the shaky table which hung on rusty hinges under the narrow window-sill, and took out my maps of Peru and a dog-eared Penguin paperback. I patted the orange cover of Hiram Bingham's *Lost City of the Incas* and opened it to the middle pages.

After an hour or so I lowered the book, slid closer to the window and contemplated the rapidly changing landscape. A large herd of llamas moved slowly down an invisible mountain path followed by several dogs and two women with long walking sticks.

The train was now moving alongside the Urubamba river whose waters swirled and rushed down the gorge, giving the impression that the train was standing still. A frayed yellow rope bridge swung in a steep dip across the abyss and I held my breath watching two red-clad figures actually making their shaky way towards the other side.

The train suddenly tilted dangerously towards the outer bank but righted itself just before going into a mountain pass. I lost sight of the rope bridge and the two Indians. I rested my forehead against the window and let the train rock me to sleep.

I was rudely awakened by loud shouts from Ivanovich now wearing a wide-brimmed hat and a red poncho.

"We're getting out," he exhorted, "let's be first on the bus!"

Everyone crowded into the aisles. The Robinsons looked excited and prepared for a day of tourism while Elsa Bronski seemed exhausted and Pablo Alvarez swayed on his feet, still half asleep.

The train was still moving at a fast clip but Ivanovich opened the door and flung himself out, hitting the platform with unexpected acrobatic skill. He ran as the train came to a halt and the group soon followed him. Pablo Alvarez was the last to make his way towards a short line of blue minibuses.

I descended, too, and walked along briskly, again behind the squat, bronze-skinned woman from the station in Cuzco. Two shiny black braids tied together at the ends with red rubber bands reached to the hem of her knee-length turquoise dress. Works at the restaurant, I decided, and boarded the last bus just before the little caravan took off to climb the precipitous mountainside.

Although I remembered my first trip to Machu Picchu several years ago, I had forgotten just how steeply the unpaved road zigzagged its way up the cone-shaped mountain. I looked out the window without getting too close and saw nothing but thin blue air and the twin peak of Huaynu Picchu surrounded by white clouds. Irresistibly compelled to look down, I stared straight into the abyss.

I felt goose bumps rise from my toes to the top of my head.

CHAPTER 5

THE bus driver ground the gear down into first and stepped on the gas without much result. Then, just as the bus was about to come to a complete stop, the path straightened and we slowly picked up speed. I leaned a little closer to the window. Now we were moving along a narrow, dusty trail in the midst of green foliage capped by the blue sky, and enveloped in black fumes.

The driver made one more effort and pulled up a sharp incline into the unpaved lot below the hotel at the tourist station.

My group got out and, at least the Americans, looked somewhat rattled. I lingered behind and turned to photograph Huaynu Picchu. I shot a couple of frames of a singular figure moving upwards at a snail's pace. Then I made my way up the broad stone steps to the restaurant.

When I caught up with Ivanovich at the buffet I addressed him in my pretty fluent Spanish. I went on at some length about the breathtaking nature of Machu Picchu, in general, and the culture of the Incas, in particular, and rather enjoyed his stupefied expression.

"You surprise me, Señora," he said at last. "I did not know you speak my language so well. Please allow me, you should try the eggplant . . . ." and he helped me to a generous serving.

I was just about to suggest we lunch at the same table when he acknowledged eager signs from the two padres to join them. So, I walked to a small table for two and looked down at Ms. Bronski. She cleared her red knitting from the second chair and, with a shy hesitant smile, said: "Do join me." She lowered her head towards her plate.

We ate in silence while I cast about in my mind for some suitable conversation (contemplating the subject of knitting and deciding against it, remembering how little I knew about it).

But Ms. Bronski was staring fixedly above my shoulder, her fork poised in the air.

I turned to see what was making her stare so intently.

There was a loud burst of laughter from Ivanovich, evidently caused by the skinny padre who held his beer glass high. His fingers were long and ebony white, covered with fine black hair practically down to his fingernails. His sleeve rode up on his bare arm. It seemed he was shirtless under his loosely buttoned black cassock. He smiled at Ivanovich.

Pedro Alvarez, the antique dealer, was at a table with my romantic actor, Charles Lupesco, and the redheaded Vicky Anderson.

Stanley and Sara Robinson sat by themselves as did Dr. and Sra. Hernandez. The tables at the back were filled by tourists from a different group and I recognized no one else from the train.

I turned back to Ms. Bronski and was rather alarmed to see her face flushed a dull red.

"Something wrong?" I asked.

"Oh, no!" Ms. Bronski fluttered her fingers across her cheeks as if to wipe off the blush and laughed, obviously embarrassed.

"Never mind me. I thought I saw a ghost. I do that once in a while . . . ."

She packed up her knitting and got up.

"Our guide is calling," she said. "Are you ready?"

"You go ahead with the group," I said. "I'll catch up with you later."

"All right." Ms. Bronski looked a bit disappointed but she smiled. And when she did, the blue of her eyes deepened and her face changed from just pleasantly elderly to that of a vibrant, younger counterpart.

Ms. Bronski hurried away behind Ivanovich and the two padres.

I returned to the buffet and helped myself to a large plate of fruit salad, poured a cup of coffee, and sat at my table until I was the last person in the restaurant.

I suppose I should have joined the group if, for nothing else, to observe Ivanovich in action. But I felt I had a pretty good picture of his abilities as a guide—no better but certainly no worse than others I had hired—and I had looked forward to experiencing the awesome silence at the ruins by myself.

But I did have a twinge of guilt about abandoning Ms. Bronski.

CHAPTER 6

I kept the strap of the camera bag across my shoulders to keep both hands free for the climb and set out down the broad steps. I walked until I reached the entrance to the lost city and stood quietly before the stone portal to Machu Picchu.

The doorway was just wide enough for a person and a half. The ashlar across the top was chiseled from one single piece of rock, the supporting walls leaning slightly inward.

I walked through the portal and continued up the stairway which began immediately inside. It had turned out to be a brilliant day on the mountaintop, the sky blue with puffs of white clouds hanging above and below my vision. A slight breeze fluttered through the tall grasses growing between cracks in the stone walls.

I continued walking and eventually climbed another, much steeper, flight of stairs cut directly into the mountainside. I ended up at a parapet from where I had a full view of the Machu Picchu ruins laid out before me like a topographical map. The wide expanse between the two areas of ruins was covered with a thick carpet of grass dotted with yellow and red flowers.

I sat down to rest on a stone from where I could see the two groups with their guides walking very far apart. There were no sounds.

I consulted my map, studied the specific points I wanted to re-visit, and decided to walk first to the main temple and then across to the series of compounds on the opposite side. That way I would eventually join up with Ivanovich.

I shot a few pictures and set out for the temple.

It was a long tiring climb across loose rubble and narrow footpaths, and I wondered briefly if Ms. Bronski was in good climbing condition. Then again, thinking of my own mother, athletic in her early sixties, I decided not to worry about Ms. Bronski.

The Temple of the Sun was even more majestic than I remembered. As I climbed to the stone altar at the far end of the now roofless enclosure, I thought of the royal mummies which supposedly had been displayed in the niches around the walls. Of the Incas and their Chosen Women, worshipers of the sun, the moon, and the stars. As always, I felt relief that the Spanish conquistadores never found this hidden city.

I crossed the vast grass field to the compound on the other side, feeling quite insignificant at the bottom of the valley. I arrived, not as planned between the two groups, but rather in advance of my own.

I ducked into the torture chamber through the rear entrance. Whoever had been punished here had not fared well. The back wall had three deep built-in seats with holes cut at shoulder-height through which the arms of the offender would be wedged. The cleverly engineered openings were angled to keep the body rigidly in place and make it impossible to escape.

I had never really tried to imagine what kind of torture would thereupon be administered and didn't dwell on it today, either.

I left the chamber through the outside courtyard and made the climb to the Temple of the Three Windows. Shadows had fallen on the windows but I remembered being here years ago, overnight, rising before the sun and standing, as today, in the middle of the temple.

The first rays had burst upon me from one second to the next, through the three windows. I remembered absolutely believing the legend that the temple was built in this exact position for the priests to worship *Inti*, their sun-god. I decided now that future groups would stay overnight.

I heard echoes of voices in the distance and reluctantly left the temple, taking care on the steep cliff. I continued downhill until I found a secluded ledge at the outside of a low wall. I sat down, burrowed my feet into the ground, and took out a chocolate bar and the small thermos with coffee I had brought along in anticipation of just such an occasion.

The sun was at its highest, the wind had settled, and I zoomed in the Minolta on two condors, their white-tipped wings motionless, their sharp eyes in search of prey, gliding in tandem above the abyss, until they became mere shadows in the thin mountain air.

I put the camera down and closed my eyes.

I was still asleep when the scream struck the stone walls. The sound reverberated and rolled among the ruins, and filled the vast space between the two mountain peaks.

CHAPTER 7

THE scream rang out again. This time the wail was at a higher pitch. It hung in the air, then rising and ebbing in a ripple of echoes, it died out leaving a palpable vacuum.

The reality brought me to my feet.

I scrambled off the ledge, leaving my things behind, and ran up the steep cliff. There were about fifty feet of slippery pebbles before I reached the courtyard leading to the torture chamber. I heard voices and shuffling of feet from inside the chamber and quickly entered.

Ivanovich was standing with both arms extended wide as if to envelop the group in a bear hug. Their faces were white and they turned simultaneously when I entered. Then they looked towards the torture rock and back again.

I turned around.

The middle seat was taken. The arms were stretched tightly through the holes, the head rested awkwardly against the back wall. The lips gaped bloody red spilling a thin trail down the length of the body.

I heard myself moan.

I went closer and followed with my eyes the red trail up the sturdy legs, up the length of the body, across the chin to the face. The mouth was wide open. The red ball of wool was jammed in tight. The knitting needle glittered brightly in the sun.

It was embedded in Elsa Bronski's chest.

I turned away from the body to confront Ivanovich and the group. They hadn't moved and I counted in silence. They were all there. Nine plus Ivanovich.

I read shock and indecision in their immobile, staring faces. I took a deep breath and straightened my back, glanced again at the still figure in the stone seat, at the contorted features.

"She's dead," I said and added, unnecessarily, "murdered."

My words opened up a floodgate of warbled exclamations and the group came surging forward until I was surrounded.

Stan Robinson supported Sara who hobbled on her right foot, the left being bandaged in what looked like handkerchiefs.

Dr. Hernandez had his arm around his wife. She had taken off her large sunglasses and looked frightened.

The two padres were conferring in low voices and Vicky Anderson was nestled against Charles Lupesco's chest.

Pablo Alvarez wiped his mouth with a large grubby cloth, his eyes obscured by the wide brim of his hat.

I cleared my throat before I trusted myself to speak again.

"You all know me as the owner of Prescott Travel and the organizer of this tour," I said. "What you don't know is that I'm also a licenced private investigator. This is an extraordinary situation, so until we can reach the police, I will take charge."

Ivanovich's eyes bulged and he took a couple of steps forward, then stopped. The others remained rooted to the ground.

I turned to the doctor who let go of his wife as if anticipating my next move.

"Dr. Hernandez, would you step up to the body with me?" I said. He nodded curtly and complied.

"And Mr. Ivanovich, could you hurry back to the hotel and get us some blankets. Four or five. We'll have to carry the body back."

Ivanovich nodded eagerly and looked relieved to be off towards the back exit of the torture chamber. He set out briskly for the tourist station.

"The rest," I said and turned to the group, "it would be better if the rest of you waited together on the other side of the wall and stayed there."

I stared at them so no one would mistake my admonition.

They all suddenly seemed in a hurry to get out of the torture chamber but I had to wait until Dr. Hernandez managed to send off his reluctant wife with murmured reassurances.

I stepped up close to Ms. Bronski's limp form together with Dr. Hernandez. He lifted her eyelids, felt her pulse, looked closely at the knitting needle which was angled downwards, touched nothing else, and nodded his head.

"Dead," he said. "Still warm. Not much bleeding. The needle went straight to her heart."

He looked at the knitting needle.

"A most unusual murder weapon."

"And very handy," I said and looked at the other needle sticking out of Ms. Bronski's tote which stood on the ground, gaping open.

I looked more closely at the needle in Ms. Bronski's chest. It had a slight bend in the middle. Next to the entry point through the blouse was a second hole. As if the needle had entered twice, the first time hitting an obstacle thus giving her a brief respite. Then the momentary realization by both victim and perpetrator that the second deadly stab was now inevitable. They had been face to face.

I shuddered and cursed my all too vivid imagination. But it is that quality that has made me the kind of investigator I used to be and obviously still am: Once I get involved I'm like a dog with an old bone. I won't let go.

I felt a familiar anger building up, the anger that fuels my energy.

I turned around and realized that the two padres had remained behind in the torture chamber. They now stepped forward and Father Orion said:

"Maybe the poor lady was Catholic? And if not, in any case we have been saying to one another that we would be remiss not to offer our services . . . ."

"That's very good of you," I said. "I really don't know but let's see . . ."

I tried not to look at Elsa Bronski's contorted face while with two fingers I carefully lifted the collar of her blouse to peer at her neck. She wore a thin gold chain with a cross. I dropped the collar back in place and turned away quickly.

"Maybe she was Catholic. Very likely. She's wearing a cross. I'll leave any decision to you."

CHAPTER 8

I turned to Dr. Hernandez and the two padres.

"Would you stand guard a few minutes, please? I need to recover my bag. And, speaking of bags, better not touch Ms. Bronski's. I want to wrap it."

Dr. Hernandez nodded reluctantly, the fathers eagerly, and I heard them whispering together as soon as I turned my back.

On the other side of the wall the group had spread out but they were all there.

Sra. Elena Hernandez sat dejectedly on a boulder.

Pablo Alvarez stood apart, chin up, hands jammed deep in his pants' pockets, looking across the valley.

Stanley and Sara Robinson sat side by side on the bottom step of a staircase which went nowhere. He was re-arranging the bandages around her ankle and she looked up at me, pain clear in her face.

"My wife had just fallen and sprained her ankle when we heard the screams," Stan said.

"I'm the one who screamed," Vicky Anderson announced. She was hanging on to the arm of Charles Lupesco who presented a stoic demeanor.

Vicky looked at me eagerly, dabbing a pink tissue at the corners of her eyes. They were a luminous watery blue. "It was terrible," she said. "We had all taken turns sitting in the seats and putting our arms through the holes, and I thought, oh, m'God, it's quite impossible to get free without someone helping you."

"And?"

Vicky blushed.

"Well, Charles, that is Mr. Lupesco, helped me."

"And what did you do then?"

"Well, you know, I wanted to sit outside the chamber by myself without the others and just look across the mountains and feel the quiet. This is my first visit to Machu Picchu . . . so, I left for a little while . . ."

"Did you have a view of the torture chamber from where you sat?"

The pink tissue fluttered and Vicky coughed and dabbed.

"Well, yes. I mean, no. I mean, I wasn't looking."

"And you didn't see anyone entering or leaving the chamber?"

"No, no. I was outside maybe ten minutes and then I thought, oh, m'God, I don't hear their voices, what if I'm left behind, and I hurried back to the chamber. It was empty, but I heard voices from the courtyard. That's when I turned around and saw . . . the poor woman . . . I screamed. Twice!"

"And that's all you remember?"

Vicky nodded, wiped her eyes again and pulled at Charles Lupesco's arm.

It took me only a few minutes to retrieve my things from the cliff. I returned to the torture chamber just as Ivanovich walked through the back entrance with a pile of gray blankets. He looked as if he had run the whole way.

He approached the rock and stopped uncertainly in front of Ms. Bronski's body.

"Should we not disengage her arms before they stiffen?" he said. "Rigor mortis or some such thing?"

"That will not happen for several hours," said Dr. Hernandez and shot Ivanovich a look saying you lay ignoramus.

"And, in any case, I need some five, ten minutes," I said hastily.

I reloaded my camera and shot the entire thirty-six pictures. The last one was of Elsa Bronski's bag which stood on the ground next to her swollen feet.

That done, I pulled out my notebook and motioned to Ivanovich to sit next to me on a rock.

CHAPTER 9

"Now," I said. "Tell me everything, in sequence, before you forget."

I poised my pen and thought longingly of the laptop I hadn't thought it necessary to bring on this trip.

Ivanovich looked at me gravely as if chastened, certainly not his previous defensive self. He cleared his throat.

"I had the honor," he said with a remnant of that pompous voice he adopted with me, "of escorting these distinguished ladies and gentlemen through the ruins of the sacred city built by my glorious vanquished ancestors. Some moments I hurry in front of my groups, some moments I stay in the middle, some moments I am behind to ensure I still have them all. But there were just ten today. The torture chamber has a high appeal, it makes the ladies scream and the gentlemen act gentlemanly."

"All right." Let's cut to the chase, I thought, but held back considering the recent thaw in our relationship. Instead I said: "When did you leave the chamber?"

"When I heard Señora Robinson cry out. She had fallen and twisted her leg. I left Dr. and Sra. Hernandez and Ms. Bronski inside. The rest of the people were outside already."

"Vicky Anderson, too?"

Ivanovich stared.

"I do not remember." He studied the ground between his feet. "No, she was not. And she was not in the chamber. But then I hear two screams and there she is, standing with Ms. Bronski . . ."

"She says she left the torture chamber to enjoy the view by herself. She says she returned ten minutes later and found the body."

"The screams. They were not fake. I think." Ivanovich looked puzzled.

"I would prefer to think not. Let's put it aside for a moment. Tell me what you saw outside after Mrs. Robinson sprained her ankle, before you heard the screams."

"Well. She was sitting on a stone staircase with her husband. Dr. Hernandez and his wife must have come out by then because he was telling Mrs. Robinson to have someone wrap her ankle."

"He didn't offer to help? He's a doctor, isn't he?"

"Yes, but a heart surgeon! As for myself, I am required to know first aid, so I helped."

"Were all the others present?"

"Yes, we were all there: Pablo Alvarez, the two padres, Dr. and Sra. Hernandez, Mr. Lupesco, the Robinsons, and myself. All except Miss Anderson and the unfortunate . . ."

His voice trailed off and I closed my notebook. We were about to go around in circles.

"I think that will be all for now," I said. "We'll go over it again later."

We got up and approached the body together with the padres and Dr. Hernandez.

"We'll remove the knitting needle," I decided. "When we wrap the body, the blanket might rub off possible prints."

"Surely it was wiped clean already," Dr. Hernandez said in that disdainful voice that I'd come to recognize as habitual. He studied the manicured nails of his right hand.

"Maybe yes, maybe no." I wished he wouldn't keep second-guessing me. "Do you by any chance have a clean handkerchief?"

Dr. Hernandez nodded and pulled out a snowy-white cloth, approached the body, tugged tentatively at the needle, removed it carefully by the tiny knob at the end and presented it to me. I stared at it. The point was thin and sharp. I put it carefully on top of my camera, wrapped in the handkerchief, and closed the flap of the bag securely.

Ivanovich and Dr. Hernandez placed the body on a layer of four blankets and tied the corners together at each end.

"I told the bus drivers to get ready to depart," Ivanovich said.

We all looked at the forlorn heap on the ground.

"Shall we?" I said and Ivanovich grabbed a hold of the front end while Father Orion gently lifted the back. The blankets sagged and Ivanovich tightened his grip before taking the first step out of the torture chamber.

Dr. Hernandez had disappeared to the other side of the wall and I heard him talking to his wife. I quickly followed, carrying Ms. Bronski's handbag wrapped in the last of the gray blankets.

Sara Robinson whimpered as she put her foot down and just as quickly lifted it. Charles Lupesco and Pablo Alvarez sprang to the rescue gripping each other's wrists to form a tiny seat. After some shuffling and encouragement they had Sara hoisted up, her bouffant transparent in the sunlight. She wrapped her arms firmly about the shoulders of her two heroes.

I walked to the front to lead the procession, with Ivanovich and Father Orion right behind me with the body. Then came the others. Stan Robinson was urging his wife to sit quietly in the grip of her two boy scouts. Pablo Alvarez' face already glistened with sweat whereas Charles Lupesco looked cool and unperturbed. Father Octavio constantly lost his foothold on the gravel. Dr. Hernandez held his wife's hand, and Vicky Anderson fell back to bring up the rear.

We walked slowly, single file, as we negotiated the last stairway and the steep ascent towards the stone portal.

I stood quietly before it, waiting for the others to catch up. The entire panorama of the Lost City stretched before us, the buildings devoid of roofs, their slate-gray walls weighted by solid, square perfectly fitted stones. The silence was absolute, as if one more death made no difference.

I stepped through the portal to lead the group on and was once more in the real world.

A small cluster of Indians stood on the front steps of the restaurant, staring inscrutably.

CHAPTER 10

As soon as the train was in motion I grabbed my notebook and began my interviews.

The departure from Machu Picchu had not gone that smoothly. Ivanovich and Father Orion had edged Ms. Bronski's body through the door of the second bus and placed it on the rear seat.

The rest of the group went in the first bus. I had taken Ivanovich aside and said: "Be sure they all board the train together," and watched him put on his pompous act.

"In actual reality there is nowhere to go except into the jungle, and no one is carrying equipment to survive out there. Whoever did it must take the train to Cuzco."

"I want to phone the police in Cuzco," I said.

"There is no telephone. The connection is by radio." Ivanovich had sounded oddly pleased.

I went inside the station in search of a radio operator. The office manager, a stocky Indian man, went about the call sedately and I wasn't surprised when, after several minutes of pushing buttons, waiting, and pushing some more, he announced that there would be a thirty minute waiting period. I decided to give it up. The police would have to wait until we arrived in Cuzco.

Ivanovich was standing just outside the door and didn't look at all surprised at the news.

"Always a long wait," he said laconically.

I boarded the second bus alone, acutely aware of the body on the back seat. We moved slowly and were just about to make a U-turn around a low stone wall when the woman in the white stove-top hat came around the corner from the restaurant. She had a great striped bundle swung across her back and moved alongside my bus, waving.

We had crunched to a halt to let her board. She dumped her red bundle on the front seat and placed her square frame next to it, her feet several inches above the floor. She turned around and grinned at me. One front tooth was missing, her plump cheeks were crisscrossed with burst capillaries, and her eyes were bright and inquisitive.

While the bus zigzagged its way back down the mountain the woman had spoken under her breath to the bus driver and turned her head intermittently to stare at me. Each time she gazed at the back seat.

At the train station Ivanovich had scared up the engineer and the conductor and stood surrounded by an excited group of Indians who must have abandoned their stalls at the nearby market place.

Elsa Bronski's body had been placed in car No. 6 in an empty compartment where I could watch it through the window in the sliding door. Our group had settled in and we were on our way.

Ivanovichs' words echoed in my head. Whoever did it would be on the train.

The other tour group had been so far removed from ours that its members were beyond suspicion. It had to be one of ours.

I looked at them one by one and realized I knew nothing about them whatsoever.

I now motioned Vicky Anderson to an empty seat.

"Have you remembered anything at all in addition to what you already told me?"

Vicky shook her head and looked at me with over-flowing eyes.

"No, nothing. Can't think of a single thing to add. And I'm not crying," she said, "I have tear-duct problems." She dabbed away.

"Here," I handed her my notebook and pen. "Please write down your name, address, and phone number."

I looked at her address. Monterrico, not far from the American High School.

"If you don't mind, just stay in this seat until I've finished talking to Mr. Lupesco," I said and went across the aisle.

I had trouble determining Charles Lupesco's age. Somewhere around fifty was my best guess. Somehow he looked younger in profile than full face. I offered him a look at my P.I. license and he examined it for longer than seemed strictly necessary.

"I'm trying to get people's recollections down on paper before they forget the details," I said. "Do you mind?"

"I don't mind," he said and looked out the window. "What would you like to know?"

"Just whatever you remember from the time the group first entered the torture chamber."

"Yes, yes." Charles Lupesco's accent now became slightly more pronounced. "We entered together and our excellent guide, Mr. Ivanovich, explained the gruesome stories of torture. I come from a country, Madame, where torture has not been unknown."

"Where are you from, Mr. Lupesco?"

"Rumania."

"And are you with the Rumanian delegation to the UN?"

He waited until I had finished writing.

"No, Madame, I am not with the official delegation. I am an international civil servant employed by the UN as an interpreter."

"I see. And then what happened in the torture chamber?"

"Our guide showed us how to sit in the horrible seats, they all tried them as some ghastly tourist experience. All but myself. It was impossible for people to get themselves extricated and I had to help Miss Anderson, after which she excused herself and left. I followed Mr. Ivanovich outside. Then this woman stumbled and sprained her ankle. The ground outside was quite uneven. Everyone gathered around to help her. I gave her my handkerchief."

Dr. Hernandez hadn't been that generous, I remembered.

"And Ms. Bronski, where was she?"

"I did not notice. After the commotion with the handkerchiefs I took a walk with the Peruvian gentleman, Mr. Alvarez. He explained more about Machu Picchu to me, he is as knowledgeable as our guide."

"For how long?"

"I should say about ten minutes," Lupesco said without hesitation.

"And where were you when you heard the two screams?"

"Still with Mr. Alvarez." Charles Lupesco spoke with an air of finality.

I gave him a fresh page in my notebook and he wrote down his address and phone number in New York. I glanced at it. Just a few blocks from the UN.

Charles Lupesco turned away from me and looked steadfastly out the window. I made a mental note of disapproval. He didn't seem to notice that I left.

I passed by Vicky Anderson who got up and returned to sit opposite him. They leaned towards each other, heads almost touching, and began talking.

CHAPTER 11

I walked across to Dr. and Sra. Hernandez. Elena explained she made her husband try out the seat in the torture chamber although he thought her foolish, after which she tried it herself. She said Ms. Bronski was next but that she just sat there without putting her arms through the holes.

"You see," Sra. Hernandez said, "I thought nothing of leaving. Ms. Bronski didn't need help to get out."

"So, you were the last persons to see Ms. Bronski alive," I concluded.

"Except for the murderer," Dr. Hernandez' voice was icy. "She was very much alive when we left. Then there was the commotion with Mrs. Robinson and only later we heard the screams."

"Who else was outside when Mrs. Robinson fell?"

Dr. and Sra. Hernandez looked at one another but he was the one who answered:

"Everyone except Ms. Bronski."

"Was Miss Anderson there?"

They again looked at each other and shook their heads in doubt.

"I think so," he said.

I flipped to a new page in my notebook and Dr. Hernandez wrote down their address and phone number in San Isidro.

I now turned to the two padres who said they were the first to leave the torture chamber since the very idea made them uncomfortable. They had been sitting outside in the courtyard and, in fact, had seen everyone come out.

"Were you helping Mrs. Robinson after she fell?" I asked. The answer was yes, as I had expected.

"And are you sure no one left after that?"

They said they were fairly sure but couldn't swear to it.

Pablo Alvarez was sitting by himself, eyes half closed, his brown jacket folded across his knees. His story was very much the same. He hadn't even gone into the torture chamber, he had seen Mrs. Robinson stumble and had lent her one of his handkerchiefs.

"Did you talk to anyone in particular?"

"Yes, I did have a conversation with the gentleman from the United Nations."

"For how long?"

"I imagine some five, ten minutes."

"And were you talking to him when you heard the screams."

"Yes, I certainly was."

I left him, went back to my seat and summed it all up in my head. Everyone had a convincing explanation which, of course, couldn't be the truth. At least one person, if not more, had to be lying. There was a very small window of opportunity and someone had taken a chance. But how? And what could possibly be the motive?

Sara Robinson was waiving to me and I went over to their seat.

"You've talked to everyone but us!" she said. She was resting her injured leg on her tote. Stanley, his hair askew, held her hand.

"Oye, what a tragedy," she said. "The poor, dear lady. We were shocked when we saw her sitting there. And imagine being gagged with your own knitting wool. And returned on the train wrapped in a blanket instead of enjoying the rest of the trip." She sighed not altogether unhappily.

"I couldn't believe my ears! The screams were enough to curl the hair on your head." Stanley patted down a strand above his right ear. "I tell you, this is the worst thing that's ever happened to us."

"It was worse for the poor lady," Sara Robinson said matter-of-factly.

I decided to stem the flow of exclamations.

"When did you both leave the torture chamber?"

"Let me see now," Stan said. "I tried out the seat and stuck my arms through the holes and my wife had to help me out."

He pulled up his sleeves and showed me the red scratches on his wrists.

"Sara didn't want to try, so we left. Right outside she stumbled on a stone sticking out of the ground and fell."

"Was anyone else outside at that time?"

"Well, the doctor and his wife came, although he certainly didn't help much. I figured he was annoyed that he had to play doctor on his day off. No matter. Mr. Ivanovich was quite competent. Mr. Alvarez came and the good looking foreign gentleman. And the two fellas in dresses."

"I'm sure they are very nice men," Sara said and glanced sideways at me.

"How long before you heard the screams, do you figure?"

"Well, now, that's difficult to remember, there was so much going on what with Sara falling and us bandaging her foot. What say, Sara? Twenty minutes?

"It seems both less and more than twenty minutes," Sara said watching me write it all down. I got the uneasy feeling she was the kind of witness who would be in two minds about almost everything.

I returned to my seat and watched them all through half closed eyes. I must have fallen asleep because the next thing I knew I heard a loud crash and reached inside my jacket for the gun, ready to defend myself, only to confront the clumsy entry of a little man pushing a cart loaded with Inca-Cola, chocolates and chips.

I no longer own a gun and haven't used one in several years. But I guess I have no control over my reflexes. I looked around to see if anyone had noticed and, sure enough, there was Ivanovich eyeing me curiously.

I purchased a couple of colas and a bag of chips for the equivalent of almost ten dollars and offered him some. He munched noisily.

"Tell me who in the group you think knew one another before getting on this trip?" I asked.

I looked at him steadfastly wondering not for the first time why brown eyes give away so much less than blue. His lids moved heavily several times.

"Let me think!" The thought process was visible on his face. His gaze wavered from the ceiling to the view which floated by sedately outside the window. "I do not really know any of them, so how can I know if they knew one another?"

"Whom did you yourself know before this trip?"

"I told you already! Just Pablo Alvarez, personally, but really not well at all, and Dr. Hernandez from reading about him in the newspapers. That's all."

I didn't really know what I was looking for. I was beginning to feel tired and, so, I didn't object when Ivanovich left me for the company of the two padres.

CHAPTER 12

Back in my room at the Regina Inca I stepped into a tepid shower of brownish water and stood there no longer than necessary. I dried off, pulled on a warm sweatsuit and socks and fell on the bed, exhausted. The room was cold, the sheets felt clammy and the lack of oxygen made my heart pound.

I reached for the small oxygen tank the receptionist had given me after taking one look at my blond hair and blue eyes. I breathed deeply for several minutes and, slowly, my heartbeat returned to normal.

The train had pulled into the station in Cuzco just after eight and I had sent Ivanovich in search of the police. They had arrived in a flurry of excitement and a sergeant informed me with obvious relief that the police in Lima would take charge since the lady had been American. He did not know if the embassy had been informed but we were all to leave the next morning with the deceased and go directly to police headquarters to be questioned. An ambulance crew had removed the body.

I placed a call to the American embassy with the receptionist suspecting that at this hour I would need an emergency number. But I thought I would give it a shot anyway. I could have saved my breath. The receptionist came back after about fifteen minutes saying she couldn't get through to Lima at all. I told her to forget it.

I poured out a steaming cup of *mate de coca* from the large thermos which was part of hotel services, and brought out Ms. Bronski's handbag.

I emptied its contents on the bed and started going through them. A brown monogrammed wallet, matching eyeglass and passport cases, a red zippered pouch inscribed "make-up" in black letters, a yellow comb, one unopened roll of Life-Savers and one half eaten, a Parker pen in a brown leather case, pocket Kleenex, and a pair of sunglasses.

I opened the wallet. American Express and Visa cards, Washington, D.C. driver's license, health insurance card, a valid AAA card, a photograph of a dark-haired woman in her 40s inscribed on the back *"A ma chère Elsa"*, five hundred dollars in twenty dollar bills, and five traveler's checks each for one hundred dollars. The amount of money didn't quite fit my image of Ms. Bronski.

There was a business card imprinted "Mme. Therése Lecroix, l'Ambassade de France, Lima, Peru," with the address and telephone number of the residence in San Isidro. I copied the information and then opened Ms. Bronski's American passport which revealed that she was born 1940 in Paris, France.

I had downed the last sip of my *mate* when the phone rang. It was the receptionist.

"Señorita," she apologized, "you have a visitor."

"Who could it be?"

"A Sr. Ivanovich."

"Could you put him on the line, please."

"He is asking for you to come downstairs, please."

Well, for heaven's sakes, I thought, and got out of bed really slowly to conserve energy.

I lumbered down to the lobby in the erratic elevator. His reason for getting me down in my pyjamas—even if it was an ordinary sweatsuit—had better be good.

Ivanovich stood right at the elevator and, with slow emphasis on every word, said: "Pablo Alvarez has disappeared from the hotel."

"What do you mean 'he's disappeared'? He's gone with his overnight bag and all?" I sat down on a green chair whose vinyl felt cold to the touch.

Ivanovich sank down on the sofa opposite me.

"We all ate together in the dining room," he said slightly less pompous than usual. "I see them disappear into their rooms, we are all on the first floor. I go into the bar to relax. There I talk to the bartender for maybe half an hour and then I remember I have forgotten to tell them the time of departure tomorrow morning. I decide to do it right away. They were all in their rooms except for Pablo Alvarez."

"How do you know his bag is not in his room. He may have gone to visit someone . . . ."

"The door was open. I stepped in. Everything was gone."

"Any idea where he could be?" I looked closely at Ivanovich's expression trying to see if it would give anything away. But he looked as inscrutable as ever and just shook his head.

"But you said you know him," I insisted.

"I know him in Lima, but not well," Ivanovich said huffily.

"All right, we'll tell the police in the morning. It's too late to do anything about it now."

Ivanovich got up in his own abrupt fashion and left. It was now well past midnight and the hotel was as deserted as the streets outside.

I watched through the glass door as he strode briskly along the sidewalk, his ponytail swinging rhythmically. He stopped at the first side street and looked behind him, furtively it seemed to me. Then, as if on a sudden impulse, he scooted around the corner and disappeared.

I wanted to rush after him in pursuit of whatever had occurred to him but knew that my lung capacity would never allow me to catch anything, not to mention my pyjamas state.

I made my way, slowly, upstairs.

Back in my clammy bed I turned out the light after a futile attempt to read a couple of pages in a mystery. The light from a 25-W bulb fluttered from under the dark lamp shade and hit the night table straight down and nowhere near my book.

Then I just lay there contemplating the ceiling. Blue veins of cracked plaster spread across it in wide rivers and narrow tributaries. When I closed my eyes determined to sleep I saw Elsa Bronski's contorted face. The images shifted and I heard her slightly accented voice, saw her flushed face and fixed stare.

I opened my eyes and looked once more at the mottled ceiling. The rivers had widened and the tributaries seemed longer.

Elsa Bronski could have been staring at anyone of the thirty-odd people in the restaurant.

CHAPTER 13

T HE minute I spotted him on the tarmac I knew I was looking at James Quentin Brown. His sandy-haired crewcut just spelled FBI. And to his left were three Peruvian police officers in uniform.

I hurried down the stairs for once as one of the first passengers, leaving the Robinsons, Dr. and Sra. Hernandez, Vicky Anderson, Charles Lupesco, Ivanovich, and the two padres behind.

I made a bee-line for Quentin.

"Jamie Prescott, private investigator." I extended my hand and he shook it firmly.

"Jim Brown," he said. "Legal attaché."

He looked around at the three police officers and introduced me. Then he pointed towards the freight hold.

"I understand you have a problem," he said. "We're having the body transferred immediately to a morgue in Lima. The Chief of Police has requested that the group traveling with the, er, deceased, be transported to his office to give their statements. I'm to accompany you on behalf of the embassy."

"I've made some preliminary notes and taken early statements," I said. Jim Brown—too bad he didn't use his middle name. I had grown accustomed to Quentin which, in fact, gave him more of a personality. He looked at me with somewhat more warmth.

"Sounds good," he said.

"What's the procedure in a case like this?"

"Initially, it's up to the Peruvian police to conduct the investigation. They should then make a formal request for our assistance since the victim was a U.S. citizen."

The three police officers had now isolated the group under the tutelage of Ivanovich and a few minutes later we were moving *en masse* through the arrival hall much like a flock of sheep.

We were herded out a side door towards three beat up black Dodges from the 1970s.

The ride from the airport went swiftly along Avenida Elmer Faucett. Because of a motorcycle which preceded us, the Dodges followed each other blithely through intersections and red lights, forcing oncoming traffic practically onto the sidewalks. The resulting tooting added cacophony to the dust rising from the shoulders of several stretches of unpaved road.

The police station was housed in the center of town in a four-story building. Inside, we were ushered into a stuffy waiting room to sit on metal folding chairs with cracked red vinyl which were lined up along two walls.

Jim Brown disappeared behind a dark wooden door marked "Feliciano Lopez, Jefe de Policia."

I pushed away an overflowing ashtray with a few butts still glowing and grabbed copies of *El Diario* and *El Comercio* which were sitting on the table. I flipped through them without finding any headlines about an American tourist murdered at Machu Picchu.

"Yesterday's papers," said Ivanovich complacently.

Just as Jim Brown returned to the waiting room, a tall man in an expensive looking blue suit entered from the corridor. His hair was silvery white in contrast to his jet-black mustache. He was accompanied by a shorter man who bustled ahead, knocked on the door marked chief of police, after which the two disappeared inside. They stayed for the best part of half an hour causing some unrest among the members of our group. They were apparently let out a different door because we were now being called into the office to give our statements.

Dr. and Sra. Hernandez went first and stayed only briefly. They breezed out the door without a second glance at their fellow travelers.

Vicky Anderson went next and came back with flushed cheeks. She waited until Charles Lupesco finished his interview and they left together.

The two padres were in there the longest and looked somehow ruffled when they left. Ivanovich stayed about ten minutes and his forehead was glistening with sweat when he reappeared.

The Robinsons were last and came straight to me afterwards.

"We wanted to continue our trip," Stanley Robinson said, "but the chief says we must stay here." And Sara added: "How long do you think it will be? And what about our reservations to Bolivia? And I can't walk around." She looked down at her injured foot.

"If I'm any judge," I said, "we'll be here several days, certainly until after the inquest. But I'll take care of your reservations."

"We'll make sure they hurry up the procedure," Jim Brown said. "You shouldn't have to stay here more than a couple of days, Ma'am." He touched an imaginary cap with two fingers and Mrs. Robinson beamed at him. He did look boyish with that crewcut.

"Well, I hope they find out who did this to the poor lady," Sara said. She stopped aghast as the thought hit her. "It's someone in the group, isn't it?" She suddenly looked quite white around the eyes. "And where's that man with the sweaty face, Mr. Alvarez? Why isn't he here?"

Sara looked from Stan to me and back.

"He stayed behind in Cuzco," I said. "The police will interview him later."

Sara Robinson, rallying, decided to dismiss the whole thing. I suggested they return to the hotel in a taxi since I would probably be with the chief of police at least half an hour.

I went inside accompanied by Jim Brown. Chief Lopez sat behind a desk burdened with stacks of tattered file folders held together with rubber bands, and the ubiquitous overflowing ashtray. A large map of Lima covered the wall between two windows with half drawn curtains. A pasty-faced young man pulled out chairs for us and sat down next to the chief, balancing a notepad on his knee.

The sight of me made the Chief jump up—no other interpretation was possible and I caught an amused glint in Jim Brown's eyes—and bustle around his desk to grasp my hand in both of his. He spoke in almost unaccented English.

"Miss Prescott!" His warm brown eyes looked searchingly into mine and a brilliant smile appeared in the midst of his curly black beard. "I'm terribly sorry to hear of all your problems. May I assure you that I, personally, will do everything possible to help you. Now, do tell me all the details."

I told him as succinctly as I could. I then offered him my notes and felt grateful for the unexpected working conditions of the photo copying machine at the Regina Inca in Cuzco.

"Ah," he said, "your notes are in English, of course. We will find a translator and you can go over them for verification. How long were you planning to stay in Peru?"

"Until Friday."

"Will a meeting tomorrow afternoon be convenient for you? At 3 o'clock?"

"That'll be perfect. I certainly appreciate your efficiency," I said, and meant it.

"We will compare your notes to the statements we obtained today. We have asked that the foreign members of your group remain in Lima for the next couple of days. Your embassy has requested a speedy inquest so that the body may be returned to the United States. Our Foreign Ministry will make the necessary arrangements. We have an interest as well from the French embassy. It seems the victim was the ambassador's sister-in-law."

"That's right," I said and wondered how he knew.

I pulled out Dr. Hernandez' formerly impeccable, now blood-stained white handkerchief with the knitting needle. I handed it to Lopez whose emotions were visible on his blanched face.

"Ah, the murder weapon," he said, and a shudder ran through him. He peeled back the cloth and bent close to the needle.

"I imagine you'll want everyone's fingerprints," I said. And when the chief didn't respond I added: "No one has touched it since I first saw the body . . . ."

Lopez nodded. He picked up the knitting needle, held it up to the light, turned it this way and that using all ten of his meaty fingers. Then he placed it rather carelessly back on the handkerchief.

I couldn't believe it. Now his prints were all over my carefully preserved evidence. I decided then and there not to hand over Ms. Bronski's handbag and, at that moment, I had forgotten about the photographs I took. Truly.

Lopez got up. Apparently our interview was over and, again, he came around to caress my hand. "I'll see you tomorrow, then," he said.

"Well," said Jim Brown when we stood on the sidewalk a few minutes later. "You made a serious conquest in there. I've never experienced such efficiency."

"Efficiency!" I said. "He put his fingers all over the knitting needle and I can't believe he didn't want to secure fingerprints!" I didn't add that Jim Brown might have taken a greater interest in the proceedings himself.

I hailed a taxi and held the door open.

"Can I give you a lift somewhere? I'm going to the Cesar Miraflores."

"Thanks, I'll come with you as far as the hotel and walk from there. I live close by."

He got in but I didn't feel like conversation and I guess he was aware of my annoyance because he didn't say much either. I certainly wasn't about to introduce myself as Bob Makowski's friend.

Back at the hotel I took out my notes and dialed the telephone number of Elsa Bronski's sister at the French ambassador's residence.

"Madame is indisposed," a voice responded.

"Please tell Madame I am the American tour leader of the group to Machu Picchu."

I was told to wait a moment. The moment stretched while I watched a TV show in which a noisy group of adults dressed as infants were being infantile. I turned off the set when Therese Lecroix came on the line.

"Madame Lecroix," I said in English, "I was on the tour to Machu Picchu with your sister. I would like to see you and to bring you her handbag."

She sobbed into the telephone and said she understood nothing, that she felt guilty sending her sister on the tour by herself, and would I consider coming to see her right away?

"I'll be there in half an hour."

CHAPTER 14

THE elevator carried me swiftly down to the lobby and I went through the revolving doors to the circular driveway in front of the hotel.

A few minutes later I was in a black sedan with a uniformed driver whose price was double that of the usual fly-by-night taxis and who transported me to San Isidro at an infuriatingly sedate pace. However, he got me there in one piece.

The French ambassador's residence sat well back in a luscious garden behind a ten-foot high wrought iron fence. An armed guard stood near the entrance to a two-car garage, his machine gun at the ready. He looked fierce enough until I caught the veiled look under his peaked cap which made me wonder whose side he was really on.

I paid off the taxi and stepped up to the intercom at the gate. I had no sooner said my name than the front door opened, a butler in black stuck his head outside, and the gate clicked open. I worked my way on the uneven flagstone path to the curved flight of stairs.

The butler beckoned me into the foyer across an impressive expanse of marble mosaic and Persian carpets, around a center display of Gladioli in a Grecian urn on a round mahogany table.

I was shown into a formal sitting room.

The silent butler pointed me towards a sofa and matching chairs upholstered in thick blue silk.

I sat down and looked around. The walls on both sides of the fireplace were mirrored and lined with glass shelves with displays of crystal and porcelain figurines. There were several signed photographs in silver frames on the mantel piece.

Therese Lecroix came towards me with her hand outstretched.

Her face had grown older since the photograph in Elsa Bronski's wallet, her eyes had lost their shine and even, it seemed, their color. Her hair was combed carelessly as if she hadn't bothered with a mirror, and she wore no lipstick

She had been crying. Nevertheless, when she shook my hand she looked composed. Her black dress hung elegantly from her straight shoulders. Her only jewelry was a pair of enormous diamond earrings matched by a ring on her left hand.

We sat down just as the butler reappeared with a large silver tray. He placed it on a side table and served us.

Once we were alone with our Limoges cups, silver coffee pot, crystal glasses, a decanter of liqueur, and an assortment of pastel colored petit fours, we looked at one another. I chose this moment to hand her Elsa Bronski's handbag. Normally, I would have given it to the police, but here nothing was normal.

"Your sister told me you are a pediatrician," I said. To be honest, she didn't look like a doctor but then, to echo Gloria Steinem, what does a doctor look like?

Therese Lecroix shifted her gaze and stared across the room through an arched doorway into a white satin salon. I, too, gazed through the square panes of the double glass doors far into the garden. Then she shook her head and her shoulders sagged.

"Yes," she said. "My sister will not, would not, forgive me for abandoning my work. But then she never had to choose between a husband and a career. She did not understand what it is like." She looked again across the room towards the garden.

"Why didn't your sister understand?"

"Elsa was very sheltered. She never married and she didn't know me that well. She lived all her life in the United States, while I was in France."

"I didn't know that. How did that come about?"

"Well, not all her life, of course. She was thirteen years old when I was born and she was eighteen when she went to America. I was a small child and I must confess I soon forgot her."

"Why did she go?" I asked.

"She was invited by some friends of my parents. She was supposed to stay only one month. But she never returned to live with us and I did not see her again until six years ago."

Therese Lecroix served us another cup of coffee and poured herself a triple shot of liqueur from the crystal decanter. I declined, and she left the decanter next to her plate. She emptied her glass without looking up.

I busied myself adding cream and sugar to my dainty cup. "Did you sister live in Washington, D.C. all those years?"

"Yes, she did. She took care of Mrs. Douglas for over thirty years."

Now the Georgetown address suddenly made sense to me. Of course! Elsa Bronski had been a companion/secretary and not an office worker.

"Elsa was her secretary, nurse, and companion rolled into one," Therese Lecroix confirmed. "When they came to Paris that time six years ago they stayed at the Ritz, very luxuriously. Elsa seemed happy in a placid sort of way. Always busy with her knitting."

Therese Lecroix stared at me with stricken eyes obviously remembering the role her sister's knitting needle had played at the end.

"And this Mrs. Douglas, she treated her well?" I asked.

"Yes, yes." Therese wiped her eyes. "She treated her well, almost like a relative but not quite, of course. Elsa was paid real money and had her own apartment in Mrs. Douglas' house. I visited her two years ago on my way to Peru."

"And your parents? Didn't they miss Elsa? You mean, she never returned to visit them?"

Therese Lecroix twirled her diamond ring around and around, and I wondered how she ever got it off past the bony knuckle.

"Our parents died within two years of each other, my father first, then my mother when I was ten." She picked up the decanter and was poised to pour when a voice boomed in the foyer and almost simultaneously a man's form filled the mirror to the left of the fireplace.

Therese's eyes remained riveted on his face in the mirror. Then, smoothly, she got up from her chair, deftly pushing the liqueur behind the coffee pot.

She turned to introduce her husband to me.

George Lecroix, Ambassador *Extraordinaire and Plénipotentiaire*, stepped into the room. His silver hair gleamed. I found him to be taller and better looking than he had appeared during the short glimpse I had of him at the police station earlier that morning.

He obviously didn't recognize me and seemed eager to be released from his wife's afternoon coffee company. He was about to retreat when Therese said: "George! Miss Prescott was on the tour with Elsa to Machu Picchu!"

The ambassador stopped in his tracks and refocused his attention on me.

"Really," he said. "And that's why you're here?"

"I invited her, George."

"What is your interest in this?" he asked me.

"I took charge of getting Ms. Bronski's body transported to Cuzco."

"That was the job of the police." He looked stern.

"Well, there were no police officers at Machu Picchu, and no radio communication, I might add. I took charge in my double capacity as the owner of the travel agency which arranged the tour, and in my capacity as a private investigator."

My words were allowed to hang in the air for several seconds before Therese and George Lecroix exclaimed in unison:

"A Private Investigator?"

George turned abruptly to Therese.

"Did you know about this?"

"No, George, of course not. But Ms. Prescott is being very kind. She was one of the last persons who ever spoke to Elsa. Maybe she can help us find out who did . . . it."

"The police will be in charge," George said curtly and extended his hand to me indicating that my visit was over.

"Thank you for dropping by, Mademoiselle."

I shook his hand since it seemed rude not to, but it was Therese I addressed.

"I'll be at the Cesar Miraflores for the rest of the week if you feel you need my assistance," I said. But she shook her head faintly.

The butler appeared out of nowhere and, *tout de suite,* I found myself on the sidewalk outside the residence before realizing I should have called a taxi. I contemplated ringing the bell but instead decided to walk across Avenida Javier Prado to hail a cab in the street.

That's when I saw him out of the corner of my eye. There was no mistaking him, same slicked-back black hair straggling around the collar of his brown jacket. The only thing different about Pablo Alvarez was the large briefcase which weighted down his right arm.

I lowered the hand I had raised to flag down a taxi and stepped up to the brick wall behind me. I sidled back crabwise until I had a full view of Alvarez hurrying along the street.

I watched him pass the front gate of the French ambassador's residence and stop at the side entrance.

I retreated but he never turned around.

Someone inside the residence clicked the gate open and Alvarez hurried towards the kitchen entrance next to the garage.

I stepped away from the wall and walked briskly down the opposite sidewalk under the watchful eye of the armed guard who now stood at the curbside leaning against a stunted tree. I kept my steps even until I reached the corner.

I now had the choice between continuing out of sight or turning around and retrace my steps. I chose the latter.

The armed guard had moved back to the recess in the wall, his gun on the ground against his leg. As I reached the corner of Avenida Javier Prado I glanced back just in time to see Pablo Alvarez emerge. He disappeared down the street in the opposite direction and I was too far away to catch up with him.

I acknowledged defeat and hailed the first taxi that came along. I hardly noticed the bumpy ride on non-existing springs as I sat wondering about the connection between Alvarez and the French ambassador's residence.

At the hotel I had three messages. One from chief of police Lopez requesting that I present myself the next morning rather than in the afternoon. An invitation from the Robinsons to have dinner with them. And a similar request from Ivanovich who said he would call for me at eight.

I rang up the Robinsons to decline their dinner invitation and we settled for a rendezvous for breakfast instead.

I went through my exercise program of one hundred jumping jacks and had finished showering and dressing by five minutes to eight. Ivanovich called from downstairs forty-five minutes later.

He, too, had changed. He had on a white shirt with laundry creases, a brown vest of rough wool with a single silver button at the waist, blue jeans, and a pair of running shoes that had seen better days. His black braid was held together by a narrow woven band whose ends hung to his waist. I felt a waft of some unidentifiable sour-sweet essence escaping from his mouth followed by a whiff of pungent after-shave lotion.

He didn't apologize for being late. Forty-five Peruvian minutes constituted an infinitesimal drop in the ocean as I had told myself with a mixture of resignation and irritation while sitting in my hotel room.

I waited for him to explain the purpose of our dinner date.

CHAPTER 15

W<small>E</small> went to the pizza place across the park. The pavement under my feet led a life of its own. The rectangular cement blocks heaved and rolled and were occasionally missing altogether which left spaces filled with sand and gravel. I could taste dust rising in the air with every step.

As soon as we approached the entrance to the restaurant we were assailed by a group of noisy, barefooted boys in tattered clothes, all shoving their hands towards me.

I dug into my jeans pocket where I customarily keep change for these occasions. I distributed several coins into each eager hand and gave one a sharp smack when I felt it worming its way into my handbag.

Ivanovich didn't offer coins or acknowledge the children in any way. He just took my arm and propelled me through the door. Waiters in white shirts and black aprons scurried about carrying enough food on each tray to feed ten street children.

"Table for two," Ivanovich ordered and we were shown to a small round table near a window. But there was no view of the street outside or of its poverty-stricken inhabitants. The glass against the closed shutters reflected only the cozy candlelight in the restaurant.

"There are more and more street children each time I come," I said.

"Ah, the piranhas, they are a problem," Ivanovich sighed and picked up the leather-bound menu.

"You mean they *have* a problem," I said. "Sleeping in the streets, sniffing glue, eating out of garbage cans, unwashed, sick, abused. The youngest one out there looked five years old."

Ivanovich glanced up briefly from the menu.

"We all have problems here," he said. "Would you like to share a large pizza?"

I grabbed the menu rather more brusquely than I intended. Piranhas? Of course, I realized it was easy for me to feel righteously upset. I would be leaving for the comforts of home while Ivanovich had to make his financially insecure way in the unstable world of Peru.

"Pizza with anchovies and black olives sounds fine," I said. "And a carafe of house wine."

While we munched on garlic bread, Ivanovich came to the point. He had lost much of his initial haughtiness and took a hearty swallow of wine before speaking.

"I do not know how many more opportunities we will have to talk," he said. "I would like to know whether you have decided to avail yourself of my services as a highly recommended and experienced tour guide for your agency?"

I pondered an adequate response. The fact was I hadn't had time to consider one of the main reasons for my trip to Peru.

As I was turning it over in my mind, he looked at me with a strange expression. I wondered, did I want to hire him or not?

"I am very thoroughly familiar with my own country, of course," he added. "And also with Bolivia, Colombia, Ecuador, and Venezuela."

He practically bowed across the table.

"Andean expert. At your service. I have traveled a lot. I am a real busybody!"

I choked on my wine. I knew I shouldn't laugh but I was hard put to keep a straight face. Busybody, indeed!

"You know what," I said. "I'll give you our preliminary tour schedule for next year. Then let me know which tours you can manage without jeopardizing your work for Mundotours. How does that sound?"

I was surprised to realize I had just offered him a job.

"What do you have scheduled, if I may inquire?" Some life had returned to his eyes.

"There will be twelve tours during the first half year. Lima two nights, Cuzco, Ollantaytambo, the Pisac market and Machu Picchu overnight. Then train to Puno with one day to see the Uru Indians and their floating reed huts, the catamaran across Lake Titicaca, bus to La Paz stopping at Tiahuanacu, and from there back to the States. That's one example of a two-week excursion."

"I am interested," Ivanovich said emphatically.

"Once we have decided how many tours you will manage, we will send you a contract."

The pizza was sizzling hot and we chewed away in silence for a while. Ivanovich ate as if he hadn't seen food in days.

"So, what do you hear about Pablo Alvarez?" I finally said. "Did the police find him?"

Ivanovich stopped chewing.

"I do not know about the police, but it so happened that I did. At the airport this afternoon where I had some business. He stepped off the last flight from Cuzco."

"I'm amazed! What did he say? Why had he disappeared?"

"He said he had no obligation to stay in the hotel, that I had no right to control his movements and, of course, he is right. He said he did not need to explain anything to me. And, of course, he is right."

"You said he's an antique dealer. Does he have a shop?"

"In Miraflores."

"Where?"

"Two blocks from here on Canseca."

That was around the corner from the hotel. I was just wondering whether to ask Ivanovich about a possible connection between Pablo Alvarez and the French embassy when he said:

"Are you investigating the murder case, maybe?"

I decided not to take him into my confidence. Of course, when I answered: "Not at all, I have to be hired by someone in order to start an investigation. I'm leaving this to the police," I knew myself well enough to look away guiltily.

Ivanovich took a furtive look at the bill and agreed to let the pizza and wine be my treat.

I let him walk me back to the hotel and hung around the reception area while I watched him disappear down the street, as usual looking as if he had a sudden urgent appointment.

I went to the middle of the lobby and casually studied a display of crafts making sure Ivanovich wasn't coming back. Then I walked out of the hotel and turned left on Canseca.

As expected, the antique shop was closed. A heavy iron grill was pulled down in front of both door and window. The window was decorated with several dusty looking ceramic vessels sitting on a faded striped poncho. There was an elaborate ceramic cathedral and a colorful *retablo* surrounded by decorated gourds and silver jewelry.

I shadowed my eyes and peered into the dark interior. A faint light seemed to flicker towards the back of the shop. I moved to get a different perspective. A sliver of light came through a curtained doorway. I lifted my hand and knocked on the door through the lattice-work.

Now there was a definite show of light inside. But that was all. No one appeared and I began to feel foolish. I had no business here other than my innate curiosity but as I started to walk away I heard hurried steps around the corner.

Looking down the alley I saw a shadowy figure disappear, no doubt about it, a woman wearing a stove-top hat. There must be hundreds of women in those hats, I reminded myself.

At this point I also heard a voice, sounding curiously like Bob Makowski's, telling me to rein in my imagination.

Another voice, this one sounding like my accountant's, told me to heed the line I had given Ivanovich about not investigating unless someone paid me.

CHAPTER 16

BREAKFAST with the Robinsons was a cumbersome affair.

Sara couldn't walk to the buffet and Stanley had to scurry back and forth to change her orders. Grapefruit juice instead of orange, herbal tea instead of Earl Grey, Danish instead of blueberry muffin.

I had almost finished my orange juice, two slices of toast with guava jam, and coffee, when Stanley Robinson finally sat down to his own burgeoning plate. He shoveled in his food with remarkable concentration and washed it down with great gulps of tea, his face color heightening in the process.

"How's your foot," I asked Sara.

"Much better, thanks," she said. "The bandage I got from the doctor at the clinic did the trick better than all the handkerchiefs and scarves people lent me at Machu Picchu. Imagine the way they ran around to collect them. Even that swarthy man, Mr. Alvarez, helped and when he returned he brought me the large handkershief that held all the others together, and . . . ."

"Returned," I said. "Returned from where?"

Stanley Robinson patted his lips with a handful of paper napkins.

"He didn't return from nowhere. He just went and came back."

I looked at Sara.

"But you just said he returned. Where did he go?"

"He went to get the scarf."

"How long did that take?"

But Sara was more interested in surveying the other guests in the breakfast room.

"I love luxury," she announced to no one in particular.

I contemplated her round, happy face and eyes that darted about the room with disarming curiosity. I tried to revive our conversation.

"So, do you remember how long it took Alvarez to get back to you? You might try it this way: what did you have time to do before he returned?"

Sara finally turned her attention away from the two expensively dressed women at the next table.

"Let me see, dear. I tell you, trying to remember every little situation is very difficult. Stan! Why don't you help me. You were there!"

"So I was there. So I can't remember everything. He left and came back, that's all I know. It couldn't of took more than a few minutes. We was messing around with all those handkerchiefs and took them all off and re-did your foot before he brought us the one that tied it all together."

He looked at me in triumph and pronounced the verdict: "Ten minutes!"

But which ten minutes? Before or after Alvarez had the conversation with Charles Lupesco which seemed to established their mutual alibis?

"We're taking the morning tour of Lima with Mr. Ivanovich," Sara said. "Are you coming with us?"

I explained that I must travel to Cuzco that same afternoon to take care of unfinished business but that I would return tomorrow afternoon. They were to take the tour to Nazca with Mundotours.

I had another cup of coffee before setting off downtown to meet with the chief of police. For some unknown reason, my second meeting with Feliciano Lopez was a lot less pleasant than the first. In fact, he was brief to the point of rudeness. In essence, he only wanted clarifications of a few points in my notes and offered no clue to the way his investigation was going. The only positive information was that the inquest would be in two days, on Thursday.

I took a cab to the airport directly from the police station. The departure hall for domestic flights was overcrowded with a volatile mass of people shoving and pushing.

I elbowed my way to the counter where I won my argument with the airline employee to the effect that I did, indeed, have a confirmed reservation. And, yes, my ticket had been issued this very day by their very own office in town. I stared down a man in a limp business suit with a shopworn briefcase who had no reservation but who, nevertheless, was on the verge of usurping my seat.

I raised my voice, waved my ticket, invoked higher authorities, and the airline official retreated. Instead, she bumped three Indian women from the flight. They took it without a murmur and returned to their bulky belongings which were stacked against the wall wrapped in striped shawls. I boarded the flight feeling responsible even though it wasn't my fault.

I made my way down the aisle towards my seat in row 26 but only got as far as row 20, where my eyes met those of Pablo Alvarez. He sat at the window next to an empty seat.

I slid into the aisle seat, planted my overnight bag on the floor, searched successfully for my seatbelt, snapped it in place, and leaned back to smile at the captive Pablo Alvarez.

"Señor Alvarez! What a pleasant surprise!"

He didn't exactly look pleasantly surprised. And he looked different. A recent haircut had eliminated the thick curls at the nape of his neck, making him look oddly vulnerable. His mustache had been trimmed as well and he seemed not quite as self-assured as he had looked heading into the French ambassador's residence in San Isidro.

"It seems you've taken his seat," he said and pointed to a reedy youth in jeans and a brown alpaca sweater with stylized llamas, who squinted at his boarding pass and then at the numbers above my seat.

I searched in my pocket and brought out my assignment to 26A.

"Here," I said and offered him the card. "I'm sure you won't mind swapping places with me. You'll get a window seat!" I pointed to Alvarez. "We'd like to sit together!"

The youth scooted happily down to 26A even before the passengers behind him had a chance to become impatient.

I beamed at Alvarez whose Latin chivalry prevailed.

"I am honored, Señora," he said faintly.

Once we were airborne Alvarez relaxed in his seat and, after drinks were served, took two large swallows of neat whisky.

I took a sip of coffee and contemplated his lumpy profile.

"What did you think of the murder, Mr. Alvarez, it must have upset you?"

"Sure, it upset me." He looked out the window and swirled the whisky around in his glass.

"You disappeared pretty fast once we reached Cuzco!" I said, knowing him well enough by now not to expect an explanation. And sure enough, he ignored me completely.

I took another tack.

"I could use some advice on where to take other groups in Cuzco. Maybe antiquing," I said tentatively.

Alvarez straightened up.

"I could take you around to a couple of shops in Cuzco. How long will you be there?" he said.

"Just until tomorrow afternoon. I imagine you'll be going back yourself for the inquest Thursday morning?"

"Of course."

"What was your impression of Ms. Bronski," I said.

"I had no impression of Ms. Bronski."

"I remember you saying you spent the time when the murder

was presumably committed in the company of Mr. Lupesco. I wonder at which point you brought another handkerchief for Mrs. Robinson's ankle?"

Pablo Alvarez leaned back in his seat and closed his eyes. I kept my gaze fixed on him until his eyelids flickered and he squinted at me.

"Yes?" I said.

"Listen." Now he looked me full in the face and there was some steel in his voice. "I have discussed this with the police, they told me not to talk to anyone. Nothing personal." He tried to disarm me with an unexpected smile. "But if you want me to show you antique shops in Cuzco, I am at your service. Antiques are more satisfying, wouldn't you say? I am staying at Las Cruces."

"So am I," I heard myself saying, hoping that would turn out to be all right with Las Cruces, and with the Regina Inca where I had made reservations.

"I'll be free first thing in the morning," I said.

CHAPTER 17

HE met me in the lobby of Las Cruces at eight-thirty. I had spent the previous afternoon and early evening placating the management of the Regina Inca by making reservations for twelve tour groups starting in early spring. I had mapped out a walking tour of Cuzco and had persuaded the ticket offices at two museums and a church to charge local fees instead of the triple price usually demanded of tourists.

Alvarez took me walking from the hotel across the Plaza de Armas towards the Museum of Religious Art.

The sun was just gaining power but, as always, the air was cool, crisp, and insufficient. We walked along streets paved with finely hewn stones and bordered by colossal stone walls, even more impressive than those at Machu Picchu.

Indian women in long black wool skirts, flat red hats, and large bundles tied across their shoulders, hurried past us with purposeful steps and at a much faster pace than I could muster in the thin air.

Indian men, barefoot in their sturdy car-tire sandals, their backs painfully bent and eyes fixed on the ground, carried even larger burdens than the women.

We made our way up a steep terraced street past houses painted bright yellow, bright pink, and bright green, under overhanging balconies and red, tiled roofs.

Alvarez stopped and knocked on a richly carved wooden door.

The door squeaked open into a dark interior.

The woman in the doorway smiled broadly. One front tooth was missing. She wasn't wearing her white stove-top hat but otherwise she was the same.

Had she really been in Lima last night?

"This is Gomercinda. Gomercinda Flores." Alvarez motioned for me to step through the door and Gomercinda extended a pudgy hand which enveloped mine in a strong grip.

"I remember you," I said and stepped into a small dark corridor from the end of which three steps led down to a large room. The white-washed walls were covered with gilded crosses, carved wooden panels, dark paintings in elaborate frames, and glass shelves with pre-Hispanic pottery and sacrificial knives. The floor space was usurped by chests laden with woven ponchos in muted colors, and carved chairs with high backs and brocade seats.

From there we entered room upon room with colonial and pre-Hispanic antiques and one with more contemporary crafts: carved gourds, alpaca rugs, ceramic churches, decorated candles, and nativity scenes.

Gomercinda stayed in the background and let me look around. Then she smiled her toothless grin and led us into a studio at the back.

"My son, Jesus!" she said and pointed to a young man in a white shirt and stained pants sitting at an easel. He was putting the finishing touches to an "antique" painting of a Spanish caballero in a black suit and hat and a ruche of white lace around the wrists. There were scores of paintings leaning against the walls around the small studio, some already in gilded frames.

"Good business!" I exclaimed and coughed. The smell of turpentine was overwhelming.

"We sell genuine reproductions," Gomercinda said. "Jesus is an artist."

Jesus nodded briefly in my direction and continued to paint quite unperturbed by his mother's praise.

"I remember seeing you at Machu Picchu," I said as I followed Gomercinda out of the studio.

"Si, Señora," she said placidly.

"Do you have a stand at the train station up there?" I tried again.

"No, Señora."

Gomercinda then explained in a monotone that she would give me a fifteen percent commission on all purchases made by my group members. I thought briefly that I'd have to warn them it was illegal to remove genuine pre-Columbian antiques from Peru. Always supposing that *any* of Gomercinda's antiques were genuine.

"Do you ever get to Lima?" I asked on the way back to the front door.

She glanced at Alvarez who raised his shoulders in a non-committal way.

"Si, Señora, sometimes."

She shut the door behind us and our visit was over rather abruptly.

Alvarez walked me back to the hotel at a brisk clip, a bit faster than proved good for my breathing.

"Quite a character, your friend Gomercinda," I tried for the last time as I hurried along beside him. "Is she a relative of yours?"

"No, Señora."

"I had a chance to visit with Ms. Bronski's sister yesterday," I said and watched his face from the side. He didn't answer but speeded up.

"Did you know that her sister happens to be the wife of the French ambassador?"

The expression on Alvarez' face didn't change. He just kept walking and lifted his hand in greeting to an elderly man standing outside the hotel. When that exchange was over he was five steps ahead of me and had successfully avoided my question.

Out of breath and somewhat tired of the one-syllable answers I'd been getting all morning, I excused myself as we entered the lobby and went upstairs to collect my bag before heading to the airport.

I told myself I should leave it to the police in Lima as I had been requested to do several times.

But, really, where did Gomercinda find her antiques and where, for that matter, did Alvarez?

And what had Alvarez been doing on the tour to Machu Picchu? He was no tourist.

And what had Gomercinda been doing at the ruins?

And, last, but not least, what business did Alvarez have at the French Ambassador's residence?

CHAPTER 18

FELICIANO Lopez, Chief of Police, stood with me near the exit from the court house where the inquest into Ms. Bronski's murder had just wound up. I squinted against the mid-morning sun, waiting for Ivanovich, the Robinsons, and Vicky Anderson. Pablo Alvarez bounded down the stairs two steps at a time and disappeared without so much as a nod to anyone. Dr. and Sra. Hernandez came out trailing behind the Ambassador and Therese Lecroix.

The conclusion of the court had been first degree pre-meditated murder by person or persons unknown. The body, accompanied by the French ambassador and his wife as the next of kin, would be transferred to Washington, D.C. for burial. The police in Peru would continue their investigations.

"I don't understand," I said to the chief. "Weren't you expecting everyone from the tour group to be present at this inquest?"

"Of course, Señora," Lopez said. "Except under extenuating circumstances. The gentleman, Mr. Lupesco, from the United Nations left Wednesday morning. He traveled on a diplomatic passport and we could not insist he stay."

Lopez' car was being driven up at the curb and he started walking.

"And the two padres?" I speeded up next to him. "Why weren't they here?"

Lopez, halfway into the back of his chauffeur-driven car, shook his head.

"They should have been here. I have no explanation right now. But, believe me, I'll find out!"

"And fingerprints?" I shouted. "What about fingerprints on the murder weapon, did you find any?"

"No," he shouted back. "No, we did not!" And his black Chevrolet drove off in a cloud of exhaust fumes.

At the inquest, Dr. Hernandez had given himself haughty importance as the chief medical authority at the scene of a murder without mentioning my role. During my own testimony I had deflated his self-made image somewhat and he now brushed past me without a second look.

Vicky Anderson had given the judge a dramatic account of her discovery of the body. She was still on a high from the excitement.

"How did I do?" she exclaimed. "I thought, oh, m'God, I don't want to make a fool of myself in Spanish, that's why I had written down my statement."

"You did fine," I said and waited for the Robinsons and Ivanovich to reach me. Sara Robinson's foot was noticeably better.

"I'm getting a cab back to the Cesar," I said.

"We'll join you." Stanley Robinson looked flushed and wiped his forehead.

"How about you, Vicky?" I said. "Would you like to have lunch with me at the hotel?" I looked into Vicky's shiny eyes and she nodded eagerly.

Ivanovich said he had business to transact and disappeared into a separate taxi.

Back at the hotel the Robinsons decided to have a late lunch and went upstairs to their room. I sat down with Vicky in the breakfast room which had now been converted into the luncheon room with linen tablecloths and napkins and a buffet with layered cakes and a huge fruit salad.

When the waiter had taken our orders Vicky put her elbows on the table and I could tell something confidential was about to come my way.

"Charles Lupesco called me last night!" Vicky's milky-white face flushed easily. "He wants me to visit him in New York."

"And are you going to?"

"Do you think I should?"

"It's not for me to say. But it seemed to me you two hit if off on the trip . . ."

"He's rather dreamy, don't you think? I just loved his accent, didn't you? So European, so gentlemanly."

I attacked my grilled swordfish. "Did he tell you how long he has worked in New York?"

"A year, I think. He says he doesn't have a lot of friends yet." Vicky dug into her fettuccini and salsa con carne. "I've decided to go visit him on spring break in three weeks."

"Sounds like fun. The police didn't say they still needed you here?"

"No!!" Vicky looked startled. "Why would they?"

"No reason, I guess. I was just wondering how they mean to solve the case."

"Well, I'm sure I don't know. All I did was find her and I can tell you I still wake up at night in a sweat."

"So, you haven't remembered anything additional about the time you were sitting out there admiring the view? You're sure you didn't see anyone?"

Vicky mopped up the last of the tomato sauce with a piece of bread and stuffed it in her mouth.

"Quite sure," she said definitively and declined both dessert and coffee, suddenly in a hurry.

I signed the bill, left a tip, and watched Vicky as she departed by the direct exit from the restaurant to the street. She disappeared into a beat-up Volkswagen Beetle with a hand-made taxi sign perched on the dashboard. One of those moonlighting taxis I avoid.

84

I spent the rest of the afternoon at the offices of Mundotours planning two excursions in Lima proper for the spring tours. At eight-thirty in the evening I departed for the airport to catch the night flight to Miami.

CHAPTER 19

"WHAT!? You mean you didn't know?"

Five pairs of eyes stared at me across the dining room table.

I felt myself flush.

Dinner at Topsy and Jack Bannister's was usually a mixed pleasure for me since Jack is a Republican with some—to me—strange notions about women's choice, equal rights, and so forth. But I tolerate him because of Topsy and, in truth, apart from his conservatism he's a nice enough guy who worships the ground she walks on and does more than his share in the house.

The guests around the table mostly turn out to be interesting although Topsy has this weird idea that she cannot invite a single woman without securing a similar male to even out the score. I've told her *ad nauseam* how antiquated this attitude strikes me.

Nevertheless, when I arrived at their house I found myself paired off with Walter D. Hughes III, a partner in one of Jack's rival law firms. The other guests consisted of an art dealer and his decorator wife whom I'd met on a previous occasion.

"Jamie just returned from Peru this morning," Topsy had said as we were finishing dessert. "We're introducing tours to Machu Picchu."

"We've been there," the decorator said, "fabulous view, impressive stone work."

"Overrated art work," her husband said. "And don't try to take out anything pre-Columbian. Not that there isn't a tremendous illegal trade both here and in Europe. But they only catch the slow-witted tourists."

"So, did everything go according to plan?" Topsy asked. I knew she was just trying to keep the conversation moving and I didn't mind helping.

"Not really," I said. "One of our tour members got herself murdered on the mountaintop."

I wouldn't say their jaws actually dropped, but just about, and I immediately felt bad about using Ms. Bronski as a story to dine out on.

"Murdered!" Topsy waved her spoon in the air. "Who was it? Why didn't you tell me? Couldn't you have called me from Peru?"

"I tried," I said, "but you weren't in, and I didn't want to leave that kind of a message on the answering machine."

Walter D. Hughes III, who looked like Woodrow Wilson, blinked his practically bald eyelids behind his gold-rimmed glasses and stared at me strangely.

"It wouldn't have been a Miss Elsa Bronski, by any chance?" he said.

This time the jaw that dropped was mine.

"Huh? How on earth did you know? I thought it hadn't reached the papers yet."

Walter Hughes carefully scooped up the last of his peach Melba before answering.

"Well," he finally said smugly. "Without divulging any confidentiality, I can tell you I'm the executor of her estate. I received notice two days ago from her sister in Peru that they're bringing the body back to Washington this week for burial. It seems providential that you can now fill me in on what happened."

I was stunned.

I don't believe in such coincidences, but there it was. And

even stranger than that, why would Elsa Bronski need such a high-powered executor?

"I've heard of her," Topsy exclaimed and looked at me. "You don't know who she was, do you?"

"I thought I did!"

"No, seriously. It was all over the newspapers a couple of years ago."

"What was?"

"She inherited an ungodly amount of money from this woman she'd been nursing for forty years!"

"Thirty-five years, and it was only ten million," said Hughes. "The rest went to charity."

The decorator and her art dealer husband nodded in concurrence.

And that's when they all turned to stare at me.

"I must have been out of the country," I said lamely.

"And she wasn't really equipped to handle so much wealth," Hughes said and looked down his nose.

That was probably true, I thought, as I struggled to revise my false interpretation of Elsa Bronski's situation and to wonder why Therese Lecroix had failed to mention the hefty inheritance.

"How did it happen?" the art dealer asked.

"She was stabbed to death with her own knitting needle in an ancient torture chamber," I said. "I'm actually surprised it didn't reach the papers here."

"Well," Hughes said, "Unfortunately it will, sooner or later."

"So, who gets her money?" Topsy asked.

"Confidential information," he said.

"Probably her sister," I said, ignoring him. "Her name is Therese Lecroix."

"Why have you spoken to *her*?" Hughes looked at me disapprovingly.

"You don't know Jamie," Topsy said. "Always getting involved in her other job as a private investigator."

"*Private investigator*?" Now Hughes looked at me not only with disapproval but with some mixture of distaste and reservation that I was unable to gauge.

"I thought you were just a travel agent," he added. He might as well have said "just a housewife." Honestly, in this day and age. Another of Topsy's match-making attempts down the drain for more reasons than one.

"So, there you see," Topsy trampled on, "there's more to Jamie than meets the eye."

"Mmm." Hughes was silent before addressing me again.

"Any idea who did it?"

"The police told me not to discuss my findings with anyone. They are still investigating."

This wasn't strictly true but I didn't care for his patronizing manner towards his late client and, so, with a mental bow to the memory of Ms. Bronski, I decided to withhold further details of her death and the subsequent events. An example of what Topsy so charmingly labels my pigheadedness.

The dinner party broke up and I wasn't sorry to see Hughes disappear in his black Mercedes.

The next day was Saturday and I kept a luncheon date with my mother—Ellen Prescott, Esq.—who met me on the doorstep of her house. It's a three-story red brick townhouse on P Street in Georgetown and is not strictly my childhood home.

My mother moved here after my father died, and after I had married and moved to France. My mother had just been accepted to law school. She was fifty and had decided to start the career she had missed early on. My father was twenty years her senior and she had given up her studies to marry as a good woman did in those days. But, as she herself says, the sequence of events really doesn't matter as long as you get it all together in the end. And she certainly did.

I handed over a bouquet of yellow tulips, my mother's favorite flower, and followed her into the kitchen where a light lunch stood ready to be served in the dining room.

My mother's home is strictly Danish. Royal Copenhagen

porcelain, George Jensen silver, and furniture and paintings from the old country. There is always dinner by candlelight, classical music playing softly, food attractively displayed.

After lunch we settled down in the living room over coffee and her famous butter cookies.

"And what's happening in the world of immigration?" I asked.

My mother laughed and reached out to retrieve her knitting from a basket under a low table next to the sofa.

I watched in dread fascination. The steel needles glittered and wound their way in and out of the wool as my mother recounted some of the horrendous experiences of her clients.

"Where did you get those knitting needles?" I said.

"Oh, they're ancient, they're from Europe, you've seen them before. I've had them all my life. Steel. Handle so much better than plastic except you have to be careful with the sharp points." The needles clicked sharply. "Why the sudden interest? Surely you're not taking up knitting?" She laughed at our family joke. As a child I had been better known for handling hammers and saws and building tree houses.

"No, I'm not taking up knitting," I confirmed.

And I told her the story of Elsa Bronski.

"I can't believe it!" My mother thrust her knitting away. "And I must say, you have a remarkable talent for getting in the way of mysterious incidents, not to mention murders. Who could have done it, any idea? It certainly sounds as if it was one of the people in the group."

"Yes, and everyone has an alibi. Someone is obviously lying. When I find the motive, I'll know."

I thought of Pablo Alvarez disappearing into the French ambassador's residence.

"I'll go to the funeral," I said.

"Are you investigating?" my mother asked.

"Not at all!"

CHAPTER 20

THERESE Lecroix stood flanked by her husband and Walter D. Hughes III, at the far end of the funeral parlor in front of the flower-bedecked casket.

Small groups of people stood about, some talking in hushed voices without smiling, others speaking louder as if taking advantage of an unexpected social occasion. They lowered the volume only when they happened to remember where they were.

The ambassador was in black pinstripe with a discreet gray silk tie and a pair of gold links at the cuffs of his starched, white shirt.

Therese wore the black dress I had seen her in at the residence in Lima. She exuded Parisian chic, with diamond earrings, a diamond ring and a glittering jewel on her left shoulder.

She looked surprised to see me although I don't know why. The funeral had been announced in the *Washington Post* and, not only that, the headlines had been quite sensational.

"Thank you for coming, Miss Prescott," she said and held my hand with the clasp of a drowning woman. "Thank you for coming."

"Yes, indeed," Walter Hughes said. "I had no idea Ms. Bronski was this popular."

I looked around the crowded room and saw a group of women and men who could easily be pictured behind the counters of various deli, dry-cleaner, shoemaker, and bakery establishments. Off to one side was a cluster of women who might be neighbors. I moved over to join them, looking for someone young enough to have a six-year old named Toby. I found her in a short, dark-haired woman who introduced herself as Geraldine Harris.

"Your son came to say goodbye to Ms. Bronski the day we left for Peru," I explained. "He asked her to bring him an elephant."

"Yes, he told me. I don't know how to explain this to him. He absolutely loved Elsa. I just can't believe what's happened. And to think that I made fun of her premonitions."

"Premonitions?"

"Well, you know, superstitions. She was always imagining things that had nothing to do with reality."

"What kind of things?"

"You know, thinking someone was following her or that she was seeing a 'ghost', as she called it."

"Yes, that's exactly what she said to me when we ate lunch together at Machu Picchu. I didn't know what to make of it," I said.

"If I were you, I wouldn't try to make anything of it."

"But did she ever say whom she was expecting to see? Was it someone she was afraid of?"

"No, no. Not afraid. More like she wanted to see the one she called the 'ghost'. As if she was nostalgic for someone. I used to think it was a long-lost lover." Geraldine Harris looked at me somewhat defiantly. "She must have been beautiful when she was young."

I nodded in agreement remembering Elsa Bronski's lovely blue eyes.

"She was just too good," Geraldine Harris went on. "So unselfish, always ready to help, treated my son real well." She thought for a moment."Mind you, she could also take a violent dislike to someone. And, when she did, she was quite implacable."

"Anyone in particular?"

"No, no. Just in general." She turned around to talk to a couple of other women, and I checked my watch.

I realized I had to leave in order to pick up my film downtown before going to my Women's Defense Class at five-thirty. The film lab is located on Pennsylvania Avenue near H Street and is the one Bob Makowski uses. They can be relied upon for sharp details and close-ups.

I said goodbye to the Lecroixs and Walter Hughes, and left.

The next morning I spread out on my dining room table the 36 photographs of Ms. Bronski's face, body, chest, knitting needle, red wool, and her handbag next to her dangling feet.

I studied each picture carefully but, of course, could find no special significance in any of them that would point to the murderer. They simply constituted a minute record of a gruesome act.

The telephone rang just after eleven.

Therese Lecroix's voice was raspy but firm.

"I am in the office of Mr. Hughes, my sister's attorney," she said. "I am wondering if you could possibly join us. Something has occurred which I would like you to hear."

"Hold on a second," I said while I took the portable phone with me into the den. I flipped down the top of my desk which is built into the bookshelf unit, pulled up a chair, and poised my pen above a yellow legal pad.

"Mrs. Lecroix, let me speak to Mr. Hughes, please."

"Yes, but before you do I wish to ask you . . . I want to hire you to investigate my sister's death."

When I didn't answer immediately she continued: "I have just now sent you a check by special messenger, a retainer you call it, no? You should receive it within half an hour. Five thousand dollars. I hope that is satisfactory. Please, Madame, say you will do it!"

Before I could react, the telephone at the other end changed hands.

"Ms. Prescott, er, Jamie, Walter Hughes here. Before you make up your mind maybe you should come over to my office to get the facts. If Mrs. Lecroix still wants to go ahead, she can do so later."

"May I ask if you are acting on behalf of Mrs. Lecroix or as the executor of Ms. Bronski's estate?"

"As the latter," he said smoothly, "and I'm advising Mrs. Lecroix in that capacity."

"But only as far as the money, not as far as the murder." I paused. "Would you put Mrs. Lecroix back on the line, please."

I heard a muted conversation on the other end and then Therese Lecroix spoke.

"Oui?"

"Mrs. Lecroix. I'll wait for the messenger and then I'll be on my way to Mr. Hughes' office. It will take me half an hour from that point on. But we need to talk before I make a commitment, okay?"

"Oui, oui, but hurry!"

"I will. Just relax and wait for me. Maybe you shouldn't discuss this any further until I get there."

"Very well. I understand."

The telephone clicked and she was gone.

CHAPTER 21

I waded across the thick carpeting as if through sand.

The receptionist got on the phone and almost immediately a tall woman in a severe dark suit came to escort me to Walter Hughes' office.

He was seated in a high-backed leather chair behind a solid mahogany desk almost completely devoid of paper. A shiny chrome stick-figure sculpture had just hit an invisible golf ball. There was one telephone with a battery of buttons but no computer hardware.

Walter Hughes got up and shook my hand across the desk.

Therese Lecroix was sitting on the edge of a chair and jumped up when I came in. Looking as elegant as ever, she extended her well-manicured hand and shook mine firmly.

"Madame, you received my retainer?"

"I did."

"And you will investigate?"

"Why don't we sit down and you tell me what brought this on," I said. "I thought the police were investigating?"

Therese pursed her lips in dismission and wafted her hands around in a Gallic flurry.

"The estate cannot be settled because of the fact of the murder investigation," Walter Hughes said stiffly.

"And there's one other problem," Therese said.

"As I've just informed Mrs. Lecroix," Hughes said, "Ms. Bronski had not had a chance to sign the codicil to her will which would have added Mrs. Lecroix as one of the beneficiaries. She had indicated to me just before this unfortunate trip that she would sign the papers upon her return. Alas, that was not to be."

Hughes swivelled left and right in his chair, looking too smug, I thought, considering he had just dealt a rather devastating blow to his late client's sister.

"I take it you were also the executor of Mrs. Douglas' estate?" I said.

He nodded briefly.

"But she was my sister," said Therese, "and she told me I was to inherit almost everything. She wanted to leave some funds for two charities, she didn't say which, but the bulk of it was to be mine."

Hughes got up.

"You would have to submit such a claim through the proper courts, Mrs. Lecroix. For that you would need your own legal counsel."

Therese and I got up simultaneously. She squared her shoulders and shook off whatever indecision had been there before. We shook hands with Hughes and the same woman who had shown me in appeared on cue to take us back to the reception.

We waded towards the exit and the elevator.

"We could go back to my house and discuss this further," I said and pressed the button to the garage.

"Yes, that will be fine. My husband has gone out for the day and I'm free until six."

"Where are you staying?"

"At the Mayflower, just across the street."

"I'll get you back here long before six."

In Bethesda I fixed a quick lunch of quiche, Caesar salad, and glasses of chilled white wine which we consumed without discussing either murders or wills.

After lunch I left Therese for a few minutes while I got on the intercom to the travel agency downstairs to make sure they didn't need me, and returned to serve coffee in the living room.

"Now, tell me all about it." I looked at Therese over the rim of my cup.

She rummaged through her Louis Vuitton handbag and came up with a pack of Gauloise cigarettes and a small silver lighter. She looked around in vain for an ashtray.

I shook my head.

"Afraid there are no ashtrays." I looked at her hand which held a trembling cigarette to her lips and felt almost sorry for her. "I'm so sorry, but this is a smoke-free house."

"*Zut,*" she coughed with that tell-tale nicotine rumble. "I forget about you Americans. We Europeans have no self-discipline, we change more slowly, we don't care if we all die of emphysema!"

She put away the cigarette and looked around the room rather desperately.

"I sympathize," I said. "Maybe I can offer you a Remy Martin or an Amontillado instead?"

"Amontillado," she said, drained the first glass and held it out for a re-fill. I shuddered as she gulped down a second helping of the dreadful stuff.

She put down the glass.

"George does not know," she said. "But I am going to leave him."

I stared.

"Elsa saw what is happening to me, she understood immediately, and that is why she was leaving me money. She wrote that she had already put me in her will. She also said she would give me an advance of two hundred and fifty thousand dollars so I could re-establish my practice in Paris."

"Very generous."

"Yes, but she wanted me to divorce George first, she was afraid he would take control of the money. And quite right. She did not like George."

"I can tell!"

"But now I am very much afraid." Her hand reached instinctively for her bag with the cigarettes, and she looked flustered.

"What if it takes years before I get the money? You would probably argue I could just leave, return to Paris, seek any hospital position, rent a tiny inadequate apartment, travel on the Metro, sell my jewelry to survive the first six months, but be free."

"No, why should you? Surely you have earned half of George's income over how many years? Ten? Twelve? How much did you give up? Eighty thousand a year, net? Well, there you have it. Take off thirty thousand a year for 'maintenance' and you should walk away with half a million. You've earned it the old-fashioned way!"

Therese leaned back in the sofa and, whether it was the liqueur or my elegant speech, she gave herself up to a loud explosive laugh.

"Mon Dieu? This is exactly what Elsa said! It is strange, is it not, but she had been in the same position without being married. She had been a housekeeper, companion, and nursemaid for that Mrs. Douglas her whole life. True, she had her salary and she could close her door behind her at night. Still, she was a dependent. And when she finally got her reward she did not live to enjoy it."

Therese paused and added emphatically: "I do not wish such an end for myself."

"So, what will you do now?"

The Amontillado had put two hectic blotches in Therese's cheeks and loosened up her smile in tandem with long strands of hair at her temples.

"Divorce George. Return to Paris, maybe find a staff position at my old hospital. Find a lawyer to contest Elsa's will. And have *you* solve the murder. Voila!"

I got up and moved towards the den.

"In that case, I have a letter of agreement for you to sign," I said. "My fee is five hundred a day plus expenses. You have given me a retainer of five thousand which will carry me through ten days. I will need a ticket to Peru, my hotel and per diem for food and transportation, say another two thousand. Depending on how many days I need there, I'll let you know when I need another advance."

Therese nodded in agreement and twirled her diamond ring around just below the bony knuckle. Then she sat down at my desk, pulled out a new green-speckled Mont Blanc fountain pen and signed the letter of agreement with a flourish and a determined dot over the i.

Then she made out a check.

"From my New York checking account," she said and stood up. "Elsa gave me a gift. She transferred a hundred thousand dollars the day before she left for Peru. George does not know, and neither does Mr. Hughes."

But Hughes soon would, I thought.

CHAPTER 22

T HE Robinsons lived in a comfortable Maryland town house on a dead end street off Rockville Pike, just south of Rockville proper, a twenty minute drive from Bethesda.

I parked in front of the house and contemplated the bright red front door with its shiny brass knocker.

Yesterday, after returning Therese Lecroix to the Mayflower and her charming husband, I had sat down to make a list of priorities and a listing of all the individuals I had met or observed as either directly or indirectly connected with Elsa Bronski.

First of all, naturally, the members of the tour group. Sara and Stanley Robinson, Charles Lupesco, Vicky Anderson, the two padres, Dr. and Sra. Hernandez, Pablo Alvarez, and Ivanovich.

The list had grown a little longer as I added Therese and George Lecroix and Gomercinda Flores of the white top hat from Cuzco.

To sources of information I had added Geraldine Harris.

And then there was Walter Hughes III.

I had made an appointment to see the Robinsons and here I was. I let the metal knocker fall smartly.

"How are you, how are you?" Sara Robinson was all delight and surprise and curiosity. "Never thought we'd see *you* again!"

"Well, here I am!" I looked around the overstuffed living room. The impression was brown. Brown checkered upholstery on matching sofas, a dark brown recliner. Wallpaper in two tones of brown stripes alternating with silver, and matching draperies. Thick brown and gold contoured wall-to-wall carpeting.

"We have told everyone about you," Sara gushed, "how you ordered all of us around and told the police what to do. Bert and Sonia, that's Stan's brother and his wife, they live next door, we bought at the same time twenty-five years ago so our kids could play and we'd be close, we play Canasta twice a week. Well, Bert and Sonia said they want to meet you, they'll be home at five, can you wait?"

"I'll try," I said and looked around at the walls which were hung with oil paintings of winter and summer landscapes framed in dark wood. A shelf above the recliner was crammed with souvenirs. It appeared at a hasty glance that the Robinsons had visited Disneyland, the Statue of Liberty, the Eiffel Tower, and at least one Caribbean island. Their recent trip to Peru and Bolivia had rendered carved gourds, ceramic churches, and dolls in ponchos.

Stanley Robinson reclined his chair and said: "So, did they find out who did it?"

"The police apparently have not made a break in the case," I said carefully. "But you may remember that Elsa Bronski had a sister in Lima."

"Yes, yes, the ambassador's wife!"

"Therese Lecroix," I said. "What's happened is that she has hired me to look into the death of Ms. Bronski. So, I'm here to ask you a few more questions, if you don't mind."

Stan tipped forward in the recliner as if on command, and Sara sat down on the edge of the checkered sofa, her feet primly together, her hands clasped in her lap.

We went over the sequence of events one more time. There was no big variation except that the details were becoming blurred. As Stan said, the entire trip seemed like a bad dream which had taken place ages ago.

"Now," I said at last in desperation, "you're sure you didn't notice from where Pablo Alvarez 'returned' when he left you and came back with another handkerchief for your foot?"

Stanley looked at Sara for several long seconds and then shifted his gaze towards the ceiling. He shook his head imperceptibly.

Sara twisted her hands until they looked like white puckered dough. She shuttled back and forth on her seat.

I leaned towards her.

"It's just that I remembered something after we left you in Lima," she said. "But then we never talked to the police again and Stan said it would make no difference anyhow, and I thought, why make trouble for such a nice young man. It was nothing. Even as I speak, I think why do I even bring it to your attention . . ."

"There you go rattling on anyway, Sara, just count me out. I didn't see nothing."

Sam leaned back in his chair and snapped the footrest up with a bang. He stared out the window and patted the top of his head gingerly.

I concentrated on Sara who'd had thirty-five years experience ignoring her husband.

"You see," she said and unclasped her hands, "it was like this. We'd just come out of the torture chamber where Ms. Bronski was still standing by herself looking at the three seats with those horrible holes where they put the hands of the people before they began to torture them. And there was all that gravel on the ground, really, they ought to sweep it clean, next time someone will break a leg and not be lucky like me, it was only a sprain."

Sara stretched out her foot to demonstrate that her ankle was slim again.

I opened my mouth to get her back on track but Sara was still on it notwithstanding her digressions.

"Anyways," she said, "there I was on my hands and knees and then on my side with my leg twisted under me. Stan helped me up and I hobbled to a little staircase, so strange with a staircase in the middle of nowhere, I remember thinking, but then of course everything up there was in ruins . . ."

"Sara," I exclaimed, but I couldn't staunch the flow of words.

"So, there I am on the staircase with Stan on his knees in front of me and all of the people from the group so nice suddenly, even that Peruvian doctor, he told them to give me their handkerchiefs, although he didn't have one himself, but his wife did, and the two priests and also the tour guide . . . ."

My throat was beginning to hurt from the effort of restraining myself while Sara forged ahead with her extraneous details, oblivious to the agony of suspense she was creating in me.

"So, anyways, there I was leaning back on my elbows on the upper step, there were only four in all anyway, with Stan at my feet, when I see that nice young European gentleman, he had the same last name as that actress, you remember her, Ida was her name, Ida Lupesco . . ."

"Lupino, Sara, her name was Ida Lupino," Sam said from his superior position in the recliner.

"Oh, well, that's how I still remember his name, I do that, try to associate by using famous names, and I got that from one of those women's magazines at the hairdresser's, you know, telling you how you can improve your memory by associating . . . ."

"Mrs. Robinson!" I practically shouted. "What was it you saw that involved Mr. Lupesco?"

"As I said, there I was sitting on the staircase looking across Stanley's back, waiting for more scarves or handkerchiefs, when Mr. Lupesco comes out in the open from behind that wall to the torture chamber, not from the doorway, mind you, but from behind the wall, and walks towards me."

I moaned audibly.

"And just a few seconds later that other man, Pablo—I remember his name because it made me think of the man at the hardware store in the shopping center, his name is Pablo Gonzalez—this Pablo comes out from behind the same wall. He sort of hurried until he caught up with Mr. Lupesco. Then they came over together and Pablo gave me a large handkerchief."

"Now she's gonna ask you how many minutes that took!" Stanley looked at me as if he'd just remembered a mutual joke.

Sara didn't wait for me to ask.

"Well, you know, it's hard to tell, I didn't sit there in the middle of nowhere in horrible pain counting any minutes."

I finally found my tongue.

"But do you remember seeing them outside the torture chamber before you fell?"

Sara squeezed her eyes shut and when she opened them she shook her head.

"No, not really."

"Well, let's say it must have taken at least five minutes for your husband to help you up and another five minutes to start the bandaging . . ."

"I told ya!" Stan bellowed.

"Probably ten minutes, then," Sara said and watched as I wrote it all down in my notebook. "So, what do you make of it? I hope I haven't made trouble for that nice Mr. Lupesco . . ."

"I'm sure you haven't," I said and got up to leave.

"No, no, wait, you must stay for coffee, it's ready, and you could wait until Bert and Sonia get here, they won't be long."

"So sorry, but I'm afraid I must get back to work. Give them my regards, though, and thank you for taking the time to speak to me."

Stanley descended from his seat and, reluctantly, Sara let me go.

Just as I pulled out from my parking space a large white Chevrolet ambled up, passed me, and waited to back into my space. I saw Sara Robinson in my rearview mirror waving and shouting, but I was already on my way to the corner of Rockville Pike feeling only the slightest pang of remorse for depriving her of her five minutes of glory in front of Bert and Sonia.

So, unless Sara was confusing the sequence of events, Lupesco and Alvarez had covered for each other.

Now, why would they have done that? They supposedly didn't know one another. And Dr. Hernandez and the padres had confirmed that both Alvarez and Lupesco were present all the time. How could they all have been mistaken?

Even Ivanovich had confirmed their presence but I distinctly remembered him saying he bandaged Sara Robinson's leg because he found Stanley, in a word, clumsy. Wouldn't Ivanovich then have had his back to the rest of the group members those ten minutes?

I felt a rush of adrenaline as I swung into the driveway in front of my house.

Then I went upstairs and called Bob Makowski.

CHAPTER 23

"HERE'S to Peru," Archibald Brewster said and raised his glass of red Burgundy.

I clinked my glass to his and took a long satisfying sip, letting the ruby liquid roll around my tongue before swallowing. Somewhat to my surprise, here I was, sitting opposite Archibald Brewster at a small corner table in a dimly lit restaurant in Chevy Chase.

"To Peru!" I echoed and took another sip.

I had been downstairs all morning making airline reservations, issuing my ticket, and faxing the Cesar Miraflores to reserve a room. I had called Therese Lecroix to announce my arrival two days hence. She had barely arrived in Lima herself and sounded cheerful although our conversation didn't touch upon my investigation.

"So, how did it go, have you heard from that gorgeous Archibald Brewster yet?" Topsy had asked when we sat in my dining room having a quick sandwich and coffee for lunch.

Before I could answer, the telephone had rung and when I heard his voice I was grateful for the invention of portable phones.

"Yes, of course I remember you," I had said and repaired to the den, leaving Topsy at the table by herself.

"Dinner on Friday? I'm afraid not, I'm off to Peru tomorrow

morning. What am I doing tonight? Well, you can imagine, all kinds of last minute things. Like packing? That's right. Don't I have to eat dinner anyway tonight? Sure, but it will be on the run and God knows at what time."

I paused and listened. "Do I think I'll be hungry by seven-thirty? Yes, probably. In Chevy Chase?"

I had put down the phone and returned to be grilled successfully by Topsy whose antennae, as usual, had picked up something in the air.

And, so, here we were, having dinner.

"I thought you had wrapped up the spring program already?" He looked at me mockingly.

"I'm wearing my private investigator's hat," I said and gave him a quick run-down of events as they had happened at Machu Picchu and in Cuzco. I also told him about Sara Robinson's observations. My account carried us all the way through appetizers, entrée, and dessert.

"When are you planning to see Ida Lupino's almost namesake at the UN?" he said when we had ordered the cappuccino.

"I called Charles Lupesco in New York at the number he had written down for me. But it turned out to be his work number. Someone in the Translations Department informed me he's still on annual leave."

"He could be gone another three weeks! You're aware, I take it, that international organizations give their employees at least five weeks of paid vacation?"

"Well, yes. I left a message on his voice-mail. That's all I can do for now."

"I called Bob to take a look," I added.

"Who's Bob?"

Brewster suddenly straightened up and I thought, oh, no, is he the jealous, possessive type?

"Good question! Who's Bob?"

I almost laughed as I thought of good ole' Bob. I slaved for him for seven years after earning my graduate degree in criminology from Georgetown University. That was after my divorce and my return from France.

"He's my former boss," I said.

"Ah!" Brewster looked relieved, but not much.

"Bob became an FBI agent in 1980 and always bitches about not getting to know J. Edgar Hoover in person."

"Yeah, what a loss," Brewster said.

"Anyway, Bob resigned after ten years on the job to set up his own agency."

"And is Bob married?"

"No, not any more. Resigning from the FBI couldn't save his marriage. His wife had become tired of sleepless nights waiting for him to turn up dead by the morning. They didn't have children and, so, one day she went off to marry a university professor. The only excitement in her life these days is waiting for his slow advancement towards tenure."

"And then you became Bob's girlfriend?"

"No, I did not become Bob's girlfriend. Why are you so obsessed with that?"

"Oh, sorry, really none of my business."

You're so right, I thought, but said:

"I was one of his first operatives. He taught me a lot."

I thought fondly of Bob. I must say he has a good sense of humor, his voice booms and he has this crooked smile which shows off his perfect row of capped teeth. Capped because, some years ago, a suspected felon turned around instead of fleeing and smacked Bob full in the mouth.

We drank our coffee in silence for a while.

"Tell me," I said, "would you be able to help Therese Lecroix contest Elsa Bronski's will? Is that the kind of thing your law firm deals with?"

Brewster didn't hesitate.

"Absolutely! Tell her to send me a notarized copy and a translation of her birth certificate. She must establish her kinship to Ms. Bronski. The best way to do that would be to produce Elsa

Bronski's birth certificate showing the same parents. We can get that from Walter Hughes. Smooth sailing from there on."

"I'll set that in motion as soon as I get to Lima and then you'll work out the terms directly with Mrs. Lecroix. Give me your card and fax number."

"I'll need the original documents, too."

"I can bring them. I really appreciate your help."

I wrote down Therese's address and telephone in San Isidro as well as my own at the Cesar Miraflores and handed them to Brewster. He put the note in an inside pocket and leaned forward. He looked at my face so closely that I began to feel self-conscious.

"What?" I said.

"Will you go out with me when you return?"

I began to pull on my jacket which had been draped over the back of my chair.

"I'll give you a call," I said.

He laughed and got up. I knew he recognized my line as a convenient way of maintaining control. He had probably used it himself countless times.

He walked me to my car which was parked at a meter on Jenifer Street. When we shook hands his felt dry and firm, even bony.

That night I slept soundly, dreaming of a herd of sheep on a mountainside, hopelessly ensnared in their tethers.

The following morning I settled into my window seat and contemplated the thick carpet of woolly clouds miles below the 747, and the vast blue universe above. This suspension in space usually clears my muddled thoughts and brings problems into perspective. But not today.

I picked half-heartedly at my lunch and decided to forgo the yellow dessert which quivered on a blue plastic plate as if shaking its head in warning. The coffee was bitter and made me shudder.

I then slept most of the way between Miami and Lima waking only briefly during a short stop in Guayaquil where we were assaulted by a trail of mist from aerosol cans wielded by health department workers.

At the Cesar I left a message for Ivanovich at Mundotours. Then I took a quick shower before calling Therese Lecroix and setting up a meeting the next morning. She spoke in a furtive voice, telling me to arrive after eleven since George might be leaving late for the office.

I asked Pancho, the stocky driver of the black Dodge from the hotel, to keep the car waiting for me outside the residence. The butler led me through the foyer into the blue sitting room. A door to the right was open to a library with black tomes embossed in gold, an empty fireplace with pink marble facing, a gilded Rococo clock on dainty legs, and an equally dainty desk on an oriental rug.

The butler placed a silver tray with two cups, a coffeepot, and a plate with biscuits on the table. A few minutes later I heard the faint hum of a powerful vacuum cleaner and the sound of several women's voices amid the closing and opening of doors.

Today the double doors leading to the dining room were open, and I glimpsed a heavy sideboard, a long dining table with chairs upholstered in rose-colored velvet, a crystal chandelier.

A draft swept along the floor and curled up my legs. I walked around the room and looked through the large bay window which was hung with two layers of curtains: a white voile in deep folds framed by floor length blue satin under a scalloped valance. Outside, a squat Indian man in green cotton pants and a frayed straw hat, uncoiled a roll of garden hose and directed a reluctant stream of water towards a rose bed.

I turned at a sound and stopped in my tracks.

Therese Lecroix looked disheveled. She wore a wrinkled beige knit dress, tied carelessly with a thin belt, and had bare feet in pink mules. No diamonds.

She didn't offer her hand, just sank into the nearest upholstered chair. A strand of hair hung down her cheek and a heavy coat of make up couldn't conceal the deep purple shiner.

"I was hit by a tennis ball," she said and got up to pour coffee and fetch two glasses and a bottle of Remy Martin. She poured a generous amount for herself and somewhat less in the second glass, ignoring my protest that it was too early in the day for me.

"I've found a law firm to represent you in contesting your sister's will," I said. And I explained what she had to get. I gave her Brewster's card.

Therese took it and poured another glass of brandy, which she drained.

"Someone at the embassy will translate and notarize my birth certificate," she said. "I have told George you are helping me but not that I have hired you to investigate Elsa's murder."

"Won't he realize it at some point?"

"He doesn't know anyone in the group except maybe Dr. Hernandez."

"Dr. Hernandez?"

"Or maybe not. It's really Sra. Hernandez and I who are acquainted. We serve on the hospital's fund-raising committee together."

I mentally filed away this information and looked at Therese's bruised cheekbone.

"Still, maybe it would be better for you to tell George before he finds out from an outsider?"

"What have you discovered?" Therese said, ignoring my question.

"So far nothing much. I did want to ask you if you happen to know a Pablo Alvarez. He has an antique shop in Miraflores . . . ."

Therese sat up suddenly on the edge of her chair, bent forward and stared out the bay window.

"*Merde*," she exclaimed loudly and got up. "George is back, he always forgets something or other."

The butler must have been standing close by because the iron gate swung open immediately and I saw George Lecroix stride over the garden hose on the paved path.

Once inside, he asked the whereabouts of Madame and, in

another five seconds, he was there in the blue room towering above us in double edition. One in the mirror on the wall and the other, very near, in the flesh.

"Therese," he said, "did you see a large envelope on the table in the hall . . ." He stopped short before Therese could reply and turned to me in surprise.

"Mademoiselle Prescott, what a surprise. What brings you back to Peru?"

"Business always brings me here," I said.

"George, she came by to tell me how to contest Elsa's will." Therese had developed her two hectic cheek patches one of which blended unattractively with her shiner. She took a deep breath and added in a rush: "And she's investigating Elsa's murder for me . . ."

She shrank back in her seat as George took a step towards her.

"What do you mean 'for you'? What foolishness are you up to now? I demand to know why you go behind my back."

"The police are doing nothing, George. And I told you what the lawyer said, Elsa hadn't signed the will, and until the murder case is solved I won't get any money. So, I have hired Ms. Prescott."

I knew she would never have gotten up the nerve to tell him if it hadn't been for my presence. But she looked as if she was running out of steam.

"And how do you propose to pay for these services? Not with *my* money! I forbid this nonsense. I, myself, will take care of this problem."

George suddenly seemed to remember I was in the room and tried unsuccessfully to put his face back in diplomatic folds. Therese mustered her last bit of courage and stood up, towering surprisingly as tall as her husband.

"Elsa is paying, George," she said in a voice so quiet that it sounded like a menace. George looked amazed, obviously unaccustomed to lip from his wife, and in front of company, too.

"What do you mean?"

"I mean, George, Elsa gave me a gift before she died and I'm using that. It has nothing to do with you."

George's face went beet-red.

"Nothing to do with me? Of course, it does. What's yours is mine. Where are you keeping this secret money? I demand to know!"

Therese just shook her head and sat down again. I decided to remain seated as well. This was not the time to abandon my client. George stood there without moving, uncharacteristically undecided, and I took advantage of the respite.

"As part of my investigation I was asking your wife if she knows Pablo Alvarez, the antique dealer from Miraflores, who was on the tour when Ms. Bronski was murdered. Do *you* know him, Mr. Ambassador?"

George Lecroix's color deepened between his well-groomed white hair and incongruous black mustache.

"Certainly not." He turned and walked towards the foyer.

"In that case I wonder who he was calling on at your house the day after the murder?" I said.

George Lecroix retraced his steps and looked down at me.

"I'm sure my wife has not hired you to investigate me, her husband," he said.

"Of course not, George," Therese mumbled.

"Therefore, when I tell you I don't know any Pablo Alvarez, I assure you, Mademoiselle, this is my last comment on your amateurish investigation." He stared at Therese with the weirdest expression.

Then he was gone before I could formulate a biting reply.

Therese had lost her last remnant of energy and reached for the brandy.

I waited until I saw George leave the house with a large brown envelope and had himself chauffeured away. Then I finished my coffee in three large gulps and stood up to go.

Therese didn't bother about the butler but accompanied me to the front door herself.

"Get your birth certificate translated," I said. "Then I'll take the original with me to Washington."

I looked closely at her face.

"And be careful with those tennis balls. Get yourself a racket so you can hit back."

Therese smiled for the first time.

"I will."

"I'll give you a call every day to keep you informed."

And to make sure she was all right, I added to myself.

CHAPTER 24

I was leafing through the local English-language newspaper when I noticed an announcement that the American High School was presenting *Plaza Suite* this very week, directed by its drama coach, Vicky Anderson.

I dialed Vicky's number but got no answer.

Then my international call came through and Brewster's optimistic voice reached me above the faint static.

"So, what's new in Peru?"

"Just a couple of things, so far. You should be receiving Therese Lecroix's notarized translation of her birth certificate within a couple of days . . ."

"And I've been in touch with Walter Hughes," he said. "Strangely enough he said he couldn't locate Elsa Bronski's birth certificate in his files. Said he'd have someone call me back. I'm still waiting."

"And if he doesn't have a copy?"

"I'll unearth one somehow!"

We hung up with assurances from Brewster that we'd be seeing each other soon.

It was almost four in the afternoon and I ordered café con leche and toast from room service. Then I changed into a gray linen pants suit, a gray and white striped shirt and black loafers, stuffed the tape recorder and notebook in my shoulder bag and went in search of my taxi. Pancho, the driver, grinned broadly and held open the door with a flourish.

We came to a slow halt in front of the Hernandez residence in San Isidro. The house looked like a misconceived museum. The facade was pink, the flat roof bordered by a delicate wooden railing with tiny carved posts a foot apart. Windows of different proportions were scattered across the pink surface, presumably matching hidden nooks and crannies inside the house. There was no attempt at symmetry.

I opened the ornate gate, stepped through and clicked it shut behind me. The curved marble steps were flanked by perfect Grecian urns alternating with statues of nymphs in flowing garments. The mahogany door was shaded by a jacaranda tree whose vermilion branches enveloped me like a tent.

I rang the bell.

A diminutive maid dressed in black with a white frilly apron opened the door just wide enough to reveal half her figure.

"Señora?" Her voice signaled that no one of my description was expected at this hour. I stuck my hand through the crack in the door and she took possession of my card.

"Please tell the Señora I need to speak to her," I said firmly and the maid disappeared for the longest time. When she came back she was all smiles and asked me inside.

As the door swung open I remained standing on the doorstep in surprise. As if swept by a magic wand the cluttered 19th century exterior opened up into a bright, sunlit, modern interior.

I could see straight through to the terrace which was covered by a blue and white striped awning, to a green lawn dotted with round flower beds. A small fountain gushed water into a shallow basin.

When Elena Hernandez appeared I hardly recognized her

without her sunglasses. She was dressed in a clinging, flowered sun-dress and wore high-heeled silver sandals. Her auburn hair hung loose, her eyelids were brilliant turquoise, and her lips swelled crimson around her too long teeth.

"Miss Prescott! From Machu Picchu! What a surprise, I did not realize you were still in Peru. How did you find me? But I am glad to have your company, I still have two hours to kill before my husband returns from the hospital. . . ."

I followed her through a room which led into several more. The white marble floors were punctuated by patches of color from upholstered chairs and divans. There were glass shelves from floor to ceiling with pre-Columbian ceramic vessels in the shape of grotesque heads and promiscuously twisted sculptures and masks.

One long wall was hung with maybe thirty fragments of ancient textiles framed expensively and well. My first thought was: a museum, followed by another: didn't all this belong in a real museum?

Mrs. Hernandez settled me in a comfortable lounge chair on the terrace and the maid brought out an extra glass, more lemonade, an ice-bucket, and gin and tonic. I agreed to the latter and popped a handful of cashew nuts in my mouth.

Mrs. Hernandez watched me somewhat furtively while fiddling with a book which lay spine up on the glass-topped table. She wriggled her toes and contemplated her nails.

"I'm surprised myself to be back here so soon," I said. "I just arrived yesterday."

"Yes?"

"Mrs. Lecroix, the wife of the French ambassador tells me you do such excellent work raising funds for your husband's hospital."

"She's very gracious." The color rose in her cheeks. "We give a dinner-dance next week and then my husband and I leave for Miami to celebrate my brother's silver wedding anniversary . . ."

"And do you have another wonderful collection of pre-Columbian art in your house there?"

"Oh, no, certainly not, such antiques are not allowed out of

Peru. In Miami we have American art, you know, Pollock, Warhol, Lichtenstein . . ."

I gulped down my gin and tonic. On his salary as head surgeon? Funds had to be flowing in from some other source. Drugs brought into Miami on their frequent trips? Hardly. Independent wealth? That was certainly a possibility.

"Mrs. Lecroix has hired me to investigate the murder of her sister," I said and kept my eyes on Elena's face. There was no reaction, just a slight narrowing of the eyes.

"And are you finding anything?" She picked up her book from the table, dog-eared it carefully, closed it, and rested it lightly in her lap.

"Some. Did you know Pablo Alvarez, the antique dealer from Miraflores, before the trip?"

"No, only from the tour to Machu Picchu. Lima is not a village. We do not all know one another."

"No, of course not, I didn't mean to imply that you do, but it did occur to me since you and your husband are collectors of antiques . . ."

"If we had known each other don't you think we would have been speaking on the tour?"

I looked at her thoughtfully above my drink. The answer could be either yes or no. Yes, if it was all on the level, and no, if they had something to hide.

I was just about to give a non-committal reply when the maid announced the Señor was on the telephone.

Elena excused herself and I got up to wander back into the house to take another look at the antiquities. Standing in front of the wall with the framed textiles I could hear her on the phone.

"José, she's right here in the house. How could I? Louisa had already told her I was home. I'm not saying anything, she's leaving in a moment." There was a long pause and then she said "we'll talk later," and hung up.

I scuttled back to my seat on the terrace.

Elena Hernandez remained standing when she returned. I looked up at her and, on a sudden impulse, lied casually: "Mrs. Lecroix tells me you and your husband met Elsa Bronski at the hospital fund-raiser last May . . ."

My heart leaped at the trapped look on her face.

"It wasn't at the fund-raiser, it was at the Diplomats' ball . . ."

I decided to proceed down the same path of improvisation.

"And then you gave a lunch for Mrs. Lecroix and Elsa Bronski came along?"

"That's right, but I didn't really get to know her at all."

"Not well enough to speak to her when you saw her on the tour?"

"Oh, but we did speak to her, it is just that she was such a strange and quiet person, it was impossible to converse with her . . ."

"Surely you had seen her again after she lunched at your house?"

"Only on the plane to Miami."

"You traveled together? When was that?"

"No, we did not travel together. We just happened to be on the same flight." Elena Hernandez looked at her watch.

"My husband will be home soon, I hope you will excuse me," she said and led me rather briskly from the terrace towards the exit. She looked back occasionally to make sure I was following and although her good-bye wasn't exactly hostile, it wasn't friendly either.

Back at the Cesar I arranged for Pancho to be available the following morning and put in a call to Therese Lecroix. I got her on the line almost immediately.

"I'm calling to ask you a couple of more questions about your sister. How well did she know Elena Hernandez?"

"Oh, she just met her a couple of times. First, I think, at the Diplomats' ball last spring. She didn't want to go at first but I persuaded her, she even bought a new blue dress and looked quite lovely."

There was a pause as if she was thinking.

"And she accompanied us on a tour of the hospital with the

other members of the fund-raising committee and, after that, to a lunch Elena gave for the committee."

"I got the impression there was some tension between your sister and the Hernandez couple?"

"That was so ridiculous. My sister was easily offended. There was some mix-up in Miami. One of their suitcases got wheeled through customs with my sister's. She had to wait until they got through with the rest of their luggage and she almost missed her flight to Washington. It was the kind of thing my sister got very impatient with. She wasn't very easy-going, you know."

"No, I gather she wasn't. Well, that at least clears up something for me," I said, and we hung up after exchanging a couple of general niceties.

Smuggling, I thought to myself, though on a most amateurish level, taking a chance that the luggage of an elderly lady wouldn't be searched? I had to dismiss the idea.

I was fairly exhausted by now and, after an unsuccessful attempt to get through to the office of the chief of police, I showered and changed and took a nap.

When I woke up it was dark outside and I had room service bring me dinner. A glass of Chilean wine helped me relax, and a cup of strong black coffee picked me up.

It was only seven by the time I finished and I decided to go down the block to see if I could catch Pablo Alvarez at his shop on Canseca.

CHAPTER 25

THE temperature had dropped and I pulled on my jeans jacket as I started briskly down Avenida La Paz.

Some shops were still open and, as usual, there was competition from vendors scattered along the sidewalks. They had their wares spread out on the ground in cardboard boxes: hairbrushes, combs, safety-pins, plastic toys, cheap shoes, t-shirts, socks.

I stopped in front of a woman in a coarse black skirt, a striped shawl, and bare feet in worn ballerina shoes. She had a baby at her breast half hidden by the shawl, and a toddler in a skimpy cotton dress next to her on the sidewalk. I pressed a handful of small bills into the woman's hand and hurried on knowing that any help was useless in the larger scheme of things.

The antique shop on Canseca was open. Pablo Alvarez stood at the back behind a glass display case talking to a customer. He recognized me immediately and acknowledged my presence briefly but remained behind the counter.

I walked inside and surveyed the scene. There was hardly room to move. Every available space was crammed with small display cases with dusty lids, stools and stacking tables on wobbly legs piled with folded ponchos. I ducked around odd garments, Indian hammocks, and bows and arrows hanging from the ceiling which limited even the airspace.

The lone customer left and Alvarez came forward to greet me.

"Señorita," he sighed in resignation and went to lock the front door. "I am closing for the evening. How may I help you?"

I gave him my explanation which by now rolled off my tongue without effort. I pulled out my license to give weight to my authority and noticed a certain air of formality settle over Alvarez. He straightened his shoulders, pulled in his stomach, and smoothed back his hair. His eyes were wary, his smile insincere, but he seemed resigned to spend some time with me.

He motioned me to the back of the shop and held open the grubby curtain to a back room. There was a desk piled with bills, papers, an old Underwood typewriter, a calculator, an over-flowing ashtray, a cup half full of cold coffee, and a stack of hard-cover ledgers and several spring binders. A green glass-shaded lamp spread a ghostly pall across the desk.

Alvarez pulled out a chair with a curved, slatted back, wiped it down with his sleeve and indicated that this would be my seat. He sat down opposite me on a wooden stool and rocked back and forth.

"I talked to Mrs. Robinson in the States," I began, having decided against using my tape recorder. "She observed something interesting while she was having her foot attended to."

Alvarez rearranged himself on the stool and looked at the floor between his large flat feet.

"It seems you went back to the torture chamber a few minutes before Ms. Bronski was found murdered," I continued.

He moved his right arm violently. A stack of loose papers sailed to the floor and settled down without distracting much from the general disorder. He got up, pushed back the stool and leaned against the desk, looking down at me. He made no attempt to pick up the papers.

"Señorita," he protested and spread his hands, palms up, to the ceiling. "I did not! I had nothing to do with the poor lady."

"But you do not deny you were not with the group at that point?"

"It had nothing to do with Ms. Bronski."

I took a shot in the dark.

"Were you back there searching for something to show the French Ambassador, maybe?"

"The French Ambassador? No, no, no. I've told you, I do not know the French Ambassador."

"Was it something to do with Dr. Hernandez, then?"

Alvarez finally looked defeated. But he had obviously decided that between the police and myself, I was the lesser of two evils.

"You must understand," he said in a barely audible voice, "I have known Dr. Hernandez for a long, long time and he has his little quirks. He's a good customer so I humor him. He has it in his mind there's gold up there."

"What!?"

"Yes, he thinks there are still unopened graves at Machu Picchu. I do not believe it, of course. And I am not a grave robber."

"But you did leave the other group members to go back to the torture chamber?"

"This is confidential?"

"Absolutely," I lied.

"Very well. Dr. Hernandez suggested we should join the tour to Machu Picchu so he could show me where he thinks the gold is buried. I humor him, I agree to go to Machu Picchu, I even agree to the charade of joining a tour and pretend not to know him. On the train he slips me a map which tells me to search on the other side of the torture chamber and says he will meet me there."

"And that's where you went just around the time of the murder?"

"Most unfortunate." He looked miserable.

"And did Dr. Hernandez join you?"

"No, he did not." Alvarez coughed. "But when I pass the north entrance I see the lady, Ms. Bronski, she is sitting down in the middle seat twisting her arms through the holes. She is smiling, she is looking up. And just as I hurry past the opening I see a shadow, only a shadow, moving opposite her, so I feel assured someone is there to help her out of the seat."

"And when did you have your conversation with Mr. Lupesco?"

"Well, first I went back to see how the lady with the injured foot was doing. Then the European gentleman walked up and we spent some time together. Until Ms. Anderson screamed, and then you know the rest . . . ."

"And the shadow? For God's sakes, man, don't you have any idea who it was?"

"I regret very much, but no."

"But did it look like a man or a woman?"

"I could not tell, Señorita." Alvarez spread his hands in dismissal and took a close look at his gaudy wristwatch.

"If you will now excuse me, please, I have work to do upstairs."

I got up and stretched my legs which had gone numb from their cramped position in the wooden chair.

"Just one more thing and I'll let you go."

Alvarez looked trapped again. The man must have a permanently bad conscience.

"Now that we understand one another better, and you know you are speaking to me in the strictest confidence, tell me with whom you were visiting at the French ambassador's residence when you returned from Machu Picchu. I did see you, you know."

He contemplated my face from under half-closed lids. Then he looked away.

"A woman friend," he said and bent to scoop up the pile of papers from the floor. He jammed everything into a yellow file folder which he tucked under his arm.

"She works there," he said with emphasis on every word and walked to the front door. He opened it just wide enough to let me out.

"I'm at the Cesar Miraflores," I just managed to say as he locked the door and lowered the iron grill with a crash.

I stood on the sidewalk for a moment, undecided, mulling

over the weird account of the supposed obsession of Dr. Hernandez with Inca gold. I decided to cross the street to the pharmacy to purchase a Swiss medication reputed to give super effective relief for Montezuma's revenge. To add to my kit, just in case.

The pharmacy had an old-fashioned air about it with wooden counters and heavy cupboards. There was an early century cash register which let out a nostalgic ping just as I walked in. The pharmacist was a slight European-looking man with a wispy mustache and glasses.

I paid for my purchase and had my hand on the door knob when I saw the light go on in Alvarez' shop. The grill was cranked up slowly, just enough to let a man enter, his head and shoulders hunched low.

The man turned his head to the left, then to the right, as if scanning the street. His profile was unmistakable.

The man was Charles Lupesco.

CHAPTER 26

I opened my eyes in the dark, wide awake. The electric clock on the bedside table showed 5:30 a.m., too early to be up, too late to go back to sleep.

I turned on the two bedside lamps.

I had rushed into the street outside the pharmacy the previous night when Pablo Alvarez let Charles Lupesco into his shop.

The grill had been cranked down immediately and there was no further sign of life by the time I crossed the street to look in through the dirt-encrusted window.

The six wooden shutters on the first floor were closed but faint shafts of light showed through the two in the middle. Presumably Alvarez' apartment.

After waiting over thirty minutes in the increasing darkness as the pharmacy closed and the stream of pedestrians petered out, I had returned to my room at the Cesar.

I had lain awake wondering about the surprise appearance of Charles Lupesco in Lima. Then I had tried to make sense of the gold story and fitting Dr. Hernandez into the profile Alvarez had sketched. Not entirely unthinkable, of course. Plenty of people looked and acted normal until their veneer was scratched. And one

126

of the maids at the French ambassador's residence might be Alvarez' girl friend, although the coincidence didn't sit well with me.

I had slept fitfully.

I now picked up my paperback mystery and leaned half way out of bed to catch a ray to read by. After a few unsuccessful minutes of that I propped up the ceramic lamp on two telephone books, sliding down in bed on only one pillow until I could see three quarters of the page. When my neck muscles cramped up I finally capitulated and turned off the light.

It was daylight when I woke up, and within another half hour I had showered and dressed and ordered breakfast from room service.

At eight I called the number Vicky Anderson had given me. She answered on the first ring.

"Oh," she said not very enthusiastically when I announced myself. "I didn't know you were back in Lima."

"Just here on a private visit," I lied. "I happened to read in the newspaper that you are giving *Plaza Suite* at the school. You won't believe this but I actually had a part in that play myself years ago. In the third episode, that is, I was Mrs. Hubley, the mother of the bride! And I thought I'd love to see your production . . . ."

"Well, of course! And that's exactly the episode we're doing! I'll leave a ticket for you at the entrance!" Vicky's voice had regained its breathless quality.

There was what you might call a pregnant pause.

"And you won't believe this! Another coincidence for you! Charles Lupesco is here and he'll be at the play, too!"

So, it was as simple as that. Lupesco had returned to see Vicky and was taking the opportunity to buy something from Alvarez.

While I finished the last piece of toast and a second cup of tea I debated how to go about detecting the state of the police investigation.

At nine I called the American Embassy and asked for James Q. Brown. He came on the line almost immediately and didn't sound surprised at all.

"I was expecting your call," he said. "Bob Makowski called

and asked me to assist you if I could. But I can't! The police have been very close-mouthed and I suspect very little is being done."

"I'm not surprised," I said. "You remember, there was no attempt at finger-printing, the chief handled the murder weapon very cavalierly and let several witnesses leave before the inquest. I'm going to attempt another meeting with him."

"Well, good luck and let me know what you find out." I couldn't help feeling, again, that he didn't much care.

"Are you involved in any official capacity?" I asked.

"No, not yet. We're still waiting for the request from the government. Everything takes its sweet time here."

He was obviously being polite only because of Bob Makowski. So be it.

Fifteen minutes later I was downstairs in search of Pancho and his black Dodge. He was there polishing the hood with a soft white cloth but stopped the minute I came around the corner, ready to be of service and looking rather pleased to see me. He maneuvered into traffic across Avenida Larco to Paseo de la Republica and we were on our way to the main police station. It took almost half an hour.

I went to the second floor and found the waiting room I remembered from my last visit. I approached the chief's limpid assistant at his desk but he didn't seem to recognize me and looked distinctly disinterested.

"Good morning, Sir," I said, "is Chief Lopez in?"

"No, Señora, he is not."

"When do you expect him?"

"I do not expect him."

"What do you mean, you do not expect him?"

"He will not be coming in anymore."

"He's dead?"

The assistant allowed himself a tiny smile. Maybe there was a human being in there after all.

"No, Señora, he is not dead, but he is no longer chief of police."

It shouldn't have surprised me. I've had plenty of experience with appointed officials being replaced at a moment's notice. Still, it was inconvenient, to say the least, having to start over with a new person in charge. I obviously needed an ally at this point, and the assistant was the closest I had.

"I'm sorry we weren't properly introduced the last time I was here," I said and held out my hand. "I'm Jamie Prescott."

"I'm Victor," he said.

"Yes, Victor, you may remember I was here about the Elsa Bronski murder, the murder at Machu Picchu, just a couple of weeks ago?"

Victor nodded and I took out my PI license. It took me only a few more minutes to convince him I should see the new chief without a prior appointment.

Victor got up, buttoned his ill-cut jacket, smoothed back his hair, picked up a pile of orange folders, and went across the room. He knocked on the chief's door and listened deferentially a brief moment, his head tilted. Then he entered and was gone an eternity.

I walked over to look at the new name on the door: Jorge Bustamante.

When Victor beckoned me inside I found that Jorge Bustamante looked and acted curiously like his predecessor, Feliciano Lopez. He had not yet put a personal imprint on the shabby office, assuming that was possible. The same worn map of Lima hung on the wall and the curtains were their previous grimy selves.

Bustamante continued leafing through the orange folder before stretching out his arm above the ashtray to shake hands with me. His face had the look of well-tanned leather.

I presented him with my card and my license and sat down. I quickly sketched out the story of the murder while Bustamante followed my account in the case file, flipping the pages back and forth, stalling from time to time to bring his eyes closer, and jotting down notes on a separate piece of paper.

When I stopped talking, Bustamante pulled out several sheets of paper stapled together which I recognized as the notes I had made in Cuzco.

Bustamante read through the English notes and I wondered if he'd taken police training in the States. But when he spoke, it was in Spanish.

"And what is the additional information you say you have for me?"

"I thought you might want to see these," I said and pulled out the second set of prints of my photographs of the murder scene.

Bustamante spread out the pictures in front of him. He exclaimed under his breath as he studied each one carefully.

"These photos make the crime very vivid! It was probably fortunate you were there. Since I have just recently taken responsibility for the Department I have been able to study only our most urgent cases in detail."

And this wasn't urgent?

"I would be interested to know what you have discovered so far?" I said.

"Would you, indeed?" He flipped through the file folder once more. "In that case you will want to know that your tour guide, Boris Ivanovich Garcia, was pulled in for questioning last week in connection with two Ecuadorian Jesuits trying to smuggle a group of political prisoners out of the main prison in Lima."

For once I was speechless. I had seen absolutely no indication that Ivanovich had known the two padres prior to the tour.

"And have you any proof that he's guilty?" I said.

Bustamante tapped his pen on the desk.

"He denies it, naturally," he said. "But we will prove it. It might be healthier for you to stay away from him."

"And you've arrested the two padres?"

"My predecessor detained them for questioning but released them after pressure from the Jesuit Order. They have left the country." Bustamante looked as if this wouldn't have happened under his command.

"But what does this have to do with the murder case?"

"Ah, we shall see!" Bustamante smiled.

"But what about other members of the group. Dr. Hernandez and Pablo Alvarez, for example?"

"Dr. Hernandez? Of course not!" Bustamante looked as if he'd swallowed something particularly ill-tasting. "Dr. Hernandez is a most respected chief surgeon. He is also my brother-in-law."

"Elena Hernandez is your sister? A charming woman." I admit I sounded most insincere but as it turned out, it didn't matter.

"No," Bustamante said, "I am married to Dr. Hernandez' sister." And he might as well have added that there was going to be no police investigation into *his* family.

Bustamante shuffled my photographs like a deck of cards and dropped them into the file folder without asking if he could keep them.

My interview with him ended as abruptly as it had begun. Victor had disappeared from his desk, hopefully not in the footsteps of his former boss, and I was thankful to find Pancho waiting for me at the curb right outside the building.

The rush hour was on and provided ample time for me to reflect on my conversation with Bustamante.

Ivanovich a member of a terrorist organization? The inept padres conspiring to smuggle political prisoners? Somehow I couldn't believe it.

Back at the hotel I left a message for Ivanovich at Mundotours.

CHAPTER 28

THE American high school consisted of a collection of one and
two-story red brick buildings connected by paved footpaths which
spread out across a generous expanse of green lawns dotted with
trees. The lights were on in most buildings and floodlights lent a
silvery sheen to the trees and lit up the path leading to the
auditorium.

Pancho let me out at the front gate and drove off to park the
Dodge behind a slew of Mercedes Benz's, BMWs and Volvos, while
I followed on the heels of a throng of parents and students in the
direction of the auditorium.

At the entrance I was handed the promised ticket and pointed
towards the middle section where the first three rows were marked
"Reserved".

Charles Lupesco was in the fourth row. As I approached him
from behind I thought that his head really was proportionally too
large for his body. I eased into the seat next to him and he turned
abruptly.

"Miss Prescott!" He blinked his blue eyes rapidly, a most
annoying trait I had forgotten until now.

"How are you?"

He blinked again.

"Good. Good."

The auditorium was filling up and the noise level neared the ten-decibel point. The shouting was done in both English and Spanish, back and forth across the hall, and the excellent acoustics didn't help the matter. I tried to catch Lupesco's eye.

"It's a real surprise to see you," I shouted. "When did you get here?"

"Yesterday," he shouted back. "From Buenos Aires. My tour was supposed to take me to La Paz, but I decided to visit with the fair Vicky instead."

"Yes, she certainly is fair," I replied. If not literally, I thought.

The noise level went up another notch and I saw Lupesco's lips move but heard nothing. It wasn't until a teacher climbed to the stage in front of the crimson curtain and pointed a fierce hand at one group on the balcony and another on the far left, that the noise subsided enough for me to make myself heard.

"I actually called you in New York and left a message. I didn't know I would run into you so soon."

Charles Lupesco coughed.

"The day after tomorrow I would have returned your call. I'm leaving for New York tonight. I will report to work on Monday. To what did I owe the pleasure of your call?"

"I'm not sure how much information you managed to get about the murder of Ms. Bronski before you left. She was visiting with her sister who happens to be the wife of the French ambassador. Her name is Therese Lecroix. She feels the police aren't doing enough to solve her sister's murder. She has hired me to investigate."

"I remember you are a private investigator."

"Yes. So, as a matter of routine I'm revisiting with all the group members just to go over their stories once more. That's why I called you in New York."

Charles Lupesco had his head bent towards me so I could speak straight into his ear. He kept nodding to signal he heard and understood. He smelled of plain soap and water, fresh from the shower. I pulled away without getting more than several more nods from him.

The curtain went up and an expectant silence descended on the audience.

The applause after the first act was as thunderous as only family and friends can muster but, in truth, the seniors hadn't been half bad and both Charles and I clapped enthusiastically. The audience got up in a great scraping of chairs and trooped noisily towards the foyer with its coffee and soft-drink bar.

"Do you need coffee or something or could we stay here and talk through the intermission?" I stayed firmly in my seat and Charles Lupesco sank back in his with a gentlemanly nod.

"Certainly! It will be our only chance because I must say goodbye to Vicky during the next intermission. My flight to Miami leaves at midnight and I must drop off my rental car first."

He stretched his legs way under the chair in front of him. He wore gray and green Argyle socks and black Gucci loafers.

"I'll get right to it, then."

I moved to the edge of my seat so I could look him full in the face.

"You remember Mrs. Robinson?"

Charles nodded.

"Well, once Mrs. Robinson settled down after the double trauma of injury and murder she remembered something she failed to report at the time."

Charles looked at me blandly.

"She seemed to think that both you and Pablo Alvarez left the group between the time she fell and the moment Vicky screamed."

Charles Lupesco sat very still.

"Did you actually stay in the clearing outside the torture chamber the entire time?" I watched as his face relaxed and his pale lips stretched into a half-smile.

"Madame," he said. "You are taking a burden from my shoulders. I know there were some things I should probably have told the police myself. It is not that I meant to hide anything, it just seemed to have no relevance . . ."

He wet his lips.

"But let me tell it from the beginning."

"Do."

"It was always my dream to tour Latin America, and after being employed by the UN for a year I had accumulated five weeks of leave. It gave me the chance to make my dream come true. I never guessed when I signed up for the tour to Machu Picchu that I would also meet my dream girl."

He glanced at me.

"Maybe you don't believe in love at first sight, and I never thought it could happen to me, but there it is! Vicky is my dream girl. We met, we talked on the train coming up, we ate lunch together, we walked, we talked, we laughed."

Lupesco cleared his throat.

"In the torture chamber I helped Vicky out of the seat. I must admit I felt a little hurt when she went off by herself to 'meditate' but, of course, I did not insist on joining her. She left the chamber through the back and I went outside with the group. And then, after Mrs. Robinson injured herself but had plenty of attendants, this is when I must confess to you I left for just a few minutes to make sure Vicky was all right." He paused briefly before he continued: "I walked around the wall outside the torture chamber on quite a narrow path and saw her sitting high up on a ledge. I didn't want her to see me so I turned around and went back. Later I felt foolish, she might have thought I was spying on her. Then I couldn't tell anyone else either. It really made no difference to the murder case."

He put his hand on my arm and squeezed. I shuddered and thought, I really don't like him! We sat silently while people began to filter back into our row, stepping on our toes and apologizing.

Then Charles Lupesco turned to me and said: "I still haven't told Vicky. Are *you* going to?"

"It doesn't seem necessary although I don't see how it would matter to her. In fact, at this point in your, ah, relationship, she might find your concern for her safety flattering. Anyway, I wanted to ask you something else."

Charles straightened up and looked at me.

"What was your impression of Ms. Bronski?" I said.

The auditorium was almost full again, the lights dimmed and a hush fell over the hall. Charles frowned and looked at the ceiling briefly before answering.

"Well, she was old and I paid no real attention to her at all. I did notice she seemed to know the doctor, I forget his name, because they were arguing on the bus coming up the mountain. And afterwards, at the Temple of the Sun, I noticed she had an exchange with the doctor's wife. The old lady looked cross."

"Did you hear what they were arguing about?"

"I'm afraid not. I was mostly interested in talking to Vicky."

"Did you see anyone else outside the torture chamber while you were looking for Vicky?"

"No, I'm afraid not."

"Elsa Bronski was buried last week," I said.

Lupesco blinked.

"I do not like funerals," he said with a tiny smile.

"I'm sure no one enjoys them," I said dryly. "You don't like inquests either, I take it. You left Peru in a hurry."

Lupesco's smile faded and he stuck a hand in his pocket.

"I was not needed at the inquest, Madame, or so I was assured by the chief of police. Surely you do not question his judgment?"

I was about to say that I certainly did when the curtain rose and the second act began. I could no longer see Lupesco's face and, watching the action on stage, I forgot about him and instead was transported back to my own high school days. I remembered my parents sitting in the audience watching me perform. But when the curtain came down it took me only a few seconds to return to reality.

I addressed Charles Lupesco again.

136

"And have you seen Pablo Alvarez this time around?" I asked. He looked straight ahead.

"No, I have not," he lied and turned around. Vicky came floating down the aisle exclaiming in her breathless voice, "Charles, dear! Jamie! Are you enjoying the play? Weren't the kids wonderful? Must you really leave, Charles? But you are staying, Jamie?"

Charles got up briskly and put an arm around the ebullient Vicky who snuggled up and purred. She lifted her face and planted a kiss on his cheek.

"I must catch my flight," Charles said and disentangled himself hurriedly. Vicky appeared not to notice his impatience but bubbled on:

"I'm seeing you to your car. The intermission is twenty minutes but they can't start until I return!"

Charles clasped my hand briefly and left with Vicky's arm around his waist.

I missed most of the last act, thinking of the previous evening when Lupesco had entered Alvarez' antique shop. Facile lie, but why? More smuggling? Easy to do on a diplomatic passport. Alvarez certainly hadn't wasted any time identifying Lupesco as a likely customer. I shook my head in disgust.

The play finished just before ten and by ten-thirty Pancho had taken us to Vicky's small house which sat behind a tall brick wall a ten minute ride from the school.

Vicky invited Pancho in for a cup of coffee and a sandwich and, after a lot of coaxing from me, he finally agreed. Once inside the kitchen he ate the cheese on rye with lettuce and tomato which Vicky put together rapidly, and drank down the scalding hot coffee. He left with many thanks and disappeared out the door to the safety of his car, his hunched shoulders signaling his discomfort.

I helped carry a tray with cheese and cucumber sandwiches and a bottle of white wine to the coffee table in the small living room. Vicky put glasses and plates, poured the wine, kicked off her shoes, and curled up in one corner of the three-seater, with me in the other.

"Here's to Plaza Suite!" Vicky raised her glass. "Was that fun or what! Makes me think I should go back to the stage in New York!"

"Back to the stage?"

"Back-stage, actually," Vicky giggled. "I started out with a teacher's certificate from Columbia, then I switched to drama, did three years of summer stock, was a stage hand off-Broadway, and got back to teaching when it became a choice between starvation and survival."

"I had no idea. Just goes to show you . . ."

I finished my sandwich and listened to Vicky reminisce about New York, about the stage, about not making it, about a failed marriage, and then about meeting Charles Lupesco.

"I've never been lucky in love," Vicky declared at last, "but I'm the eternal optimist. Whenever I meet someone a small voice says, Oh, m'God, maybe this is it, and it is for a while, and then it fizzles out, how about you?"

"It's a wilderness out there, all right."

I put down my empty glass.

"Let me explain to you what my problem is about the murder case."

Vicky immediately looked somber, her expression a mixture of apprehension and defensiveness.

"You were sitting there on the ledge, high on a rock, meditating, I imagine, on the life of the Incas. The quiet of the scenery was so intense that you could have heard the proverbial pin drop."

Vicky nodded.

"The merest shifting of a stone, say by someone stepping on it, would have sounded as loud as a firecracker."

I paused but Vicky didn't move.

"I feel there's something you haven't told me. I remember the spot you sat in. An Inca command post of the entire area."

Vicky lifted her face.

"Now," I said, "now I think the time has come for you to come clean. And before you make up your mind to the contrary, let me tell you I think you did see someone up there."

Vicky blushed and clattered her wine glass down on the table. When she spoke it was in a fretful, defensive voice.

"You didn't even give me a chance to tell you that I *have* remembered hearing something. Instead you make me feel guilty as if *I* did something wrong."

Right you are, I thought and suppressed a satisfied smile. Nothing like smoking people out by putting them on the defensive. Works every time. The down-side is that when you're on a case you can't afford to be nice to anyone.

"I'm glad you were planning to tell me and I'm sorry if I made you feel guilty." I looked at Vicky without remorse.

"So, what *did* you want to tell me?"

Vicky turned to plump up the cushion at her back, picked up her wine glass, took a long sip, curled her legs back under, and looked straight ahead, away from me.

"You said if I recalled anything at all, to tell you. Well, when I did remember, you were gone and, anyway, I didn't think it mattered one way or the other because I didn't *see* anything, I just *heard* something."

Vicky drained her glass, put it down and looked at me briefly before she continued.

"I had been sitting on the rock for some time. I felt almost sleepy from all that silence. Then, very faintly, I heard gravel shift as if something was moving carefully, real slow-like. I turned my head but saw nothing so I thought to myself, oh, m'God, it's a snake. Are there snakes up there, do you know?"

I shook my head meaning either 'I don't know' or 'there aren't', and Vicky continued.

"Well, whatever, I didn't hear it again so I stayed put. Then a little later, just as I was getting up to leave I heard steps moving really fast, and I don't know why I got scared, maybe the place and because I couldn't hear the voices from the group, I felt suddenly isolated, and that's why I rushed through the opening to the torture chamber even though I had meant to just follow the wall around to the other side. And then I found her. I swear, I still have nightmares."

Vicky's eyes brimmed over either from tear-duct problems or emotion, it was hard to tell with her. Her voice hadn't been particularly emotional so maybe it was the tear-ducts.

"Well, I'm glad you cleared that up for me," I said. "Have the police been back in touch with you?"

"No, no. And I wish you wouldn't tell them what I just told you. It couldn't make a difference since I didn't see anyone."

"You're absolutely sure about that?"

"Swear to God!" Vicky raised her hand. "So, you won't tell?"

"Probably not. Let's see what else develops."

Vicky refilled our glasses.

"I can't tell you what a relief this is," she said, "to have talked to you, I mean. I just don't want to be involved in this anymore."

"A natural reaction. Murder is so unpleasant!" The ironic tone was lost on Vicky so I picked up my glass and, instead, talked about the subject closest to her heart.

"You have certainly conquered Charles Lupesco," I said.

"Yes, I can hardly believe it myself! Imagine, he changed his entire schedule to spend more time with me."

"And are you still planning to visit him in New York?"

"You bet. Spring break comes up in two weeks. I'll stay with him at this fabulous apartment on 48th and First Avenue he's renting from a colleague. He's on the 19th floor with this awesome view of the UN and the East River. When I sat in my shared loft in SoHo I never thought my next stop would be the East side with a doorman."

"I imagine Charles is interested in antiques from Peru, you know pre-Columbian . . . ?"

"Yeah, well, he loved the Gold Museum."

"I had a feeling he would! Anyway, do you happen to have his phone number just in case I get to New York while you're there?"

Vicky looked indecisive.

"We could go to a show or dinner," I added and Vicky got up to write down Charles' home number.

"That would be fun," she said and handed me the note.

"Vicky, did you by any chance mention the footsteps to Charles?"

Vicky looked surprised.

"No, I don't think I did. He had left already. And I really didn't find it important."

"Well, I'd better be going." I stood up and prepared to leave. I followed Vicky into the small foyer where a wooden chest covered with a striped Indian poncho stood next to a small carved chair.

A faded kelim rug on the tiled floor shifted dangerously under my feet. Vicky caught my arm and we stumbled together towards the front door.

"Darn rug, I meant to put foam rubber under it!"

"Do that!" I said. "And let me know if you have any new revelations about Machu Picchu. I'm at the Cesar for another few days."

Pancho, possessed of a sixth sense, was on the sidewalk holding the door open to the back seat.

The streets were totally deserted, there were practically no street lights and neither sight nor sound from the villas hidden behind tall walls and chained gates, protected by armed guards and police dogs.

A suburban life style I was definitely not hankering for.

CHAPTER 29

T HE Cesar's lobby was deserted except for two couples in evening dress on their way into the elevator. A porter sat slumped and apparently sleeping on a bench in the corner opposite the reception.

I bypassed the unattended desk where the room keys hung in plain view. I carry mine in my handbag, being a firm opponent of announcing to the world: 'I'm out, please feel free to burglarize my room.'

The elevator was slow coming back down. I watched the lights on the panel change at every floor until five, then at three and two, until the doors opened.

I stepped into the small cubicle decorated with gilded fleur-de-lis and smokey mirrors all around. I pressed the button to my floor and the doors sailed together smoothly until they were a hand's breadth apart.

Their movement was stopped when an arm in a grubby sleeve pushed through the narrow crack and widened it enough for the entire arm, followed by the body of a man, to squeeze inside.

The doors snapped shut behind him and the elevator started upwards with a slight bump.

I made an instinctive move towards the corner with the control panel just as the man brought his other hand out of the pocket of his long dirty trench-coat and lurched against me.

"What the hell!" I exclaimed and my hand automatically shot up to the control panel reaching for the alarm button.

I only had a second and took valuable time to avert my eyes from the man. In that second my arm was caught in a steely grip and I missed the button.

My reaction was instantaneous, noisy, and completely subconscious. I jerked my arm towards my body and it slipped out of his grip easily. My hands flew up, I pushed him sideways, my foot connected with his knee cap and within two seconds the man lay on the floor whimpering, both hands clasping his right leg. A pair of green John Lennon sunglasses sat askew on his mottled face. A black leather cap lay next to his head.

I bent down to look at his closed eyes and the long braid of hair which had escaped from under the cap.

"Ivanovich!"

I shook his shoulder.

"For God's sake, Ivanovich, I thought you were a mugger or worse."

His face was discolored, an ugly red line ran from his left eye, which was all but shut, across his cheekbone down the jaw. His lower lip was swollen translucent and looked about to burst.

Ivanovich opened his eyes, grabbed the gilded handrail and hauled himself up just as the doors opened on the eighth floor.

I stepped out of the elevator quickly and he followed me into the deserted hallway. His leg buckled.

"Come on!" I said and pointed down the hall to my room. He stood close to me while I got out the key, and practically fell inside with the door, stumbling to the middle of the room. I locked the door and fastened the chain before turning to him.

He looked lost in his long coat, rubbing the arm I had twisted to the point of breaking and pulling up the knee I had kicked.

"Sorry about that," I said.

"You are strong," he grimaced.

"Why don't you take off your strange garment and sit down."

He did as he was told. Under the coat he wore filthy jeans, ripped at the knees and covered in what looked like red paint caked with mud, and a torn t-shirt with an imitation Coke sign saying *Kora-Kola*. The laces were missing from his running shoes which also looked as if they'd been dipped in mud.

He slumped into one of the upholstered chairs, his hands, looking lifeless, hanging down over the armrests.

He shook his head slowly.

"What happened to you?" I asked.

"The police." He touched his swollen lip and tapped his cheekbone gently. "They took me in for interrogation two days ago. They accused me of being a terrorist."

"And are you?"

"Would I tell you if I were?" His swollen lip made his smile lop-sided and he shook his head. "No, most sincerely, I am not."

"The new chief of police, Jorge Bustamante, warned me not to associate with you. I was there having an apparently civilized conversation with him yesterday while they must have been busting you up in another part of the building."

Ivanovich looked at me pitifully.

"He also told me the Ecuadorian padres are helping political prisoners escape. Is that true?"

"It may be." Ivanovich looked tired and contemplated me out of his one good eye. "Yes, it is true."

"And you are assisting them but you're not a terrorist? How does that check out?"

"Check out?"

"Yes, how can you be helping and yet be innocent? Aren't they planning for terrorists to escape?"

"No, certainly not. They were trying to rescue three Ecuadorian prisoners. They have been held for months without a trial, without being charged, and may suffer a disappearing accident at any time. The padres are taking a dangerous risk."

"For you it is even more dangerous because you can't run off to

Ecuador. I imagine you don't have the Jesuit Order to run interference for you."

"Interference?"

I would have to speak basic English. "Yes, help you. Look how the police treated you. What are you planning to do now?"

"I am leaving for Ecuador in the morning. They will come for me at four."

Ivanovich stretched his leg and grimaced with pain.

"Karate," he said and shook his head at me. "I very much regret I surprised you in the elevator. I waited for you for more than two hours. I could not go to my cousin or anyone else I know. I need a place to sit, just in this chair, until the morning. And you are a tourist, so they will not come here."

I didn't feel at all confident about that and thought wryly of the notice posted conspicuously on the inside of the entrance door: 'Guests are forbidden to entertain members of the opposite sex in their room!' The moral righteousness was in some contrast to torture of prisoners and beating of suspects.

"Of course, you can stay," I said automatically, "and not in the chair either."

I eyed the chair to evaluate how I could best curl up in it while Ivanovich occupied my bed.

I got up. "We don't have that many hours. Why don't you take a shower and I'll clean the worst off your pants, even give you the laces from my Reeboks and a clean t-shirt! And if you promise to stay out of sight until I tell you the coast is clear, I'm ordering room service. Coffee or tea?"

"*Mate de coca.*" Ivanovich got up, limped to the bathroom and turned to me: "My heart wishes to thank you from the bottom."

"Oh, no need to!" I said rather startled.

I tossed him my bathrobe. "Here, use that."

The twenty-four hour room service produced cream of tomato soup, chicken and rice, a large slice of honeydew melon plus a pot of scalding *mate*.

I knocked on the bathroom door as soon as the waiter left.

Ivanovich appeared barefoot in the Cesar's short white bathrobe, his long hair hanging loose in wet strings around his shoulders.

He looked unusual to say the least.

While he ate every scrap on the tray I fashioned an ice-pack for his face from a towel and miniature cubes from the small refrigerator, and found some Tylenol. I pulled the bedspread off the bed, and pointed him to it. I set my alarm for 3:30 am, a mere two and a half hours away.

Then I got to work on his jeans with soap and water and my hair-dryer, threaded laces through the eyelets of his worn sneakers, and brought out my largest t-shirt.

Ivanovich was in deep sleep flat on his back, the blanket tucked under his chin. The enigmatic expression on his face, with its swollen lids and broad cheekbones, its long flattened nose, was curiously evocative of the pre-Columbian masks in the Hernandez' collection.

I changed into a sweatsuit in the bathroom, pushed the two armchairs together and settled down quite uncomfortably.

In what seemed like two minutes the buzzer went off and I rooted around in the chair to find the alarm, then the stopper. By the time I had wedged in a fingernail and moved the recessed button two notches I was more or less awake.

I got up and looked at Ivanovich. It was obvious he would require some rigorous waking up and I padded around the bed to shake him as hard as I thought his injuries would allow. He fended me off with one arm, moaned and groaned, but finally swung his legs to the floor and sat on the edge of the bed.

"*Caramba!*" he mumbled and slowly opened one eye.

"You have twenty minutes," I said brightly and turned on the lights in the entrance, then in the dressing room and bathroom.

It was still pitch dark outside.

It took Ivanovich several minutes to get into his jeans which, in spite of the cleaning process, were quite stiff, and my Hard Rock Café t-shirt. My shoelaces gleamed Ultra-Brite in his dirty sneakers. When he was fully dressed in the black leather cap, his braid out of the way, sunglasses in place, and his body hidden under the yellowing trench coat, he looked unrecognizable to someone looking for Ivanovich but strange enough to provoke the curiosity of anyone else.

I hoped darkness and distance would protect him.

"Wait a minute! What about money?" I asked.

Ivanovich shook his head and made no sign of protest when I pressed a mixture of dollars and Peruvian bills in his hand. He just stuffed the money in his pocket, embraced me awkwardly, and went to call the elevator.

The last I saw of him was a raised hand as the doors closed. The panel showed the elevator stopping on the first floor before it reached the lobby.

I chained the door, turned off all lights and hurried to the window. But as time passed and I saw no movement whatsoever on the short stretch of side street visible from my room I went to bed.

I had to assume Ivanovich had made a successful escape. I realized he hadn't told me who was picking him up and how he was leaving. By car? By plane? By sea?

I lay churning over a thousand questions in my head but finally fell asleep from sheer physical exhaustion.

CHAPTER 30

THE bell wouldn't stop ringing. I groped for the clock before realizing it was the phone. I picked it up with a great clatter and was rewarded with the voice of Therese Lecroix at the other end.

I listened without opening my eyes while Therese explained the reason for her call in a newfound optimistic voice. She was inviting me to accompany her to a fund-raising ceremony at the Miraflores General Hospital where the ladies of the committee would present two dialysis units and a check to Dr. Hernandez in his capacity as chief surgeon and interim director general. The ceremony would begin at eleven and Therese would come by in the embassy car to pick me up at ten-thirty.

I opened my eyes and looked at the clock.

"I think I could make that," I croaked.

It was only nine and a trip to the hospital might give me a chance to talk to Dr. Hernandez without making an obvious appointment which he would probably refuse.

I pondered my limited wardrobe and came up, again, with the gray linen pants suit, the white silk blouse and gray shoes, all quite hospital-like.

The black sedan pulled up in front of the Cesar punctually at ten-thirty and the agile chauffeur sprang around to open the door for me.

Therese had successfully made up her face to conceal any remaining signs of her so-called tennis ball accident, at least sufficiently for indoor scrutiny.

She looked elegant from the black raw silk suit, a full set of diamonds, and a string of pearls blending softly into the folds of an egg-shell silk blouse, down to her slim feet in snake skin shoes.

"I have not heard from Mr. Brewster in Washington," she said.

"Early days yet," I said as the sedan rolled away from the Cesar.

"And you, Madame, are you getting closer to the murderer?" Therese said this in a peevish voice I hadn't heard from her before. Was she suddenly counting the hours and the money?

"Early days yet," I repeated.

Therese looked up, obviously wanting more, but changed her mind when I just looked straight ahead past the broad back of the driver.

"Tell me about the fund-raising," I said.

So, instead, she outlined the difficulties the fund-raising committee had encountered in obtaining an exemption from customs duties for the importation of the two dialysis units from France.

"Wouldn't you think the government could encourage such gifts rather than try to profit a few *Intis*," she asked rhetorically.

The hospital was a three-wing, four-story building with a large noisy main hall where people scurried back and forth, in and out of slamming doors. Therese led the way past two public elevators blocked by a multitude of grim-looking visitors to a private elevator which took us slowly and noiselessly to the fourth floor.

Up there the atmosphere was indicative of a successful fund-raising program. Wall-to-wall beige carpeting stretched across a reception area furnished with fine mahogany chairs, a French escritoire with an abundant bouquet of fresh flowers in a large copper bowl, and a round table stacked with magazines. The

Venetian blinds were closed, the room softly lit through rose-colored lamp shades on expensive brass bases.

The receptionist, a dark-haired young woman in a tight-fitting white suit with a very short skirt hugging her rear, tripped out behind her desk and beckoned us down the corridor to a heavy wooden door.

The large executive meeting room faced a park at the back of the main hospital wing. The windows were open and a slight breeze billowed through the sheer curtains.

The oval conference table was fitted with individual microphones, a pad and pencil at each seat, and surrounded by swivel chairs upholstered in gold tweed. Several silver trays with cut-crystal water carafes and matching glasses were placed down the middle of the table.

I paused to study the eight impressive oil paintings of former and present male chief surgeons and directors general of the hospital. The portrait of Dr. Hernandez was placed prominently in the middle of the wall.

Eight women clustered at the far end of the room under an architectural rendering of an idealized version of the hospital. They were dressed to the hilt in what I would have hesitated to wear at Ascot. The air around them glittered and glimmered with diamonds, emeralds, and rubies on satin and lace backgrounds. All this made me feel decidedly humble in my silver lapel pin.

Two waiters in black trousers and short, white jackets with brass buttons, offered soft drinks and canapés.

Therese introduced me to the ladies of the fund-raising committee but they shifted their attention from me abruptly when Dr. Hernandez entered the conference room. He was followed by Elena towering above him on stiletto heels.

I watched from the sidelines and was surprised by Dr. Hernandez' ruffled appearance. He, in turn, looked startled when he spotted me. His hair stood on end as if he had just roughed it up with his hands. His tie was loose under his soft shirt collar.

The ceremony could have been brief but wasn't. Each member

of the committee got a chance to speak, and speak they did, with an eloquence and fluency which totally belied their appearances as glamour hostesses. I was floored.

Therese Lecroix spoke in all but fluent Spanish of a proposal for new maternity and pediatrics wards, presenting a detailed budget for a building and equipment nearing the two million dollar mark. If the purpose of Therese's invitation had been to impress me with her organizational skills, her mission had been accomplished.

While the members of the group spoke I caught Dr. Hernandez' veiled glance several times. Whenever that happened he would blink and look away. Still trying to figure out what I was doing in his conference room.

The official donation was made by Therese who handed José Hernandez a check whose amount was announced as a stunning two hundred and fifty thousand dollars. Dr. Hernandez had good reason to look pleased so why did he look so distracted?

He did make an acceptable thank-you speech and placed the envelope with the check in a leather portfolio before announcing that the second part of the ceremony was about to begin in the dialysis department.

On our way down I pushed my way in front of two committee women into the elevator which could hold only five persons. I descended in the company of José, Elena and two others.

"Dr. Hernandez," I said loud enough for everyone to hear, "I would like a few minutes of your time in private after the ceremony."

He shot a look at his wife and nodded less than gracefully.

"Five minutes," he said.

"Just long enough for you to confirm something Mr. Pablo Alvarez has told me," I added, probably unwisely since it would give him time to think, but I had the satisfaction of seeing him acutely discomfited.

The two units were sitting in several crates in the hallway outside the dialysis department, waiting to be unpacked. There wasn't much the committee members could do except bend down to inspect the black lettering on the crates and exclaim how wonderful it all was.

After another few minutes the group dispersed. I explained hurriedly to Therese Lecroix that I needed some time for a conversation with Dr. Hernandez and she put on a white coat and said she would visit the pediatrics ward in the meantime.

"Take half an hour if you wish," she said and disappeared behind a door marked 'No Entry'.

José Hernandez beckoned curtly for me to follow him into a small examining room.

"Yes, what is it you want now," he said impatiently, fingering his wristwatch.

I got right to the point.

"Gold treasures at Machu Picchu."

"What?" He looked livid. "Miss Prescott! I am a busy man."

I sank down on a plastic covered stool. Seemingly he had no clue what I was talking about. But I still gave it one more shot. I pointed to a chair.

"Won't you sit down for a minute, Dr. Hernandez. I feel I must speak to you at some length."

He looked undecided but then sat down on the edge of the seat. He stared at me.

"I was told," I said softly, "I was told yesterday by Pablo Alvarez that you made him join the tour to Machu Picchu, made him pretend he didn't know you, and made him play a childish game following a map pointing the way to a hidden treasure. The gold of the Incas."

I paused and Dr. Hernandez shifted his gaze. My voice dropped even lower.

"Could he have made up such an improbable story, Dr. Hernandez?"

I tried to catch his eye but he wouldn't let me.

"*Loco,*" he said hoarsely and stood up. "He is a crazy man. Look at me, I am the chief surgeon and director general of this hospital. Are you going to believe a down-at-the-heels art dealer over me? He is not of a sound mind, everyone knows his crazy ideas about the gold of the Incas. A crazy *loco*. A subversive. A communist."

"So, you now confess you know him?"

"Confess!" he spluttered. "I confess nothing."

"Alvarez also said he saw Ms. Bronski in the torture chamber, sitting in the middle seat, looking at someone . . ."

"Well, it wasn't me!" Hernandez exploded. "Just ask my wife. I didn't leave her side for an instant."

Which was hardly true as far as I recalled.

There was a loud knock on the door to the small examining room where we were now standing staring at one another, he furious, I confused. Elena Hernandez' head appeared through the crack in the door.

"José! Are you ready to leave?"

"I most certainly am," he said to her. And to me he hissed: "You will not repeat any of this to anyone. I will sue you for libel!"

And with this final salvo he stalked out.

Therese Lecroix was waiting in the main hall. When we sat in the sedan heading back to the Cesar I complimented her on her work on the committee. I then sat silently the rest of the way while she outlined her plans for the new wards, saying she hoped to advance the cause considerably before leaving Peru for good. Somehow she now sounded as if that was far into the future.

At the last moment I remembered the request from Bob Makowski for more details on the group and said: "Would you happen to know the Hernandez' address in Miami?"

Therese looked surprised but got out an address book just as we drove up in front of the hotel.

"I have it," she said and wrote it down for me. "How much longer do you think you need to stay in Lima?"

"Just until tomorrow," I decided on the spur of the moment. "I may as well give you my report now in case I don't see you. I've re-visited everyone who was on the tour. The new chief of police may become more actively involved in the case. I can't promise you, though. And I'm waiting to receive a background check on the group's members."

"Not much progress," Therese said.

I ignored that.

"When I get back to Washington I'll keep you informed of the results. Do you happen to know the names of any close friends of your sister's in Washington?"

Therese shook her head.

"I never met any," she said categorically. "The only person she ever mentioned was her neighbor. Her small son sometimes spent the afternoons with her."

"Geraldine Harris," I said. "Anyone else?"

"No, she never talked about anyone else. Except, of course, for Mr. Hughes. I always thought she had a small crush on him."

No accounting for taste.

Therese extended her hand.

"Call me soon," she said and I assured her I would.

I went upstairs and changed into jeans and walking shoes. I felt hungry but decided food would wait.

It was almost three-thirty when I walked down Avenida La Paz to Canseca and Alvarez' shop.

CHAPTER 31

I hurried past a pile of evil-smelling garbage festering in the deep gutter and made my way around several street vendors.

The iron grill had been raised halfway in front of Alvarez' shop and I could see light shining through the curtain from the room at the back.

I ducked under the grill and pushed the front door open which produced a faint tinkle from a cluster of brass bells. I stepped into the now familiar musty interior.

A single tube of neon brought a cold sheen to the counter at the back, showing up the grime on the glass shelves and flattening the contours of the colonial interiors in three oil paintings high on the wall. The hand of Gomercinda Flores' son, Jesus, was unmistakable.

I turned around sharply as a sudden draft moved the door open a few inches before slamming it shut. The curtain to the back room was sucked inside and the green lamp shade on the disorderly desk showed up briefly.

The draft rippled across the ceiling making its way like a giant hand tugging on a forest of strings. The marionettes came to life with a faint whistling sound which raised the hairs at the nape of my neck.

I suppressed an exclamation as I felt a clammy bone caress my cheek and looked up at the stretched neck and protruding eyes behind half open lids of a parched llama fetus. The gutted and dried skeleton was hung by the neck and turned slowly on a string, its front legs curled against the chest and the back legs pulling the skin taught around the rib cage. The fetus swung against another, then another, creating a domino effect of swishing skeletons.

I had always hurried in the marketplace when I noticed llama fetuses hanging from wooden beams or lying jumbled in cartons waiting for Indian customers. A fetus buried under the floor of a new construction supposedly protects against the evil eye.

I moved rapidly towards the back of the shop and stopped at the glass counter. I was looking down at four tiers of trays crammed with coins, filigree jewelry, and silver spoons.

I rapped sharply on the glass.

"Señor Alvarez!"

I waited an inordinate amount of time before moving around the counter and pulling the curtain to look inside. The silence continued to envelop me as I stepped through the doorway. The bulb under the green shade fluttered as if at the end of its tether.

The piles of dusty papers, torn envelopes, and old ledgers on the desk looked as if no one had disturbed them since my last visit. A few pages were still scattered on the floor where they had fallen around my feet. A disorderly heap of Indian shawls and ponchos lay near the wall at the far side of the desk.

The overflowing ashtray and the cup half full of cold coffee were still there. But there was something new on the desk sitting on top of a stack of invoices. Three glistening brown pieces of ceramic sculpture so explicitly pornographic that I felt a jolt to my stomach.

I stared in fascination and some revulsion at the crude organs, the slits and protrusions, the lewd positions, and the pre-Columbian cretinous faces with their heavy eyelids and highly polished cheekbones.

I stepped around the desk just as the door leading to the hallway, partly hidden by a black poncho with a single red border, sprang open a crack wide enough to let in another draft. The bulb in the desk lamp fluttered and dimmed twice, then snapped sharply and expired, leaving the room dark except for a faint stripe of light from the hallway.

I groped my way through the door in the near darkness and entered a cramped space next to a narrow staircase leading up. A bare bulb swung above my head from a short wire, spreading murky shadows on the peeling paint on the walls but leaving the staircase dark. I found my flashlight and turned the powerful beam upwards but not before stubbing my toe on the bottom step.

There were ten or twelve steps ending at a closed door. Each one creaked in a different voice as I ascended slowly to the top. The door looked old, painted a dull green, the round metal doorknob blackened by many layers of tarnish.

I knocked, listened to the echo rumble down the stairs, and waited with my ear to the panel for the sound of steps inside.

After about ten seconds I knocked again. Then I tried the knob.

It turned smoothly and the lock clicked. I pushed at the door and it opened wide enough for me to call inside. A musty odor wafted through the crack, a pungent smell of onions mingled with some unidentifiable spice.

"Señor Alvarez?"

I hesitated on the doorstep while shining my flashlight around the tiny entrance hall, debating the wisdom and necessity of trespassing. I groped around until I found a switch which turned on the ceiling light.

The small entrance had no furniture or rug, just three doors, all closed. The first opened into a closet stuffed with merchandise from the shop. The second led to a dingy bathroom with a torn shower curtain.

Behind the third door was the living room. It was fairly large with four windows behind tightly closed shutters. The smell of onion hung like a mist above the dour furniture: a large dining table surrounded by four sturdy chairs on lions' feet, a lumpy sofa and two side tables with mismatched brass lamps.

In the far corner stood a sagging arm chair covered by a plaid blanket still bearing the imprint of a heavy body. Next to the sofa was a low table with a portable radio.

"Señor Alvarez," I called out again but with less conviction.

I followed the onion smell to the kitchen. A large enameled pot stood on an electric plate, small puffs of vapor escaping from under the lid. The tiny window was completely fogged up and little streams of water had gathered at the bottom of the frame, dripping slowly to the floor.

I picked up a soiled dishcloth and lifted the lid. I waved aside the steam to look in. Nothing was left in the pot except for mush in a cupful of liquid. I hauled it to the marble counter and turned the knob to 'off'. The pot was an eight-quart and looked as if it had originally been full to the brim. It must have taken hours for it all to evaporate on such low heat.

I coughed up acid air, closed the door to the kitchen, and stepped back into the living room. Surveying the room once more I ended up staring at a door behind the worn armchair. I approached and knocked tentatively without expecting a response.

I knocked one more time just to be sure, and opened the door. It creaked loudly sounding like a cat in distress and I half expected one to slink out around my feet. But there was no other sound from the room and no movement.

I pushed the door open until I could see most of the bedroom. The light was on. A chest of drawers with a heavy mirror, a double bed at an angle, and a single chair heaped with clothing: a brown jacket, a pair of trousers with the belt trailing, an undershirt with short sleeves, a white shirt with the tie still knotted around the neck.

The bed was empty, the bottom sheet twisted in the middle

and pulled away from the stained mattress. An apple-green wool blanket hung half-way to the floor. One well-worn brown shoe stood next to the bed, the other lay tossed against the wall. The socks were nearby.

There was an eery silence in the room.

I took one step inside and moved to the right of the door. I saw one naked foot, then the other, protruding just beyond the end of the bed.

I was at Alvarez' side in two long strides. He lay on the bare floor dressed only in a pair of boxer shorts, one fleshy arm above his head, the other across his chest. His black hair curled at the nape of his neck but on top it was a dark bloody mass.

I didn't have to touch him to know he was dead.

I disturbed nothing in the bedroom or in the living room on my way back into the hall. But, of course, my fingerprints were on all the doorknobs and on the pot in the kitchen. Not that anyone would probably dust for them.

I closed the door at the top of the stairs without locking and went downstairs using my flashlight to guide me to the last step.

The telephone was on the desk half covered with papers and I picked it up preparing to dial 911 when I realized I didn't know the Peruvian equivalent.

I stuffed the flashlight back in my bag and was about to leave in search of help when I stumbled over the pile of ponchos stacked against the wall. Something fell across my feet. I shuddered thinking 'rats', got the flashlight out again and aimed a strong beam at the floor.

Then I got down on my knees, breathing hard.

I tore the top poncho away and grabbed hold of the hand which had fallen out from under it. I pulled frantically at the rest of the ponchos until I had uncovered the body underneath.

Gomercinda Flores' empty eyes gazed up at me. Her thick lips were parted and the empty space where her front tooth had been showed up as a black spot. Her long braids had fallen forward across her breasts. Her sturdy legs lay twisted, bare, under her turquoise cotton dress. Her white stove-top hat tumbled out from under the last poncho.

I checked her pulse rapidly but knew I wouldn't find one. I hunched over to examine the head wound. Same type as I had just witnessed upstairs. I closed her eyes gently and pulled the poncho back to cover her.

Then I turned around and threw up in the wastepaper basket.

When I recovered I looked around the room for the likely murder weapon. There were plenty of metal and wooden clubs in the shop, several heavy enough to have been used. Not that it would matter.

I locked the door and hurried across the street to use the phone at the pharmacy.

CHAPTER 32

"You forgot something, Señora?"

The little old pharmacist looked at me from the back of the room where he was counting bright orange caplets into a small white paper bag. He folded the top of the bag fastidiously, pressed sharply with his thumbnail, turned down one corner to keep the bag from opening, and placed it in a wooden stand next to a glass jar. He stared at me distractedly above his rimless glasses.

"No. No, I didn't forget anything." I looked at his florid face and wondered briefly how the crisis I was about to spring on him would affect his blood pressure. He blinked his watery blue eyes and waited for me to continue.

"I imagine you know the antique dealer across the street . . . . ," I began.

The pharmacist relaxed visibly.

"Pablo," he said. "We know each other for the past twenty years. I have been here in my pharmacy, he has been there in his antique shop, yes, I know my good friend Alvarez very well."

He kept his eyes on my face.

"Sometimes he loses customers because he leaves without anyone to take care of business. I have told him many times but he is not a businessman. If you give me your telephone number I will let him know you wish to buy from him. Perhaps something pre-Columbian? He has some fine pieces."

His face fell when I shook my head.

"I'm not a customer, exactly," I said. "I'm afraid something has happened to Mr. Alvarez."

"Happened?"

The pharmacist leaned across the counter, his voice tentative, already fending off unpleasant news. "What has happened?"

It could wait no longer, blood pressure or no.

"Mr. Alvarez has suffered an accident. I need you to call the police."

"The police?"

"Yes, I'm afraid he is dead. It looks like murder. And there's a woman dead inside, as well."

"Gomercinda."

It was a statement of fact, not a question. The pharmacist groped behind him for a wooden stool and sat down face in hands. But when he looked up again his expression was composed, his complexion back to normal. He pulled out an old-fashioned black telephone from under the counter. The only sign of stress was the trembling of his hands as he held the receiver in one and traced the phone numbers on a piece of paper with the other.

He stabbed his index finger at a number printed in red and dialed laboriously. I could hear the busy signal rasping. He held down the button, released it gingerly as if careful handling would ensure success, and dialed again. And again. I was just about to suggest trying some other number, any other number, when he seemed to be listening.

He switched the receiver to his other ear as if this would help the outcome.

"Give me the right number. Please! Wait, wait, I must find my pen."

I fished out my pen, tore out a page from my notebook, and

he wrote down a number. He handed the page to me, obviously in no condition to continue the quest.

I pulled the phone across the counter and dialed the new number. Again and again. The pharmacist rocked back and forth on his stool and hardly looked up when I finally got through to the police station in Miraflores.

"*Un momentito*," someone said and put me on hold.

A sergeant came on the line and I explained the situation. I was rewarded with instructions to meet the police outside number 210 within fifteen minutes.

The pharmacist suddenly took charge of the situation and invited me to the back where he produced some fairly hot coffee from a thermos. He kept the door open and assured me he could see clear across the street to Alvarez' shop and would not miss the arrival of the police.

He sat down on a small sofa with me in a chair and brought the coffee cup to his lips. Now that the action was over he seemed to shrink into his white coat, his shoulders sloped and his neck plunged forward, leaving a space inside the collar. He put the cup down on the floor and his entire body began to tremble. I was just about to suggest he get a tranquilizer from one of his own glass jars when he pulled out a flat metal box, extracted a tiny pill and placed it under his tongue. Presently the trembling stopped.

"I'm sorry to have brought you into this," I said. "I would have called the police from over there but I didn't know the number."

I then told him very briefly how I had met Alvarez in Cuzco and had returned in order to discuss some business with him. My explanation didn't seem to register. When I stopped talking he spoke as if he hadn't heard a word.

"Pablo and I have been more than just two business people who happened to own shops on the same street. We looked out for each other. Pablo was married but his wife left him. My own wife died five years ago and I no longer wanted to return home for lunch every day. Pablo, and Gomercinda whenever she was in town, would invite me to eat with them."

I told him about the onion soup that had been cooking on the stove and he nodded in recognition.

"She was always cooking, or working, or traveling. She had tremendous energy."

He rocked back and forth.

"Ach, Gomercinda, she was the brains behind his business, she could find the antiquities his foreign customers wanted and their son, Jesus, yes, I always thought Jesus was Pablo's son, although he never said so and I would not pry into his private affairs. Gomercinda, sometimes she was like a wife and sometimes she was the business partner. These women from Cuzco are tough, don't marry if they have money. They say the Spanish law will give their possessions to the man, so they stay single. Very clever . . . ."

The pharmacist suddenly wrung his thin hands.

"How could this have happened? My friends, who would murder my friends . . ."

I tried to keep his eyes engaged. "Did you know any of Pablo's customers by name?"

He pondered the question.

"There was the French ambassador," he said and straightened his back as if in pride. "Pablo had to find him many pre-Columbian antiques."

"To take out of the country?"

The pharmacist suddenly looked cagey and shook his head. "It is forbidden."

"Did you ever hear that Pablo had dealings with the chief surgeon of the Miraflores General Hospital, Dr. José Hernandez?"

The pharmacist's face changed color again and he swallowed audibly. "I do not know for sure. Really."

"Did Pablo Alvarez ever tell you he was having trouble with anyone? Or did Gomercinda?"

He rubbed his hands together. "I will tell you this in confidence. I told him once he must be careful with smugglers, not to risk himself with the police. And he became insulted. After that I never said another word. But I was afraid greed would lead them into trouble. And now they're dead!"

He looked towards the street and attempted to get up from the sofa. I was on my feet before he was.

"Señora, the police have arrived. Do you wish for me to accompany you?"

"Thank you, but there's no need for that, you didn't discover anything, you just lent me your phone. I'll stop by later to tell you what's happening."

He stayed on the sofa while I went across the street where an ambulance was now parked in front of Alvarez' shop. A short stocky man in a blue suit got out from the passenger side of a black Chevrolet and conferred with the two ambulance attendants. He pointed towards the alley and the ambulance backed into it. He then walked up to the front door and, finding it locked, turned around and acknowledged my presence.

"Your name?" he said.

I told him.

He didn't introduce himself, just turned and rattled the door knob again.

"I locked the door when I left the shop," I said. "To prevent anyone else from entering. There's an entrance to the apartment in the alley."

The blue suit grunted and went around the corner without inviting me to accompany him. I followed him anyway just in time to see him put a powerful shoulder to the back door. It burst open without noticeable resistance and within seconds he was inside taking the stairs two at a time. The ambulance attendants and a uniformed policeman followed him up the stairs with me in pursuit.

We crowded through the tiny hallway into the living room which still reeked of onion, and into the bedroom. They looked briefly at Alvarez' body on the floor behind the bed and the blue suit told the one in the uniform to look around for a weapon. I thought he mumbled something about the *gringa.*

He then beckoned me to the living room where he sat down at the table. I took a seat without waiting for an invitation. He produced a small orange notepad with a drawing of two balloons on the cover, and made me spell out my name and address in the States. He also noted down my room number at the Cesar.

"I thought you said you found two people dead," he said curtly. "Where's the other one?"

"Downstairs." I used the same curt tone and he shot me a sour look. His black eyes didn't waver.

"Show me."

I moved towards the stairs just as the uniformed policeman appeared with the information that there was no likely murder weapon in the bedroom and should they take the body to the morgue? Permission was given and the ambulance attendants went down to get a stretcher. I suppressed a desire to question this hurried procedure. No photographs, no doctor? Needless to say, no fingerprinting.

Alvarez' office lay in darkness and I pulled out my flashlight to shine it on the heap of ponchos with which I had covered Gomercinda. The blue suit peeled them off until he got to the body.

"Same type of weapon," he grunted and looked around the dim room. He pulled aside the curtain to the shop and stuck his head through. "Plenty of weapons in here," he continued as if to himself. "*Bueno*, move her. Double them up on the stretcher. Keep everything locked up. Board up the back door."

The uniformed underling acknowledged the instructions and I followed the blue suit outside. He motioned for me to get into the back seat of the Chevrolet.

"I didn't catch your name," I said.

"Sosa, Captain."

"Captain Sosa, are you inviting me to the station to make a statement?"

"That's right." He waited for me to get in and slammed the door shut. What was his problem, anyway? Maybe he'd just gotten out on the wrong side of the bed or, improbably, he didn't like blondes. Whatever it was I had somehow rubbed him the wrong way. He sat in front next to the driver and didn't speak a word to me the entire way.

The Miraflores police station was tucked into a back street and sported the same scuffed desks and metal chairs I had seen at police headquarters in town. I was ushered into a tiny windowless office where I was made to wait until Captain Sosa showed up after more than half an hour. He had brought a larger, less infantile notebook this time and sat down opposite me at a small table.

He tapped his pencil on the table top with infuriating speed and shot his questions at me.

"What were you doing upstairs in the man, Alvarez', private apartment?"

"I had arranged to meet him downstairs and waited for quite a while before I went to look for him upstairs."

"Why did you not just leave and return later?"

"I had no time to waste. I'm leaving for the United States."

"Why were you meeting with him?"

Thanks to my solitary confinement I'd been able to go over my strategy.

"He was bringing in some ponchos for me to choose from," I said.

"And they were in a heap on the floor covering a body?"

"I don't know if they were the ones, I never got to talk to him."

"Did you know the woman?"

"Her name was Gomercinda Flores. She lived in Cuzco, had a craft shop there."

"And you've been there?"

"Alvarez took me there to visit a couple of weeks ago."

"So, you have known him a long time?"

"No, only for about a month."

"Where did you meet him?"

"On a tour to Machu Picchu."

A silence fell between us.

Captain Sosa stared at his notepad. His eyes looked like black holes. He got up without another word and strutted from the room leaving me behind. I decided to give him five minutes before going in search of him.

The minutes crept forward slowly and the small office began to feel thoroughly oppressive. I went to the door and turned the handle. Nothing happened. I rattled it to no avail and suppressed an urge to pound. He'd actually locked me in as in an act of unlawful imprisonment which probably meant nothing here.

When he reappeared I said: "Look here, I don't appreciate your locking me inside. What's the big idea?"

"Locking you inside? Nonsense, Señorita." He actually smirked. "I won't need you for much longer, just for signing a short statement."

He escorted me to a waiting room where he left me, again without further explanation. Within the next hour I approached the woman at the desk outside the waiting room about six times. Each time I was told not to worry, or to have patience, or to sit down and, at the end, impatiently, just to wait until I was called.

The call came a few minutes later.

The chief of police, Jorge Bustamante, strode into the room followed by Captain Sosa who closed the door firmly. Sosa must have recognized my name and put it together with Elsa Bronski's murder.

"Captain Sosa here tells me you have found two more bodies, Señorita Prescott," said Bustamante and sat down in one of the uncomfortable chairs. "You make a habit of this, apparently. Would you like to explain this to me?"

I took my time.

"A coincidence," I finally said.

"Didn't I warn you about interfering in police work?"

"How am I interfering in your work?"

"I am not sure, but you keep showing up in the wrong places," he said sourly. "In any event we will have an announcement in the case very soon. And an arrest."

"You must have come across many irregularities among the suspects in this case. I imagine you've found out about Dr. José Hernandez' illegal trade in antiquities?"

I thought he would explode but he managed to keep his calm. His message was unequivocal, though, and consisted of a warning about libelous allegations against a respected Peruvian citizen who had the absolute confidence of the most illustrious persons in the country. After delivering this salvo he stood up and beckoned Sosa outside.

As soon as the door closed behind them I walked over to open it just wide enough to note that they'd disappeared. I decided to stay outside just in case the door was locked on me again.

When Sosa returned he handed me a typed statement to the effect that I testified to finding the bodies, that I'd known Alvarez and Gomercinda, and that I'd met Alvarez on the tour to Machu Picchu where an American citizen, Elsa Bronski, had been murdered. He handed me a black ink pen and watched as I signed. He then escorted me to the exit without admonishing me to stay in town and left me to walk six blocks to the nearest main street.

A rusty VW Beetle with an amateurish taxi sign swerved across two lanes, setting off a symphony of car horns. It screeched to a halt at the curb three feet away from me. Throwing caution to the wind I got in next to the driver. The fare to my destination would be the equivalent of less than a dollar.

The back seat was piled high with shoe boxes, and during our brief ride I learned that my driver held down three jobs: as a night watchman in a textile factory, as a delivery service driver during the day, and as an interim taxi driver. He looked neat and clean and confessed to being a university graduate trying to beat the unemployment rate. I paid him outside the pharmacy on Canseca and returned his friendly wave as he drove off.

Although it was almost nine in the evening the pharmacy was open and the only customer left just as I stepped through the door. The pharmacist greeted me as a long-lost friend, locked the door, turned the 'closed' sign around, and took me to the back for another cup of thermos coffee.

"I left a message for Jesus," he said. "I wanted to tell him before he hears from the police. They came back just a few minutes ago to ask if I had seen anything. I told them all I did was lend you the phone." He looked at me anxiously.

"Don't worry," I said and gulped down the bitter coffee. He then turned out the lights, locked the door, cranked down the grill, and we left together, he taking a left and I turning slowly towards the Cesar.

When he had disappeared from view I made a U-turn to the other side of the street and went back to Alvarez' shop. I wanted to take another look at the downstairs without Sosa breathing down my neck.

The alley was pitch dark. The entrance to Alvarez' apartment had been loosely boarded but there was no warning sign from the police against entering. I ran the beam of my flashlight along the wall which revealed large patches of crumbling brick under peeling plaster. The beam reflected off of a large metal trash can without a lid. Garbage was piled up around it in a sodden mass.

I turned off the flashlight and was just about to pry the board loose when my foot caught the edge of the trash can lid. It swung up in the air and smacked into my kneecap. I yelped in surprise and pain and dropped my flashlight. I rubbed my knee vigorously and leaned against the wall until I was sure the noise hadn't prompted any curiosity from neighbors or pedestrians.

I resumed work on the board and managed to squeeze my fingers behind it and pull. The nails let go with surprising ease and it was just a matter of moments before I had the door open and was inside at the bottom of the staircase.

I groped my way to the small office, not wanting to use the flashlight until I was sure the curtain at the doorway leading to the shop was closed. I felt my way around the desk, shoving tentatively at the chair and the wooden stool.

I pulled the curtains tight and shone a beam of light on the desk. The pile of invoices was still there but the indecent ceramic sculptures were gone.

I heard the whooshing sound too late to turn. My flashlight rattled to the floor at the moment my knees buckled and my body pitched forward.

The blow to the back of my head plunged me into immediate darkness.

CHAPTER 33

SOMETHING wet and cold was seeping through my jeans and plastering the shirt to my body.

Lying in the alley on my back next to the trash can I looked up at a rectangle of night-blue sky. I turned my head carefully and moaned as pain shot from the back of my head into my shoulders. My left arm was pinned under my body. The only feeling I had was a burning sensation in my fingers. My right arm was stretched out and rested on top of my handbag. I eased to a sitting position and leaned against the wall.

I stayed put until the buzzing in my ears diminished. Then I turned around on my knees, grabbed a hold of the top of the trash can and hoisted myself up very carefully. I felt for the bump at the back of my head. It was already the size of a golf ball. I took a tentative step, then another, waiting for signs of a serious concussion. When no nausea made itself known, I picked up my bag and prepared to walk. My shirt was hanging outside my wet jeans and I didn't even try to stuff it back inside the waistband.

Slowly I made my way out of the alley into the deserted street. I was only one and a half blocks away from the Cesar but it seemed like ten before I reached the entrance. The doors were locked and

I had to wait for the imperturbable doorman to appear from behind the reception to let me in.

"Señorita Prescott," he said and held the door, allowing only a flicker of an eye to indicate curiosity. I decided to let him speculate in private on my peculiar behavior and struggled the half mile across the lobby to the elevator. I was shaking by the time I reached my door. Then I had another struggle to find the key and get inside my room.

I moved directly to the bathroom without glancing at myself in the many mirrors, shed my clothes, and got in the shower. It was 4:30 a.m. when I lay down in bed, on my stomach, with an improvised ice-pack on the golf ball at the back of my head.

When I woke up at nine the ice cubes had soaked the mattress and I had a massive headache. It was all I could manage to call room service for breakfast and, when it arrived, to reach the door. I took two painkillers with the orange juice and went back to bed, waiting for the results.

The only thing I recalled was standing in Alvarez' office looking for the sculptures. Thinking back I remembered my feeling of surprise that the board at the door had come loose so easily. But I had been too intent on getting inside to pay proper attention.

At eleven I felt well enough to get dressed and descended to find Pancho and the Dodge. He was there, leaning on the shiny hood, and snapped to attention when he saw me.

I told him to take me to the French ambassador's residence and got into the car taking great care with my stiff neck and bruised arm. As the Dodge swung into traffic I suddenly felt a greater appreciation for Pancho's sedate driving habits and diplomatic silence.

On my instructions he let me out half a block from the residence. I walked to the gate leading to the garage. The armed guard was sitting across the street against a wall, weapon across his knees, cap over his eyes, fast asleep.

I rang the bell several times before a door next to the garage opened and a tiny woman in a white apron peered outside. I waved her forward and the woman stepped lightly down the path to the gate.

"Señora?"

"Are you a friend of Pablo Alvarez?"

The woman raised her hand to cover her mouth. She giggled behind it.

"No, Señora!"

"But you know him?"

"No, Señora!"

"Then whom does he visit here?"

"I don't know, Señora!"

The woman turned away and I had to give up.

She disappeared inside the house and the guard suddenly woke up and came across to lean against the crippled tree at the curb.

I said 'Buenos Dias' and shook my head at my own involuntary obeisance to the persuasive power of his gun. I walked to the main gate and pressed the button vigorously. The butler appeared in record time and, recognizing me, let me in without first checking with Therese Lecroix.

He showed me straight into the blue living room. The house smelled of furniture polish and ammonia, and a cool draft flowed through from the open windows leading to the back garden.

Therese came in looking different in blue jeans and a tight t-shirt that revealed slim hips and broad shoulders. She wore no jewelry and with her hair pulled up in a ponytail she looked fifteen years younger than when I'd last seen her.

"A surprise visit," she said and wiped her palms down her thighs. "But I am glad you are here. I was about to call you."

"Yes?"

"I wanted to tell you I am leaving for France tomorrow."

"In that case I will give you an account of my expenses." I fished out my notebook and tore out the page marked Lecroix.

Therese glanced briefly at the bottom line and stuck the account in her pocket.

"And your husband," I said, "is he going with you?"

"No. George left yesterday morning, a very sudden decision. He took the eleven twenty flight, didn't even come home from the office, just sent the driver for a suitcase which I had to pack for him within ten minutes." Therese looked irritated.

"He didn't give you any explanation?"

"No, none at all. But I have my suspicions." Therese looked away. "Money. His problem is money. He has gambled irresponsibly on the stock exchange."

"Is that what he told you?"

"He tells me nothing. But I always know. That is why he was interested in my inheritance from Elsa. I will not stand for this, I will divorce him now, before the estate is settled. He deserves nothing."

"Where will you be staying in Paris?"

"At 2100 Rue du Ranelagh, just off Avenue Mozart. I have rented an apartment."

"I know exactly where that is," I exclaimed. "The Metro station is on the corner. A friend of mine used to live there."

Therese smiled. "You must visit me in Paris, my dear Jamie. Write down my telephone number as well."

I did, and after a few minutes she excused herself and returned with a check for my expenses.

I looked at her carefully.

"Did George by any chance mention Pablo Alvarez before he left?"

"Pablo Alvarez?" Therese's face looked curiously naked without make-up and the flush which spread on her face had nowhere to hide.

"Why?" she said.

"George did know him, didn't he?" I realized I had spoken in the past tense but Therese didn't notice. "It's all right, Therese," I added. "I'm not investigating George for smuggling."

I paused while Therese regained her normal color. "Unless, of course, George's money trouble ties him in with Elsa's murder."

"Oh, no!" She shook her head categorically. "George was not on the tour."

"But Alvarez was."

"Are you accusing George of conspiring with Alvarez to murder Elsa? Absolutely ridiculous. You do not know George at all."

I wouldn't say that, I thought. It's true there's a difference between beating your wife and making someone commit murder. But probably not much.

I held Therese's gaze sternly.

"I really need you to tell me if George went to see Alvarez yesterday before leaving so suddenly for Paris?"

She didn't waver.

"It is true he might be carrying something he got from Alvarez. But he could have hidden it for some time. I do not search his closets." She laughed, not exactly happily. "I do not have keys to his closets."

Really! I thought.

"He did not go anywhere the last evening he was here. We went to a reception at the Korean embassy and returned here together."

"What time did he leave yesterday morning?"

"Well." Therese looked uncertain. "He left early. I was surprised to see him up at six and ready to go."

"And his driver picked him up?"

"No. George drove his private car to the office." Therese had paled.

We looked at one another in silence.

"Look," I said at last. "I hardly know the best way to tell you this. Pablo Alvarez was murdered yesterday in the early morning hours." I held up my hand when she started spluttering. "I don't know the exact hour."

In the absence of a doctor's examination it would depend on how long it took eight quarts of onion soup to evaporate on a low fire.

"Oh, no. I cannot believe any such thing about George," she stammered.

"Did George say when he would be back in Lima?"

She shook her head. I could almost hear her thoughts racing. George had the motive and Alvarez the opportunity and later Alvarez had to be eliminated.

"Are you going to tell the police?" she asked.

"I may have to at some point."

"But not yet?"

I shook my head. I wasn't contemplating another interview with the Peruvian police.

"Just be careful," I told her. "I wouldn't discuss this with George if I were you."

She looked stunned.

Before leaving I told her I would be in touch with her from Bethesda.

It was only a matter of a five-minute drive to the Hernandez residence and Pancho got me there in ten.

The maid opened the door the smallest crack to peer at me. The Señora was not at home and, no, she had no idea when the Señora would be back. And the same applied to the doctor.

"Are they traveling by any chance?" I just managed to throw in before the door was closed and I heard what sounded like a negative answer.

I instructed Pancho to drive by the Miraflores General Hospital on our way back to the Cesar.

The main hall at the hospital was teeming with visitors and patients, the noise as deafening as on my first visit. I made my way to the private elevator at the back and ascended to the sixth floor. The well-coifed and manicured receptionist looked up from a glossy magazine without any evident interest.

"Señora?"

"I'm here to see Dr. Hernandez. The name is Prescott."

She didn't even glance at the open appointment book before she shook her head.

"You do not have an appointment," she said, implying that was the end of our conversation.

"I know. But just let him know I'm here, he'll want to see me."

She shook her head.

"He's not here, he left early."

I looked around the room at the three doors in view. I walked to the nearest which had a sign saying 'Director General' and opened it under the horrified protests of the receptionist.

The office was empty.

"Señora! He is not here. He has not been in all day."

"You mean he didn't come in this morning? Isn't that unusual?"

The receptionist nodded unhappily and looked furtively at the telephone.

"Could he be somewhere else at the hospital? Could you find out?"

She agreed a little too eagerly and picked up the phone. She spoke into it rapidly asking someone to come to the sixth floor immediately. She needed help.

I wagged a finger at her and headed for the elevator. The doors opened immediately and I descended to the hall where I held the stop button to allow two agitated security guards inside. They went up and I walked outside to the Dodge.

By now even the slightest bump in the road made my head pound and I wished I could have stayed in the hospital for an X-ray. It would have to wait.

At the Cesar I paid off Pancho and told him to take me to the airport in the morning. He looked crushed to lose my patronage and seemed only vaguely reassured by my promise of an eventual return to Lima.

A large group of tourists was checking in at the desk and I didn't notice Captain Sosa until I was almost at the elevator.

CHAPTER 34

Sosa was leaning into the shadows between the staircase and the elevators but became mobile the moment I stepped up to the doors. He was no longer in his blue suit. His gray uniform looked brand new, with black epaulets and shiny brass buttons. His peaked cap was tucked jauntily into his left armpit. His eyes shone like black marbles in his round face and, as he stepped closer, a narrow white line flashed briefly across his face. But when Sosa spoke his lips hardly moved.

He clicked his heels, thrust his right hand forward and handed me a white envelope.

"I am serving you this order in the name of His Excellency, the Minister of the Interior!"

I had no choice but to accept the envelope. I let the doors to the elevator open and close without making a move and walked towards the lights near the staircase with Sosa close on my heels.

There was a single sheet of paper in the envelope with an impressive black letterhead followed by the name of the minister. The letter was typed on a defective manual typewriter which had punched out all the o's. All that remained were perfect little holes ringed in black.

The letter contained only one paragraph dwarfed by an intricate signature made illegible by a series of tightly crisscrossing vertical and horizontal strokes. The red lacquer seal at the bottom was imprinted with an equally illegible stamp.

The message was brief. I was declared *persona non grata* by virtue of my unwarranted interference in the internal affairs of the Sovereign State of Peru. I was ordered to leave the country immediately. I would be escorted to the airport by Captain Emilio Sosa.

I read it through several times. The letterhead was obviously authentic and the defective typing didn't surprise me. I kept my eyes on the page until I felt reasonably sure I would be able to control my facial expression and my voice.

When I looked into Sosa's glowing eyes I caught his look of disappointment at my lack of emotion and felt a surge of confidence. I stuffed the letter back in its envelope and dropped it inside my handbag.

Two officers of lesser rank had materialized behind Sosa and looked at me curiously as they leaned close enough to listen in.

"You didn't have to go to all this trouble, Sosa," I said. "I'm leaving tomorrow."

Sosa smirked. "You are leaving tonight! And you will be unable to return!"

"We'll see about that," I retorted, referring to my return. He obviously had the power to send me off tonight.

"You will pack immediately. We must be at the airport in two hours." Sosa looked at his watch. "You have thirty minutes. The hotel has been instructed to prepare your bill. You can pay it now before we go upstairs."

I paid the bill which came to just over four hundred dollars. The cashier kept her eyes demurely lowered throughout the transaction and didn't insist on sending someone to the room to check the refrigerator bar. I had to suppress a sudden urge to explain that I was wrongly accused, that I was innocent. But my moment of near panic passed, I tucked the receipt in my wallet, brought out my key, and walked to the elevator once more, this time followed by Sosa and his two officers.

The four of us filled most of the space in the small elevator. I contemplated the pock-marked neck of the sergeant who stood stiffly and uncomfortably close, my nostrils filling with the odor of cheap after-shave lotion.

They crowded around me at the door.

I dangled the key in the air in front of Sosa's face.

"I'm going inside alone," I said, "or not at all."

To my relief he stepped back just enough to indicate he would let me.

"Thirty minutes," he said peevishly.

I shut and bolted the door and was at the phone in a couple of long strides. I found the number in my address book and dialed.

"American Embassy, good afternoon," said a pleasant voice. I opened my mouth to ask for Jim Brown but all I managed was 'hello' before the line went dead with a prolonged whine and two beeps.

I gave it up right there. It could be the endemic sickness of the Peruvian telephone system but more likely it was due to the machinations of Sosa.

Once back home I'd call the Embassy to launch a protest and clear my record before another trip on travel agency business. As far as the investigation, Therese and George Lecroix would be in Paris, Hernandez presumably in Miami. Lupesco was in New York, Vicky Anderson would soon be there, and the Robinsons were in Maryland. Hopefully, Ivanovich would decide to stay put in Ecuador and, equally hopefully, he would call me in the States. Collect.

It would have been pleasant to shower before leaving but by now there was no time. I dropped my one dress, the pants suit, blouses, jeans, and toiletries into my tote, congratulating myself on my economical packing methods. I pulled on a thin sweater on top of my white silk blouse, donned my jacket, checked the closets and bathroom one more time, flicked back the bed-cover and lifted the pillows. Nothing left behind.

I was ready to leave.

Sosa was leaning against the wall directly opposite my door, his arms folded. The two sergeants stood together a little further along the corridor. They managed to avoid eye-contact but it was probably too much to imagine they felt embarrassed.

The elevator doors opened on a couple dressed for a night on the town. The woman wore a white gardenia pinned to her bosom, the man a tight-fitting dinner jacket. They moved back to make room but Sosa stretched out his arm to prevent me from entering. I caught a glimpse of the apprehensive look on the couple's faces as they went on without us. The next car was empty.

On the way down Sosa studied himself three ways in the mirrors and adjusted his peaked cap with a smug expression. The uniform was doing wonders for him.

A black lorry which looked like a padded wagon obstructed the entrance. Apparently, this was to be my transportation to the airport. It had attracted a small crowd of onlookers including the couple from the elevator.

The doorman sprang to my side to take charge of my luggage and, to his credit, kept going even when he realized I was headed for the prison wagon under police guard.

"Everything in order, Ms. Prescott?" he asked anxiously. When I nodded he brought my bag to the wagon and stepped aside reluctantly.

A dark figure separated from the crowd which had shrunk against the far wall at the sight of three police officers. Pancho, with admirable disregard for the dangers inherent in tangling with the authorities, stepped up behind Sosa and spoke loud enough for everyone to hear.

"Señorita, what about tomorrow. Will you need me?"

"Pancho!" I said with feeling. "I apologize! I am forced to leave tonight instead of tomorrow and, as you can see, I have been provided with transportation!"

I stuck out an elbow to ward off Sosa and grabbed a large handful of Peruvian bills from the outside pocket of my handbag.

I thrust the bundle into Pancho's hand and said "thanks for your excellent driving!"

Pancho, looking very confused, retreated with a tentative wave of his hand as I got all the way into the back seat and we took off.

The wagon lumbered towards the airport and I watched through the barred window as streets and sidewalks, trees and people floated sedately by. Sosa rubbed his small brown hands methodically up and down his thighs and never once looked at me, not even when he ordered me to hand over my ticket.

"My ticket?" I said. "I prefer to handle the check-in myself."

"I will do it," he answered curtly. "You will get your ticket back on the plane."

I decided nothing was to be gained by an argument although I was tempted since it was so easy to goad him into a state of extreme irritation. I still didn't understand what he had against me. Men are usually attracted to me!

A gate behind the arrival hall opened with unusual speed when the prison wagon pulled up. We entered a restricted area. We cruised to the right and came to a halt at a door outside customs. Sosa and the two sergeants escorted me inside. They let me wheel my own bag and soon I was waiting in a small office. Almost immediately a woman customs officer appeared and planted herself in front of me.

"You are required to take off your clothes, down to your underwear. Strip search."

I looked at her incredulously. My reaction was instantaneous.

I was at the door in two quick steps and into the hallway before she could bar my way. Sosa was in his habitual position against a wall, arms akimbo. He dropped them and looked, for once, at a loss when I came barging out.

"That's it!" I shouted. "You will now get my bag and take me directly to the plane or I'll make a real scandal. I can become very disagreeable!"

When he just stood there I filled my lungs with stale air and let out a trial scream which reverberated along the corridor and caused several heads to pop out of doorways.

Sosa's face reddened and he put up his hands in defense.

"*Bueno*, Señorita," he said meekly. He went inside and I heard him talk to the female officer. Then he came back and handed me my bag. A second later we were on our way to the plane.

The aircraft had been kept waiting. The Boeing was jam-packed with passengers who were just dying to see the cause of their delay, and here I came. Sosa made a big production of getting a flight attendant to stuff my bag in the overhead compartment. He handed me my ticket reluctantly—his fun was coming to an end—and swaggered back down the aisle towards the exit.

I fell into my window seat as the lights dimmed and music poured into the cabin. The couple next to me entered into a whispered consultation and flagged down a flight attendant as soon as we were airborne. In short order they arranged to be transferred to first class, presumably because of acute discomfort at being seated next to a felon. It was a blessing because I could now stretch out across three seats and go to sleep.

The proceedings at Immigration and Customs in Miami were peaceful and quiet. No one questioned my right to be there and I bypassed the beady eyes of my fellow passengers, most of whom had to stand in the interminable visitors' lines.

I went upstairs to the main terminal to change my reservations to Washington and get a new boarding card. By the time I was squared away it was only 6:30 a.m., too early to call anyone.

I settled down in the coffee shop near Gate C with a huge Danish, orange juice, and coffee, and watched as bundles of newspapers were tossed on the floor in the gift shop opposite. I got up to get the *Washington Post*.

A stack of papers in the corner revealed the late edition of *Ultima Hora*, the Peruvian afternoon paper. I bent closer to look at the prominent headlines. *Police Chief Bustamante Solves Machu Picchu Murder* they screamed and, in slightly smaller letters: *Suspected Terrorist Arrested.*

A familiar face stared at me from a grainy photograph spread across the top part of the page. Ivanovich looking stunned, his body sagging against a bare brick wall, one eyelid half closed, a dark smear down his left cheek, and his braid half undone.

My Hard-Rock Café t-shirt was visible under the trench coat. Only the black leather cap and the sunglasses were missing.

CHAPTER 35

I read the newspaper account for the third time just as my flight made a wide circle above Washington, D.C.

Bustamante's photograph, a flattering picture showing him in half profile, spread across the second and third columns. He had been interviewed in his office at a press conference and had summarized the murder of Elsa Bronski in the torture chamber at Machu Picchu several weeks earlier. He described how he had taken charge of this mysterious crime immediately upon being appointed chief of police and how the Minister of the Interior had instructed him to solve the case with all possible speed. This would be in the interest of diplomatic relations with the United States of America, the victim being a citizen of that country, and with the Republic of France, the victim being related to the wife of the ambassador from that country.

Bustamante had his suspicions from the start, he said. The arrested man, Boris Ivanovich Garcia, was a known terrorist, communist, and agitator, whose father, Andrei Ivanovich, had been involved in subversive activities against the State—his name alone was indicative of his subversiveness—since his arrival in Peru in the early 1950s. It was obvious the apple had not fallen far from the tree.

And, a reporter asked, had the suspect confessed? Well, Bustamante said, not exactly, but he would soon enough when faced with the overwhelming evidence. And the Chief of Police had produced a series of photographs taken at the murder scene purported to have been found in the suspect's apartment, as ample proof that the suspect was a hardened murderer who had gone out of his way to document his dastardly deed. My pictures. The rat!

And, the reporter asked, what had been the motive? Well, Bustamante said, this would become clear once the suspect had been thoroughly interrogated and his fingerprints had been matched to those on the murder weapon.

I folded the newspaper and tried to remember if Ivanovich could possibly have touched the knitting needle at some point. Not that it would make any difference.

The strong midday sun shimmered on the waters of the Potomac River, the plane turned, the Pentagon careened in and out of sight in my small window and we settled in just above the water for the final approach. The wheels caught the landing strip at the strategic moment, the engines braked, and I was home.

A cab brought me to Bethesda and I went directly upstairs. The apartment had acquired, even in the brief time I'd been away, an uninhabited air. Topsy had watered my one surviving fern enthusiastically and a small pool had evaporated around the base leaving a gray imprint on the parquet floor. I raised the blinds and opened the windows before climbing the stairs to the bedroom. I looked longingly at my bed but decided to postpone the pleasure of sleep until the early evening.

I didn't even unpack but went downstairs to the agency. Topsy sprang to her feet. Her hair had been recently frizzed and frosted and with her freckled nose and full lips she looked amazingly the way she had some twenty odd years ago when I'd first seen her in the dorm room we were to share. Bubbly, sunny, take-charge.

She held me by the shoulders at arm's length and studied my face.

"You look awful," she declared cheerfully. "I'm taking you out for lunch and you can tell me all about it. Then you'll get an early night's sleep and be good as new in the morning."

Fifteen minutes later we were at our favorite Italian restaurant. I told her the latest development first.

"*Persona non grata*! Ha!" Topsy guffawed. "Yeah, that's how I've often thought of you when you're being really exasperating and stubborn."

"Well, now you know why I look awful. Last night I had only four hours of sleep, the night before I discovered a double murder. Later I was knocked unconscious and left for dead in the mud, and the night before that I had a subversive terrorist in my bed."

Topsy, easily baited, wanted to know about the terrorist.

"Well, he was waiting for me late one night and just followed me to my room. Before I could get him into bed I had to feed him, clean his clothes, give him pain-killers . . . ."

"What are you rambling about?" Topsy stopped eating and brandished her fork in my face.

I laughed and outlined the events of the past seven days. Topsy listened attentively. She was my familiar sounding board, eager and willing to analyze and pronounce verdicts, sometimes rash with even the rashness feeding my imagination, but most of the time thoroughly practical and logical.

"Two more murders!" She looked genuinely shocked, her eyes blurring over. "And who knocked you unconscious?"

"I have no idea."

"Could it have been Captain Sosa?"

"Could have been, but somehow I doubt it."

"And that Gomercinda," Topsy said. "She sounded like such an impressive character. How gruesome for you to find them. I don't know what you find so fascinating about the detecting business. Honest to God, Jamie, why?"

I just shook my head and concentrated on my food. There was nothing I could say. Apparently we had to have this conversation every so often. Topsy let silence reign for a while longer before she resigned herself.

"You don't for a minute believe your subversive terrorist, the ubiquitous Ivanovich, is guilty, do you? Of murdering Elsa Bronski, I mean."

"No. No, I don't." I stirred extra sugar in my cappuccino.

"The police probably caught Ivanovich the minute he stepped out of the elevator at your hotel after he'd spent a pleasant couple of hours in your bed. Was this your first experience with a man with waist-long hair?" Topsy sucked suggestively on the small straw in her coffee.

"I did notice the elevator stopped on the first floor when Ivanovich went down," I said, ignoring her. "And I never did see him in the street."

"Alvarez seemed the more likely murder suspect," Topsy said. "I don't mean to speak ill of the dead but he sounded very shady. Whose account did you believe about the Inca gold rush, his or Dr. Hernandez'?"

"The trouble is, Alvarez sounded so convincing when he first told me. But then Dr. Hernandez' counter explanation was convincing, too."

Topsy looked speculative.

"Maybe Alvarez' story was only partly true but he laid it on thick to convince you?"

"So, if Alvarez' gold story wasn't true, did he murder Elsa Bronski for George Lecroix?" Topsy said.

"Ah, so you've thought of that?"

"George needs money. Wife's sister has money. Sister books far-away tour. Wife catches cold, cannot go on trip. Alvarez agrees to kill for George (why I haven't figured out yet). George kills Alvarez to silence him. George departs for Paris. Waits for inheritance to kick in."

"Enter Bustamante to protect brother-in-law, Dr. Hernandez," I continued. "Arrests Ivanovich and, inadvertently, gets George Lecroix off the hook."

"Disposes of the annoying Ms. Prescott. Induces his superior, the Minister of the Interior, to issue a deportation order, or . . ." She looked at me expectantly.

"Or types it up himself! Don't think it didn't cross my mind. But I figured I'd rather accept a free ride to the airport than spend a few really nasty nights in a lousy jail, and I mean lousy. I just hadn't foreseen the strip search."

We laughed and Topsy paid for lunch.

"What else is new," I asked as we sauntered back to the agency.

"I had an SOS from the McCormicks yesterday. When they arrived in Hong Kong their luggage failed to appear for several days. Then, when they arrived in Singapore their bags had gone to Bangkok. Rather than waiting they decided to follow the luggage to Bangkok. Then guess what happened?"

"Their luggage was returned to Singapore?"

"Right. They're waiting for it to reach them as we speak. It's been a nightmare and it's a hundred to one they'll blame me. And they're friends of Jack's. I'll have to invite them to dinner.

"Well, count me out!"

"Even if I invite Archibald Brewster?"

"Especially if you do."

"Have you been out with him yet?" Topsy stepped faster in order to get a better look at my face. And, as she often tells me, my face is like an open book. Not the best attribute for a private investigator as she also tells me.

"You have!" she concluded. "You know you can't hide anything from me."

"Oh, okay. We had dinner the night before I went to Lima. Just food. That was all."

"I shall be watching further developments!"

I left her at the door to the agency feeling sufficiently awake to make a few phone calls before getting that early night.

It wasn't too difficult for me to get the information I needed from a friend of mine at the airline. In fact, I was able to access the entire passenger list on screen. George Lecroix had indeed been on the Sunday morning flight from Lima. After scrolling through to the end I sat staring out the window for quite a while pondering my next move before going upstairs.

I turned on the answering machine. All my new messages had come in within the past two days. My mother, sounding cheerful, just wanted to say 'Hi'. Bob Makowski said please call the minute you get back. A competing long-distance phone company urged me to switch loyalties. My Alma Mater's alumni association begged for a contribution to the scholarship fund. Somewhat surprisingly Vicky Anderson told me she was already in New York. And Archibald Brewster, all serious business, had left his cell phone number asking me to call concerning the Lecroix case.

I dialed Charles Lupesco's New York number first and got Vicky on the line on the first ring.

"You wouldn't believe it," she said. "I got here Saturday and on Monday Charles was sent to Paris to substitute at a conference, and off he went leaving me here in his lovely apartment, doorman an' all, but all by myself."

"When will he be back?"

"Hopefully before I have to return to Peru although I did take an extra week off. You said you might be coming to New York . . . I'd love to see you . . ."

"I'll do my best. I can't promise but let's keep in touch. I'll call you." I more or less doubted I'd get to New York that soon but she sounded so pitiful I didn't have the heart to discourage her completely.

Archibald Brewster picked up on the second ring but asked if he could call me back later. Bob Makowski's line was busy so I called my mother's office and was told she was in court.

Sort of at a dead end I went upstairs and ran four miles on the track while watching TV, then did a half hour of stretches and push-ups. I stood a long time in a steaming hot shower and had just put on a sweatsuit when Bob called.

He had a good laugh at my *persona non grata* story but sobered up when I told him about the two new murders.

"I've got a lot of information for you," he said. "How about lunch tomorrow?"

We agreed to meet at the Mayflower Hotel at noon and I hung up feeling satisfied that something, at last, was moving along. I pulled out my notes from the trip, turned on the computer in the den and entered the report. I printed out a hard copy and took it upstairs to bed with a cup of tea and toast. I had just reread the report when my mother rang. I frankly didn't have the energy to tell her my long story and just said I'd come to her house for lunch on Saturday.

Archibald Brewster hadn't called back but I turned off the phone, read half a page in *The New Yorker*, and went to sleep.

CHAPTER 36

Bob Makowski was late as usual and I was seated with the menu by the time he arrived. He eased himself around the table with some difficulty, dragging the tablecloth askew until we sat side by side on the half-circular leather sofa. I contemplated his still-evident, though former, FBI special agent persona: Marine crew cut, dark suit, sober tie, white shirt, and spit-and-polish wing-tips. A bulky George Washington University ring glowed ruby-red on one fleshy finger.

He waited until we had ordered before handing me a sheaf of printed pages. His gray eyes were somehow naked in his smooth, square face.

"The information you requested," he said with a satisfied smile and added unnecessarily: "Go right ahead, start reading, don't mind me."

"Can you believe it," I said, just as the food was served. I read aloud.

"Victoria Elizabeth Anderson, born Omaha, Nebraska, April 7, 1968, student at Columbia University, 1988, convicted of shoplifting, no trace of whereabouts until fall of '97 when she applied for welfare in New York City. Off welfare, then employed at art gallery on Broome Street, same place reported as domicile. Hired at American High School in Lima in fall of '99."

I stared at Bob.

"Makes me wonder how the school went about checking her background."

"Not very thoroughly!" Bob struggled with his French onion soup trying to make the cheese leave the surface and, once it did, battling to pry it off the spoon with his teeth. "I always regret ordering this," he muttered, "and I never learn."

"Vicky told me she'd done summer stock and acted in off-Broadway productions. There's no mention of that in your report."

"Is it important?"

"Guess not. By the way, she's staying at the apartment of her new beau, Charles Lupesco, in New York, as we speak. And *he's* in Paris at a conference."

"She'd better stay away from shoplifting while she's there . . ."

I picked up the second page which contained only one paragraph. Charles Lupesco had been employed as an interpreter at the United Nations for just over one year with a net salary of $51,360. I looked up and said "nice going." Citizen of Rumania, born 1961. Somewhat younger than I'd imagined.

"That's all you got on Lupesco?"

Bob shrugged. "That's the best I could do short of burglarizing the personnel files. I could try to get a photocopy of the entire record. But all you'd get would be education, former employment, and references."

"And what about Interpol in Paris?"

"Patience, woman! Still working on it!" He held up his hand. "I'm also waiting for the report on George Lecroix. And on Pablo Alvarez. You still want information on him?"

I nodded and went to the third page. Sara and Stanley Robinson. No surprises there. He had worked thirty-five years for the electric company. She was a retired clerk from the Motor Vehicle Administration. They owed one more payment on their townhouse and otherwise lived on their pensions and Social Security.

I turned to the fourth and fifth pages.

"I'm impressed," I said and looked at the information Bob had assembled on José Hernandez.

"I made my pal, Rivera, in Miami work for his money. As it happened, he had some personal knowledge of the guy. There was some newspaper mention of Hernandez a couple of years ago which Rivera remembered. But go on, read it for yourself."

José Hernandez had owned a condominium in Miami—also registered in the name of his wife, Elena—for a little less than six years. Their credit rating was excellent, they belonged to the nearby country club where they played golf and bridge. They traveled in and out of the States with rather more frequency than seemed necessary, sometimes staying no more than two or three days. Dr. Hernandez made several additional trips a year without his wife.

The brief newspaper notoriety referred to an incident about a year and a half ago when Hernandez was reportedly on a yacht owned by a Colombian national, which had been boarded by a custom's patrol. The Colombian had been arrested for possession of cocaine. His four guests, including Dr. Hernandez, had spent a night in jail without subsequently being charged. But the incident had hit the papers. In the account Hernandez was referred to as an art dealer rather than as a doctor. But the report was undoubtedly of the same person.

I stuck the papers in my handbag and watched Bob suck in the last string of recalcitrant cheese, his graying hair damp from the effort.

He threw the spoon down in disgust and said:

"You know, I've been thinking, maybe there are two sets of unrelated murders. Elsa Bronski. And then Alvarez and Gomercinda."

"I thought of that, too, but you know how I feel about coincidences."

"Dr. Hernandez with his art smuggling activity seems to tie in better with the art dealer, Alvarez, and with Gomercinda and her art forger son. Jesus!" He laughed. "An illustrious name! A man can't do much better than that!"

"Too true. Anyway, Hernandez aside, I'm left with George Lecroix. He left Peru suddenly on the morning of the two murders."

"And Charles Lupesco, just to cover the whole field."

"I haven't forgotten about him. But I can only tie him to Alvarez, if at all."

"But don't forget, you seem to dislike him!"

"Hardly enough evidence!"

"I'm thinking of your famous intuition!" Bob laughed and added hastily: "In any case, let's wait for the Interpol report."

"Which reminds me, have you heard from your friend Quentin in Lima? I thought the FBI was supposed to investigate deaths of U.S. citizens abroad?"

"Funny you should ask," Bob said. "I did talk to him and apparently there was some bureaucratic snag and the investigation was delayed."

"Well, gee, I wonder why?" I snorted. "Could it have anything at all to do with Jorge Bustamante and Emilio Sosa?"

"Probably. And now they've conveniently 'solved' the murder. The incentive for further investigation is gone."

We shared the bill and parted on Connecticut Avenue outside the hotel. I walked half a block to get my car and drove west on Pennsylvania Avenue towards Georgetown, where the avenue becomes M Street. I followed M Street to Wisconsin Avenue, then turned north to R Street. I had to circle Ms. Bronski's block three times before finding a parking space. Then I went across to the Harris house.

Geraldine Harris opened the door on the first knock.

"Yes?"

"Hi," I said. "Remember me? Jamie Prescott. We met at Elsa Bronski's funeral. Do you have a minute?"

"Yes, of course." Geraldine Harris opened the red front door while holding back a small white terrier with her foot. The hall was narrow with a solid staircase taking up more than half the width and I could see clear through to the kitchen at the back. There was a wooden bench with a jumble of children's windbreakers and sweaters and several pairs of rain boots.

Geraldine led the way into a large living room lit dimly from two windows towards the street. There was a well-proportioned fireplace, a mixture of Hepplewhite and Sheraton furniture, and colorful prints of steeplechases in mahogany frames. A genteel English country interior.

"Would you like some tea?" Geraldine inquired. "Or coffee? I was just about to have some myself."

"Thank you, in that case I'll have coffee." I followed her through the dining room to the kitchen.

"I do apologize for barging in unannounced," I said.

"I'm a little surprised to see you." She worked swiftly on the coffee.

"For the past several weeks I've been investigating the murder on behalf of Ms. Bronski's sister, Therese Lecroix," I said.

"You're an investigator?"

I nodded. It didn't seem to faze her, she just poured the coffee and put cups and a plate of chocolate chip cookies on a tray. I trailed behind her back to the living room where we settled down opposite one another on matching sofas in front of the cold fireplace.

"Tell me about Elsa Bronski's friends," I said.

Geraldine screwed up her eyes as if against the light.

"Friends?" she said. "I don't know if she had friends. While she was Mrs. Douglas' housekeeper and companion—and I knew her for ten of those years—she hardly had a life of her own. You know, didn't invite guests to the house as far as I know, although she could have. She did have a small apartment on the top floor, two rooms and a bath, but then she would have had to cook in the kitchen on her days off and carry the meals upstairs for guests. I think she preferred to leave the house instead."

Geraldine shook her head and looked as if she had a hard time remembering, or maybe difficulty visualizing the life style she had just described.

"She enjoyed a good movie and she came over here often enough, even to baby-sit while Toby was younger. And later, of course, to take him out as I think I told you already."

"Yes, you did tell me they went to the Zoo. I was wondering if you could elaborate on Ms. Bronski's seeming paranoia. You know, about the one she called 'the ghost'."

Geraldine smiled. "I already told you all I know. And I wouldn't call it paranoia. I thought she might have been reminded of an old flame. It was nothing real."

She turned her head towards the door and said in a slightly louder voice: "Is that you, Toby?"

There was a sound of clumsy feet up the stairs but Toby himself didn't materialize. I emptied my coffee cup and abstained from another cookie.

Geraldine leaned towards me and said in a hushed voice: "We don't talk about Elsa anymore. I want Toby to forget all about it as quickly as possible."

"Aren't you afraid he'll worry more if you don't talk about it?"

She shook her head decisively and said: "Not at all."

"So," I said after a short pause, "you never saw Elsa Bronski with *anyone* during all those years?"

She thought for a moment.

"There was someone several years ago, a woman she would take walks with, but I believe the woman died. And it wasn't until Elsa inherited from old Mrs. Douglas that I learned she had a sister. Therese Lecroix and her husband came to stay several times after the inheritance. I got the feeling Elsa disliked *him* although I must say I didn't quite understand why, he's very distinguished looking. And they did invite her to stay with them at the Embassy in Peru several times. It even got mentioned in the *Washington Post*. You know, under celebrities in the Style Section. It was quite funny to think of Elsa as a celebrity."

My mission was netting next to nothing. I tried one more question.

"And after she inherited, did she develop any new friendships?

After all, she now owned the whole house and didn't have to hide in her rooms on the top floor."

"You know something," Geraldine said with a small laugh, "she never got used to the idea of being a millionaire. She stayed on the top floor and just kept cleaning the rest of the house as she had before, never made it her own, if you know what I mean."

"Who helped her clean?"

"No one. Every few months Mrs. Douglas would have a cleaning company do a professional job, usually while she and Elsa traveled. Otherwise Elsa did it all. I don't think she even used the cleaning company after Mrs. Douglas died. But, then, the only one who came to see her was her lawyer."

"Her lawyer? You mean Walter Hughes?"

"The Third!" She made a face.

"You don't like him?"

"I didn't like the way he started paying attention to her after she came into all that money."

"He was the executor of the estate. He was obliged to pay attention to her."

"Yes, I know. And he did help her maintain the investments. But I didn't like it when he invited her to lunch downtown and even less when he invited her to the theater. Anyway, I shouldn't air my personal dislikes. I'm sorry I couldn't be of more help."

"On the contrary," I said as she saw me to the door. "You've been of tremendous help. My picture of Elsa is becoming clearer." And my picture of Walter Hughes as well, I might have added. The cad. What had he been up to?

Traffic was thickening on Wisconsin Avenue and it was a slow ride to Bethesda. I did some much needed grocery shopping near the Metro station and once I'd worked my way through the store from vegetables and fruits to frozen foods, dairy products and bakery, my cart was full and I'd decided to put the murder case aside at least for the evening.

I picked up some California Chardonnay and a select couple of bottles of St. Emilión. When I arrived back at the agency the lights were out and Topsy's car gone. In its place was a dark gray Infiniti. Not withstanding our huge sign proclaiming parking for customers only, the space is frequently usurped by visitors to the nearby real estate office.

When I heard the car door slam I placed my brown paper bags on the doorstep. I waited until the driver came close enough to be lectured on trespassing when he waved his arm.

"Brewster?"

"Yes! Hope I didn't frighten you!"

"No, I was on my way to give you a parking ticket. What are you doing here?"

"Trying my luck." His teeth gleamed in the near darkness. "When I called you back just before lunch today you were out. In fact, you've been out all afternoon."

"That's right," I said.

"Not that you owe me an explanation," he said hastily. "I just didn't want to keep on leaving messages. I was driving by and took a chance on your being home."

He followed me around the corner.

"Do you have some time now or are you on your way out again?"

"No, I'm not on my way out." I watched as he picked up three of the brown shopping bags.

"Allow me!" he said and prepared to follow me in the door.

He stayed close on my heels up the stairs into the kitchen where he propped up the bags on the counter. I put down the fourth plus the wine on the floor.

"Let me just put this away," I said and opened the refrigerator. "Why don't you make yourself comfortable in the living room in the meantime."

He sauntered away in the direction I indicated. When I was done I put cheese and crackers and a bunch of grapes on a tray and went inside.

Archibald Brewster was standing with his back to me, both hands in his pants pockets, looking intently at the large Haitian painting above the fireplace. He turned around at the sound of the silver tray on the glass coffee table.

"Good looking paintings," he said. "Quite a collection."

"I picked up most of them in Haiti a few years ago. I'm partial to primitive art. And color. What can I get you to drink? I'm having wine but you can have almost anything within reason."

I walked across to the corner cupboard and opened the door to show him his choices.

"I'll have Scotch on the rocks," he said predictably enough and carried the tumbler and the Johnny Walker to the table while I went back to the kitchen for ice.

I served him cubes from the ice-bucket, poured my Chardonnay, and sat down on one sofa while he took off his jacket, draped it carefully across the back of a chair and sat down opposite me.

"Mighty nice of you," he grinned, lifted his tumbler in salute and popped a cheese cracker in his mouth. I was intensely aware of his mocking eyes and taught muscles under the white shirt sleeves.

"You left me a message yesterday," I said and cut a slice of Camembert. I balanced the cheese on a cracker and looked up at him. He was watching my hands with uncanny concentration and laughed when he became aware I was aware. Then he leaned over to his jacket, pulled out an envelope, took out two papers, and pushed them across the glass top.

"Surprise," he said lightly as I picked up the pages.

The first was a copy of Elsa Bronski's birth certificate stating she was born in Paris, March 30, 1940, as Elisaveta Eugenia, the daughter of Bronislav Karel Bronski, laborer, and wife Eugenia Josefina, seamstress.

I looked up, now conscious of Brewster's eyes on my face. He had sprawled out a bit more across the sofa.

"Where did you get this? From Walter Hughes?"

"No, never heard from him. I got it from the INS."

"I didn't know you could do that?"

"You can if you've got friends in high places."

"Fair enough!"

He looked at me with an inscrutable expression which raised the hairs on my arms.

I picked up the second page. Therese Lecroix's birth certificate, translated and notarized by the consul at the French Embassy in Lima.

Therese Anastasia, I read, born in Paris, September 16, 1953, the daughter of Emanuel Marcel Bronski, bookbinder, and Natalya Therese, housewife.

I jumped up so fast that my crackers scattered all over the floor. I waved the two birth certificates in the air.

"My God! Talk about surprises," I cried out. "How can you sit there so calmly. This changes everything." I could feel color rise in my cheeks and my voice cracked.

He kept his eyes on my face as he got up and placed his tumbler on the table. He laughed and came around to where I stood.

"They're not sisters!" he said and looked hugely satisfied with my reaction.

"Cousins at best!" I exclaimed. "Their fathers might be brothers. Still, it puts a different slant on the inheritance, doesn't it?"

I sat down, and somehow Archibald Brewster now sat on the same sofa, quite close. He bent over and filled my wine glass, then his tumbler. I leaned back in my corner and looked him full in the face.

"Have you told Therese Lecroix yet?"

"I called her number in Lima but as far as I could make out with my limited Spanish, she has gone to Paris. I assume you have her number?"

"You assume right, I'll get to her tomorrow. She won't be pleased. If Elsa Bronski has living siblings or even parents, then Therese is out of the running. If not, there may be more cousins entitled to a share. You'll have to inform Walter Hughes."

"I thought maybe you'd like the honor," he smiled and slid an arm along the back of the sofa. Heat radiated into my shoulder from his hand. I leaned against it and took a long sip of wine.

"So, what else happened in Peru?" he said and, not entirely casually, touched the back of my head.

"Ouch," I said when his fingers ran into the bump which was still sore even if diminished in size. "Lots of things happened in Peru, most of them unpleasant. I'm afraid the case is getting increasingly complicated. Two more people have been murdered."

I told him about Pablo Alvarez and Gomercinda Flores, about Captain Sosa and being knocked out at Alvarez' shop and dragged outside.

"Why did you return to the place so late at night. And by yourself?" he said and shook his head.

"I needed to look around. I'm an investigator, remember?"

Then I told him the rest. He wasn't at all surprised to hear my *persona non grata* story.

"Old trick," he said. "It happened to a friend of mine in Bolivia, a Swede who was about to disclose some corrupt government scheme or other. They shipped him out of there within three hours. Never even got to pack his bags!"

"The worst thing," I said, "is that Ivanovich is now falsely accused and incarcerated God knows where."

"Yeah, he'll need some help."

"I'll call the embassy tomorrow. Oh, boy, what a day!"

Brewster looked as if his mind was on something else entirely. He put down his glass.

"Is that it?" I said and looked up.

"No." His voice was hoarse. "No, there's more."

He held out his hand. I took it and he pulled me close. His lips were softer and his muscles harder than I'd expected. And I paid no attention to the warning signals as he followed me up the stairs.

CHAPTER 37

I arrived on the 12th floor just before nine o'clock. The receptionist hadn't quite settled in behind her desk and made me wait just long enough to make her point. When a beautiful wall clock chimed the hour she acknowledged that Walter Hughes had been in his office, as usual, since eight but would not be seeing anyone without an appointment.

"Why don't you try him," I said. The receptionist looked at my card, shook her head doubtfully, but in the end decided to disturb the great man's secretary.

I was somewhat surprised to see Hughes approach me in person across the luxurious carpeting and have him escort me personally to his office. He pulled out a chair for me before he sat down at his desk. His expression revealed nothing.

"How did you hear about this?" he demanded. His voice was as dry as his sandy hair.

"Well, Archibald Brewster brought me copies last night."

The glasses glinted. "That's impossible."

"Impossible? What do you mean?"

"It's privileged information."

"If it's privileged information I'd like to know how it reached *you.* Brewster was hired by Therese Lecroix to file claim against the Bronski Estate. How did you come into possession of her birth certificate?"

"*Her* birth certificate? I don't know what you mean."

Walter Hughes stared at me blankly and I handed him copies of the two birth certificates. He studied them in silence, completely absorbed.

"Remarkable coincidence," he finally said. "Remarkable."

I moved forward to the edge of my chair.

"Remarkable coincidence," he repeated.

There was a muted knock on the door and Hughes' secretary stuck her head inside. He waved her forward and she came in balancing a tray with coffee in a silver pot and matching creamer and sugar bowl. There were two cups and an assortment of biscuits.

For a moment I thought she was going to pour, too, but Walter Hughes took over. He handed me a cup and I took it. Hughes sipped once and pursed his lips in satisfaction.

"Yesterday," he said, "I received a registered letter from a law firm in Paris. With a notarized translation of a birth certificate."

He picked out two pieces of paper from a file folder and handed them to me. The two pages were joined in the upper left-hand corner with a red ribbon locked in place by a lump of shiny red wax. It looked for all the world like the minister's *persona non grata* decree to me. The first page was a notarized translation, the second page a copy of the original.

Karel Stanislaus Bronski, I read. Born in Warsaw, Poland, November 2, 1951, son of Bronislav Karel Bronski, laborer, and wife Eugenia Josefina, seamstress.

"Oh, my God! Those are the same parents." I looked at Hughes in disbelief. "Elsa Bronski had a brother!"

"Yes! Yes!" Hughes finally allowed himself some emotion and tapped his fingers on the edge of the desk. "At this point I must make the assumption that your client, Therese Lecroix, no longer has any claim on the Bronski Estate."

I swallowed hard.

"I will naturally have to verify the legitimacy of this birth certificate and of the brother's identity," Hughes continued.

"Naturally," I said and stared into space above his right shoulder at a large black cloud hanging on the horizon outside the picture window. When I looked back at him he was eyeing me with a peculiar expression.

"Therese hired me to investigate the murder," I said. "I will continue to do that!"

Hughes shook his head.

"I have had communication from our Embassy in Lima that the murderer, a known terrorist, has been arrested and that the case is considered solved."

"There's grave doubt about that."

"The police seem satisfied." He looked at his watch, got up, extended his hand, smiled, and switched gears. "I hope to see you under less trying circumstances soon. Maybe at the Bannister's barbecue next month?"

I thought of the annual garden bash. The party was usually enjoyable and I nodded in affirmation. I shook his hand and tried to meet his eyes, which looked like tiny pinpricks amidst the concentric circles in his glasses.

"Yes, I may see you there," I said cautiously.

He accompanied me to the reception area but when I reached the front door and turned around he'd disappeared.

"Carpentier, Berlioz, Grandjean et Cie.," I mumbled to myself several times as the elevator got me to the lobby. There I took out my notebook and wrote down the name of the law firm in Paris representing Karel Stanislaus Bronski. I'm pretty good at reading upside down and I had been repeating it to myself some ten times during the latter part of my conversation with Hughes.

I drove back to Bethesda unable to shake off my dismay at this new twist. The police in Lima hadn't wasted any time, either, and I felt a rising tension thinking of Ivanovich and his chances of getting out of prison. I speeded up and made it by the skin of my teeth through several yellow lights before pulling up at my house.

I reached James Quentin Brown at the Embassy on the first try. He had the decency to be concerned about my deportation but didn't seem that interested in Ivanovich.

"Go ahead and fax me a copy of the deportation order," he said. "I'm pretty sure I can fix that for you. Ivanovich is another matter. We don't have authority to interfere in the internal affairs of the country. I'll keep my ears open, though."

"I appreciate that. Just one more thing. Could you find out if the French ambassador has returned to Lima from Paris?"

"No need to make any special inquiries about that. It was in the afternoon newspapers. The French ambassador won't be back for several months. He's in Paris recovering from injuries sustained in an automobile accident a few days ago."

"It just gets better by the minute."

"Excuse me?"

"Oh, nothing. But thanks so much for the information."

"Tell Bob I said hello!" he said and we hung up.

The time had obviously come for me to go to Paris. I looked at my watch. Not yet three. I could make a flight from Dulles Airport at midnight and arrive in time for breakfast. I went downstairs, made my reservations, printed out my ticket, and called the airport shuttle to pick me up at nine.

Quiet suddenly descended on the office. Business had a strange tendency to ebb and flow, the customers were gone, the fax and telephones were silent, there was only a faint shuffle of papers from the front desks. I pulled out my deportation order, made a photocopy and faxed it to Brown before joining Topsy in the back office.

"You're leaving!" Topsy looked at the ticket and the passport I held in my hand.

"I'll be back to take over before you go off to the Caribbean." I looked at my watch. "Better get started. I need to throw some Paris outfits together."

"Paris? Lucky dog, I'm coming with you!"

"You'd be disappointed trailing in my footsteps."

"Who said anything about trailing in your footsteps? I would be traipsing up and down the Faubourg St. Honoré and Rue de Passy."

"Good thing you're not going, you've bought more clothes this year than I have in the past ten."

Topsy made a face and turned to a sheaf of brochures of Scandinavia. Tivoli Gardens, Amalienborg Castle, and Odense, Hans Christian Andersen's birthplace. Vigeland Park, the Kon-Tiki Museum, and Bergen. Skansen, Drottningholm, and Gamla Stan. She shuffled the brochures into a stiff white folder and wrote a name on the cover.

"Where will you be staying?" she asked.

"The Plaza-Athénée . . . ."

"My, *you're* feeling luxurious!"

"You know me, I hate crummy hotels. I haven't actually made any reservations, I should probably stay with Therese—she offered—and be closer to the action. But she doesn't answer her phone."

"Action? Are you zeroing in on George?"

"Agent Brown in Lima read in the papers that George was in a car accident and won't be returning to Peru for several months. And there's a whole lot of other stuff going on that I can only check out in Paris. I need Therese for that."

I told her briefly about the birth certificate complications.

"Elsa Bronski had a brother she never mentioned? And Therese didn't either?" Topsy looked delighted.

"Seems strange. Maybe they didn't know? The supposed brother was born in Warsaw."

"Supposed?"

"It may be a fake. I'll have to find out."

I picked up the phone, dialed Therese, and let it ring. And ring.

"Still no answer," I said and wrote the number down for Topsy. "If you don't hear to the contrary I guess I'll be at the Plaza-Athénée."

"You run along now," said Topsy. "Everything here's under control. And, by the way, the McCormicks caught up with their suitcases and are back home. They are coming to dinner in two weeks. Please say you'll join us!"

I looked at Topsy's face with its mixture of irony and pleading and, against my better judgment, said: "Okay, I guess it won't kill me."

I went upstairs and packed a small bag, added paper and pens to my office kit, a file folder with a pocket Baedeker, a map of Paris and one of the Metro, put new batteries in the flashlight and the laptop, and added an umbrella in deference to Paris weather. Lastly, I left a message for my mother and resisted an impulse to call Archibald Brewster.

I ate a late dinner and at nine I was on my way to Dulles Airport.

CHAPTER 38

I wheeled my luggage up to a round marble-topped table and sat down in a cane-backed chair. I ordered a café créme and a croissant from a waiter whose rumpled looks indicated he might have been up all night, and prepared to soak up the atmosphere on the Champs Elysées before calling Therese Lecroix.

The Charles de Gaulle airport had been crowded and I'd made my way around clumps of immovable travelers to line up at a money exchange before boarding the Air France bus to the Étoile. Last night's champagne dinner of smoked salmon, beef Burguignonne, and chocolate mousse cake had put me to sleep clear across the Atlantic, and I'd resisted the early morning call for airline breakfast.

Now I leaned back in my squeaky chair and took a deep breath contemplating my very favorite city. The city of shuttered windows, wrought-iron balcony railings, and flowerpots precariously balanced on ledges and window sills.

The city of French meter-mademoiselles, in sky-blue uniforms and saucy hats, working both sides of the street slamming tickets under windshield wipers. And the city of tourists, I thought, and looked around at jeans, Reeboks, and UCLA sweat-shirts.

"*Voilá*, Madame." The waiter actually spoke as he slid a cup and plate across the marble and I took advantage of the opening to ask the location of a phone. He lifted a tired hand and pointed somewhere into the dark interior.

I sat a little too long, ate and drank, paid an exorbitant amount of money for the pleasure, and pulled my bag inside to the phone.

Therese picked up on the second ring, confused at first about my whereabouts.

"But you must not stay at a hotel, my dear Jamie," she said once she got over the surprise. "You must stay with me! I insist! I will be waiting, I have much to tell you!" She certainly sounded cheerful enough.

I walked back to the Étoile and hailed a cab at the corner of Klebér. I was taken a pretty direct route via Avenue Mozart to Rue Ranelagh.

The sun shone through the naked branches of the trees bathing them in a sheen of light green. The houses had been there for hundreds of years and looked as if they were good for several hundred more. The facades were grimy behind tier on tier of wrought-iron balconies. The doors were ten feet tall, the rooftops dotted with oval windows framed in unrelenting rococo.

I had to be buzzed through two doors before I reached the elevator in Therese's building. I pressed the button under the severe scrutiny of the concierge, a woman with gray hair pulled back in an untidy bun and dark eyes under heavy brows. Her height and weight could not be determined since only her head was visible above the wooden counter. She was in a small cubicle reminiscent of a hat checkroom. Only, instead of hats the wall behind her was lined with pigeon-holes.

The door to the apartment stood wide open and Therese was framed in the middle, arms outstretched. She no longer dressed in black silk and pearls but wore a business suit and pumps. She bustled me through the foyer to the guest room and showed me the adjoining bathroom.

"Welcome, welcome, this is a great pleasure," she said effusively. "I will prepare something for us to eat while you settle in."

I took a shower and changed my clothes. The room I was in obviously did double duty as guest room and as Therese's workplace. One wall was lined with books from floor to ceiling. A white sleep sofa was flanked by two antique side tables with Victorian lamps. Just inside the door stood a mahogany tall-boy with a slew of silver-framed photographs. In front of the window, on a small oriental rug, stood a matching table which served as a desk. A tall stack of medical books sat on the tabletop and another on the upholstered seat of an Empire armchair.

I pulled aside the voile curtain at the tall, narrow window and looked across the rooftops at the backs of buildings and inner courtyards, and at other people's bedroom windows. They were all shuttered.

I returned to the living room which was furnished quite differently from the oppressive opulence of the residence in Lima. No gilded furniture, no silk curtains, or marble floors. Instead, lightly buffed parquet floors, white rugs, chrome and canvas furniture, glass tables and white sofas.

On the white walls large paintings in browns and beige with black accents hung in narrow silver frames. One entire wall consisted of built-in cabinets with books and artifacts behind glass doors.

"How exquisite," I exclaimed and Therese flushed with pleasure.

"I am renting, but the furniture is mine," she said, and I stepped onto the narrow balcony which ran the length of the room.

I leaned on the rail and looked down eight floors. Traffic was slow and there were very few pedestrians. The building opposite was the same height, not counting a miniature cottage on the roof. I looked closer. What a fabulous penthouse! I could see myself living there with no trouble at all: close to the Opéra, close to the Louvre, close to the Left Bank.

I followed Therese to the kitchen to pick up a ready tray. The kitchen had been renovated, with new cabinets and appliances, but, being long and narrow, had retained an old-fashioned aura.

Therese served coffee and croissants and I ate slowly without mentioning I'd had the same breakfast an hour ago.

"Maybe you would like to sleep?" Therese said.

"Oh, no, better follow *your* schedule from day one or we'll never meet!" I accepted another cup of coffee and one more croissant.

"I have started divorce proceedings against George," she said. "In two weeks I begin work at the children's hospital. I will be able to support myself while I wait for my inheritance."

Oh, boy! Hadn't she heard about George's accident? I decided to say nothing for the time being. I was the bearer of enough bad news as it was.

"I take it," I said, "that you haven't heard from Walter Hughes?"

Something in my voice must have alerted her because she looked up sharply.

"Why? What about?"

I coughed and reached for my bag, pulled out the copy of Elsa Bronski's birth certificate and handed it to Therese.

"Listen," I said hastily as she started reading, "I'm awfully sorry . . . ."

"But this is wrong," Therese said. "These are not Elsa's parents. Who are they?"

"Did your father maybe have a brother?" I asked gently. "A brother who returned to Poland with his wife before you were born?"

"No, no, I never heard of anything like that." Therese's eyes were dark and shiny and she tucked her hand behind her back like a recalcitrant child.

"I'm afraid there's more bad news." I really hated my role in this. "Elsa apparently had a brother born some eleven years later and he has sent his birth certificate to Walter Hughes in Washington."

"No!" Suspicion was clear on Therese's face. "Elsa and I were the only children. There's something wrong."

"We'll find out if there is," I said. "The law firm that sent the letter to Hughes is here in Paris."

"We must see them immediately." Therese put her hands to her burning cheeks. "I wonder if my aunt Ludmila knew anything about this."

"Where's your aunt Ludmila?" I asked hoping the answer wouldn't be 'dead.'

"She lives in the eastern outskirts of Paris, beyond Ivry, on the banks of the Marne."

"How old is she?"

"Almost eighty, she's my mother's sister."

"Would she know whether perhaps your parents adopted Elsa?"

"Why would she have kept that a secret?"

"I don't know." I had another thought. "When your parents died, did Elsa inherit together with you?"

"I don't know. My parents were poor, there was nothing to inherit. I was just a child and Elsa was in America. My aunt became my guardian and I lived with her until I entered the university. She helped me with food and rent and, for the rest, I managed with scholarships."

"Could we visit her?"

Therese nodded eagerly. "She does not have a telephone but she only leaves the house to shop for food. We will need a car, though." She grimaced. "There are times I miss my chauffeur-driven limousine!"

"Surely this is a good trade-off, always assuming you had to make a choice?"

"Of course!"

"Okay, then, we'll rent a car and go first thing in the morning." I helped take the tea things to the kitchen. "I feel as if I'm running out of steam, though. I'll make a couple of phone calls, and then maybe I'll catch a few winks."

"I will get you up by eight so we can have dinner in the Créperie around the corner."

I caught Bob Makowski at home and spent a couple of minutes convincing him I was really in Paris. He enjoyed the story about the birth certificates for all the wrong reasons. And he had no trouble remembering what was in the unofficial Interpol report: A total blank on everyone.

"You don't seem to be dealing with hardened criminals," he said.

"Well, hardened or not, I know for sure there's one. And I'll find him. Or her," I added for the sake of political correctness although I believed there was no question of a 'her.'

"Okay, kiddo, let me know if you need me!"

I rented a car from nine the next morning and brought up the address of the law firm of Carpentier, Berlioz, Grandjean & Cie. on the mini-computer, courtesy of the telephone company. The law firm was located on Rue du Colisée, just off the Champs Elysées.

That done, I curled up in a blanket on top of the bed and fell into a deep sleep. I woke up in a sweat, hearing Ivanovich scream my name repeatedly, his voice a thin echo down a long hallway.

CHAPTER 39

T HE weeping willows along the banks of the Marne cast deep shadows onto the murky river. The properties ran down to a narrow red-tiled path right above water lapping at a stone wall. The houses, sheltered by shrubbery, seemingly teetered on the very brink.

The car rental agency had been slow in providing the promised Citroén and it was almost ten before we headed across to the Left Bank. We took the longer scenic route along the Seine rather than the highway leading to Porte d'Ivry.

Therese drove at her insistence, ostensibly to give me the freedom to enjoy the sights as we passed them: the Eiffel Tower, Jardins des Tuilleries, the Louvre, the Palais de Justice and, finally, Notre Dame. But I suspected she also rather enjoyed being in control of a car once more.

Aunt Ludmila's cottage sat in a garden of neglected roses and shaggy grass. We pulled up in front, and Therese hefted a wicker basket from the back seat. When there was no response to the loud noise produced by the metal knocker, she put down the basket on the front step and led the way around the side of the house.

Aunt Ludmila was at the back of the garden on a small bench, obviously a strategic outpost designed to give her an overview of the river and of her neighbors. When she spotted us she raised a cane in the air and swung it in a circular greeting. She got up quite briskly and walked towards us without leaning on the cane.

"My dear, what a surprise!" she said and embraced Therese. Her voice was firm, belying her age, her eyes blue and clear under a high unlined dome of a forehead. Her white hair was pulled back over her ears and held together in a wispy ponytail which curled up at the ends.

She turned her sharp gaze on me during the introduction and I got the impression she took in everything about me in an instant.

"Good," she said. "I will now practice my English. Come inside."

We followed her slowly across the grass along the flower beds where Aunt Ludmila picked off dead leaves which she let flutter haphazardly to the ground.

"Doesn't Monsieur Dupuis come around to do your garden any more?" Therese asked.

Aunt Ludmila swung her cane, muttered something about M. Dupuis being ill, and moved towards the house. We entered by the back porch and Therese went to the front to fetch the wicker basket.

"What did you bring me?" Ludmila looked at Therese with a mixture of pride in her niece and eagerness at the unexpected gift. She sat down in a well-worn armchair upholstered like the matching sofa in dark burgundy plush. The dull mahogany frame around the back was deeply carved.

Therese opened the basket and stacked canned and fresh foods on the pedestal table which stood surrounded by chunky dining chairs under a shaded lamp. Ludmila bent over the table and picked up each item, turned them to read the labels, and declared that these were her favorite foods and that we must stay for lunch.

She now peered at me with unabashed curiosity.

"And you, Madame!" she exclaimed. "Are you an agent of the CIA?"

I laughed out loud in surprise. She wasn't that far afield.

"Whatever gets into you, dear Aunt," Therese said. "Jamie is a private investigator."

"Works for the CIA," Ludmila said with great satisfaction and finality. She squinted at me so mischievously that I didn't know if she was putting me on or showing signs of senility.

"No, no! I brought Jamie from America to help me win Elsa's estate."

At the mention of Elsa, Aunt Ludmila's eyes clouded over. She clutched her cane with both hands and the corners of her mouth took on a blue, moist tinge. Her head began to shake, at first imperceptibly, then quite noticeably. This galvanized Therese into action.

"Here," she said hastily, "let me get all of us a small glass of sherry." She went to a heavy sideboard which took up a good deal of room at the back wall.

"Give me cognac!" Aunt Ludmila said and let go of her cane. "The Grand Marnier!"

I accepted a glass of sherry and watched Ludmila go through a sniffing, twirling, sniffing and tasting routine with her cognac. After several sips her pasty cheeks assumed some color and she sat lost in thought.

"The poor little Elsa," she said. "The poor little Elsa."

"Aunt Ludmila," Therese said and sat down close to her. "I don't mean to upset you but there are some things I need to know about Elsa, and you're the only person who can tell me. I have come to suspect that Elsa and I were not sisters . . ."

Ludmila nodded as if she had been expecting this moment all her life. She took a deep, trembling breath, emptied her snifter and held it out for a refill. Once she got it she looked from Therese to me and back again and clasped her hands tightly around the stem of her glass. At first her voice was faint but it slowly increased in strength as the story poured out of her.

"Elsa's parents, Bronislav and Eugenia, arrived in Paris from Poland before the war. He was a strong man but immature, uneducated and poor. They had come upon the advice of Bronislav's brother, Emanuel, who would later marry my sister and become Therese's father.

"Bronislav thought gold lay in the streets of Paris ready for him to pick up. He was going to make his fortune here. What fortune!" Ludmila snorted.

"But Eugenia adored him, she would look at him with those big blue eyes. Her hair was flaming red, braided and coiled around her head like a crown. She caught the men's attention, all right, and Bronislav was extremely jealous and possessive."

"You never told me any of this!" Therese's voice was almost a wail as she struggled to keep it on keel. She looked both offended and surprised.

"I am very sorry," Ludmila said and reached for Therese's hand. She stroked it for a moment before releasing it. "It happened a long time ago. I knew you might ask one day, but never did I think it would be because poor little Elsa was dead. We kept it a secret to protect her."

"But why did they leave her behind?"

"I will tell you. Bronislav had to work as a farm laborer outside of Paris. There was no other work, it was a terrible time for all of us. He only came home to Eugenia once every two weeks but managed to get her pregnant anyway. Elsa was born in 1940. Eugenia adored Elsa but Bronislav was jealous of the attention she gave to the child. He wanted it all for himself."

"And I always thought Elsa was my big sister," Therese said, and it seemed to me the regret in her voice had nothing to do with the inheritance.

Ludmila now paid no attention to either of us but was off into the far past.

"I met them when my dear sister, Natalya, married Emanuel Bronski. Emanuel was 22, and had just finished his apprenticeship with a fine bookbinder in Paris. He was a good man, a good husband to my sister, and a good father. He had encouraged his brother, Bronislav, to leave Poland maybe because he himself felt lonely and in need of family. But they did not get along. Emanuel was very disappointed in Bronislav. Only Natalya and Eugenia got along. We all loved Eugenia and little Elsa, Natalya especially because she did not herself have children. Whenever she did get pregnant, she lost the baby. Every single one before Therese."

"I didn't know. Poor *Maman*." Therese was near tears.

"So, when Elsa was two, and Bronislav decided to return to Poland, he persuaded Eugenia to leave Elsa behind. Just for a few months, he said, until he found work. Eugenia cried and cried but, in the end, she gave in to Bronislav. As always."

Ludmila asked for another cognac, which Therese hastily supplied while I was hoping this wouldn't cloud Ludmila's memory.

"Naturally, Emanuel and Natalya offered to look after Elsa, and Bronislav left with Eugenia. In the beginning Eugenia wrote but, you know, she was not much of a literate person. The letters stopped, there was the terrible war, of course, and then we heard from them only once more, in 1950. Bronislav wrote that life was difficult, he planned to return to Paris with Eugenia if they could get away."

Ludmila drank up.

"Not a word about Elsa, didn't even ask how she was. For him, all that mattered was Eugenia. They never did arrive in Paris and that was the last we ever heard from them. And we never told Elsa. She was ten by then and thought Emanuel and Natalya were her parents. Poor little Elsa. And then, when Natalya finally carried a baby to term and Therese was born, Elsa was thirteen and loved her little sister."

"Why did she go to America?" Therese asked.

"Well, it came about in a sad way. Elsa always wanted to be a nurse and at seventeen she was about to enter nursing school. That was the year she met Guillaume. Very unfortunate. Maybe Elsa was like Eugenia, her mother. Masochist, you say? She would do anything to please Guillaume and, let us say, he took advantage. Elsa had the abortion and immediately afterwards my sister helped her find the post with Mrs. Douglas in Washington. She was supposed to stay for just six months but, well, you know how it went: She stayed the rest of her life."

Ludmila looked at the empty cognac bottle.

"But she must have found out by then about her real parents," I said. "Surely she needed her birth certificate to get her passport."

Ludmila shrank deeper into her chair. "Yes, that is how she learned. And she was angry. Angry at her real parents for abandoning her, and angry with all of us for deceiving her. Said she would have loved us anyway. She never wrote from America, not until thirty-five years later just before she came to Paris with her Mrs. Douglas."

Therese was crying now.

"So, that's why she never returned. I wish you had told me about this many years ago, dear Aunt Ludmila," she said. "We should have been in touch with Elsa much sooner."

"She came when she felt ready," Ludmila said a trifle sternly and sat up as if ready to defend herself. "She came with her Mrs. Douglas, a very strict woman, and then, of course, she suddenly became very rich!"

"That is not why I went to see Elsa!" Therese protested.

"But that was why George became interested in her." Ludmila looked stubborn.

"It's none of his business. I am divorcing him, he won't get any of Elsa's money as long as I live," Therese said, apparently forgetting that she might not either.

"Did Therese's parents adopt Elsa?" I asked.

"No, they could not adopt Elsa without the consent of Bronislav and Eugenia. In 1950 they wrote to the address Bronislav had given in Poland but never got a reply. Maybe they are dead by now."

"But you don't have any proof of that?"

Ludmila shook her head.

"That means I won't inherit," Therese said.

Ludmila suddenly sat very quietly.

"Aunt Ludmila, we have discovered that Bronislav and Eugenia had another child," I said. "A son they called Karel Stanislaus. He was born in 1951, if we are to believe his birth certificate, and he is now claiming Elsa's estate."

Ludmila didn't look as devastated as I'd expected.

"It is possible, of course," she said and almost smiled. "Eugenia would have been only 30 years old in 1951. She could have had another child." Now she really smiled. "I am glad. She must have missed Elsa and it is good to believe she was blessed again. It is right that he should inherit."

When Therese got up and pushed her chair back rather forcefully, Ludmila grimaced.

"Never mind, my dear, money is not everything. You have your profession and if you could only be rid of George, you would do well. As for money, you can always look forward to the inheritance you will get from me!"

I wasn't sure what to think about Ludmila's wicked smile, but Therese didn't look as if Ludmila's money measured up to Elsa's. Without saying another word she put away the contents of the wicker basket in the small kitchen and started lunch. Aunt Ludmila ate the soup, the salad, and the crusty baguette with a good appetite, and I was feeling hungry, too.

Therese barely touched the food and soon afterwards we left with Aunt Ludmila watching from the sidewalk, now leaning heavily on her cane.

Therese drove in silence, which gave me a chance to digest Aunt Ludmila's story.

"The newspapers in Peru said George had been in an automobile accident and was in a hospital in Paris," I finally said. "That's not true at all, is it?"

She shook her head.

I didn't want to outline my new theory to her so all I said was: "We'd better go find George."

CHAPTER 40

"Let's split up," I said when we reached the center of town. "You go to the foreign office to find out about George. I'll take the law offices on Rue du Colisée. If you'll drop me off close by I'll return to your apartment by Metro."

Therese hurtled the car into the melee around the Arc de Triomphe, dodging, feinting, crisscrossing, and circling until, by some miracle, we were coasting down the Champs Elysées towards the Place de la Concorde.

"I'll never get used to this," I huffed. "Now, if this had been Washington you'd have the lanes marked so there would be no doubt where to go."

Therese laughed. "There *is* no doubt! Everyone knows you yield to traffic on the right. Why would we need marked lanes?" There was a certain Gallic logic to this, which, however, presupposed that only Parisians hurtled around the Étoile.

We pulled up at the curb just before the Rond Point and I got out. Before crossing to the opposite side I stopped at a newsstand, an architectural wonder topped by a pagoda-like roof. Inside, the vendor, in deep conversation with a man in an old raincoat and an even older beret, ignored me completely even as I waved the Herald

Tribune in his face. He put out his hand for the money without the smallest peek at me, just dropped the money into a box under the counter, and continued his conversation.

With the newspaper tucked under my arm I stayed on the corner waiting for the lights to change. I stopped in the middle of the Avenue to get an unobstructed view of the Arc and let the traffic lights change twice before I continued. Paris is such a satisfying place in the springtime. But even as I took in the scenery I knew there was something I ought to have understood about the Bronski case which kept eluding me. Everything now depended on whether I could wheedle Karel Stanislaus Bronski's address out of the lawyers. Once I had that, the pieces of the puzzle would start settling in.

Rue du Colisée ran for only two short blocks. There was a café on the corner of Franklin Roosevelt, its two red awnings pulled up. People sat at the open windows at small tables with white tablecloths. Walking past, I heard the click-click of forks and knives over the low hum of voices. There was a Laurent boutique with just one expensive dress on display and, next door, a patisserie from whose open doors wafted a warm scent of almond fillings and fresh dough.

Carpentier, Berlioz, Grandjean & Cie. were on the top floor of a venerable old building. Inside the cavernous entrance a staircase disappeared from view in the dark next to the elevator. I pushed the old-fashioned button imbedded in an intricate brass panel which set the machinery in noisy motion.

The concierge, a gnarled old man in baggy pants, appeared out of nowhere and watched me wait for the cranky elevator. When I opened the recalcitrant door and stepped inside, he said: "You must walk down. This elevator only goes up!"

I'd forgotten about this peculiarity of the old elevators and had a momentary attack of panic as the car wheezed its way up. It hesitated at each floor as if gathering strength for the next lap. I wondered what would happen if I rode down. Would I plummet to the ground willy nilly?

When I opened the door at the last stop I had to step up half a foot to reach the landing. I pressed the button and the elevator began its empty downward journey.

The walls were painted to match the dark brown cracked linoleum on the floor. The law offices were at the end of the corridor. The glass panels in the door had a frosted flower design which prevented me from seeing anything on the inside except lights and shadows.

I knocked and tried the knob at the same time. The door was open.

One of the seven dwarves was sitting behind a counter. Sleepy watched my entrance with a placid smile and a somnolent stare above rimless bifocals. His bulbous nose turned red with the effort.

"Madame?"

"Is M. Carpentier in?"

Sleepy's bifocals shook and his generous lips parted without emitting any sounds.

"Maybe M. Berlioz?" I tried.

The color in his cheeks deepened to match his nose. He leaned forward and spoke just above a whisper.

"Madame, there is only M. Grandjean left, a grandson of the original founder. As for me, I am Eduard, at your service. How may I help you?"

"I'd like to consult M. Grandjean on a private matter," I said just as a door to the right of the reception opened and a balding man in a tight-fitting gray suit ushered an elderly couple towards the staircase. The couple began their downward climb without even a passing glance at the elevator.

M. Grandjean closed the door, stopped in front of me, and listened to my partial explanation. In another moment I was seated in his office on a dark green leather sofa.

"You are an American, Madame Prescott," he stated and looked at my card. "A private investigator from Maryland. How can I help you?"

I took a deep breath. Might as well plunge right in.

"M. Grandjean, are you familiar with a Karel Stanislaus Bronski?"

His gaze wavered.

"Maybe. Maybe not."

I smiled slightly. Okay, if we were going to play cat and mouse, I'd be the cat.

"Mr. Walter Hughes of Washington D.C. received Mr. Bronski's birth certificate by registered mail from this office. Maybe one of your associates is familiar with the case if you are not?"

"I did not say that I am not."

I tried to stare him down but couldn't for the life of me catch his eye.

"All right, then, do you happen to have Mr. Bronski's address? Mr. Hughes needs to verify his identity and," I said, stretching the realities somewhat, "I am here to do it."

"Do you come bearing a letter from Mr. Hughes to that effect, Madame?"

"No, but you're very welcome to call Mr. Hughes in Washington."

I could practically see the price of an overseas telephone call in his eyes before he looked away. I also imagined he was weighing what might be in this for him.

"We do not have an address, Madame," he said. "The fact is, we acted more as couriers than actual representatives. It seemed a small enough thing to do."

He doesn't know about the inheritance, I thought.

Grandjean shuffled his body around.

"It is like this, Madame, and I can tell you this without breaching any confidences. We received a typed letter in the mail without a return address, postmarked at Orly Airport. Inside was a copy of a birth certificate, written in Polish, with a request from Mr. Bronski for us to forward a notarized translation to Mr. Walter Hughes. There was a fee included in a postal money order. Everything quite anonymous."

"Did you try to find out if Karel Bronski lives in Paris?"

"As a matter of fact, we did. But without luck. There is no such person here. We found a few entries named Bronski but, when contacted by telephone, they professed complete ignorance of a Karel Stanislaus."

"Would you let me have a copy of the letter. I suppose it was signed?"

The expression on Grandjean's face underwent a subtle change as if his thought process had finally caught up with reality. He got up from his chair and pulled ineffectively at his pants. When he didn't manage to heave them above the paunch, he buttoned his wrinkled jacket over the misery instead. He looked down at me and, from this temporary advantage, wheezed, "Ah! Client-lawyer confidentiality! You understand, Madame."

I understood, all right. The question was only how much this was worth. I got up and regained my superiority by towering almost a foot above Grandjean.

"It's a matter of a substantial inheritance," I said, bating him shamelessly: "You wouldn't regret it."

He sat down, and so did I.

"So, was the letter signed?"

Grandjean's words tumbled out eagerly. "The signature seems to have been written with the left hand. Quite illegible. Frankly it made me uneasy but the birth certificate seemed genuine enough, and I had nowhere to return the money."

"Did you keep the envelope by any chance? I'm looking for fingerprints."

"Fingerprints? This is a criminal case?"

"It could be if the birth certificate proves to be a falsification. I know Mr. Hughes would appreciate your collaboration in finding out."

Grandjean fairly bounced out the door and returned moments later with a file folder from which he extracted a white envelope. Holding it by one corner he placed it on the desk in front of me. The address was typed, there was no return address, and the envelope was clearly postmarked Orly.

Grandjean placed a piece of white notepaper in front of me with the same care. Also typed, the letter contained only a few lines. Considering previous handling it would be a miracle to find meaningful prints, but it was still worth an attempt. I made a quick calculation about the time it would take for me to call Bob in Washington and for him to contact his friend, Clarisse, at Interpol, located as far as I remembered in St. Cloud.

Five minutes later I hurried down the stairs clutching a plastic folder with the original letter and envelope. Both Eduard and Grandjean watched me anxiously from the landing.

I walked quickly to the Franklin D. Roosevelt metro stop, purchased a ticket, and followed a stream of passengers down a tunneled walkway. I slowed down to make sure I was heading in the direction of Pont de Sévres and got to the platform just as a train disgorged half its contents—a multitude of harassed-looking Parisians with far-away expressions in their eyes.

I rode rocking from side to side in my seat in a deafening clatter of metal wheels and emerged in Rue Ranelagh about a hundred feet from Therese's apartment.

I stopped at the grocery store on the corner where an ill-fated attempt had been made to convert a mom-and-pop store into a mini-supermarket. Only one-way traffic, no passing, and no back-tracking in the narrow aisles. I selected some fresh crunchy bread, Camembert, and a great bunch of dewy green grapes, all of which I subsequently carried to the apartment building and into the elevator past the inquisitive eyes of the concierge.

Therese arrived ten minutes later. She threw her handbag across the hall where it landed with a thud on a tooled leather stool, pulled off her Hermes silk scarf and stormed into the living room with me close on her heels.

"So, what did you find out at the foreign office?" I said.

"George!" she said. "That George! George has taken leave of absence. And of his senses. He told a colleague he was going to the south of France. What would he be doing there? He sold the house on the Riviera two years ago."

"I suppose he could go there anyway? But why?"

"I don't know. I can't think anymore." Therese wiped angrily at her eyes. "What did you find out at the law office?"

I pulled out the letter from Karel Stanislaus Bronski and placed it carefully on the coffee table.

"Look at it without touching," I warned. "I don't suppose you recognize the signature?"

Therese squinted at it.

"It's illegible. And why would I recognize the signature?" She suddenly looked wild-eyed.

"Can you find me something recent with George's signature?"

Without a word she disappeared into the guest room and returned with a letter from George addressed to her.

I looked at the signature: one large circle petering out into a straight line which ended in a downward hook. More an initial than a signature, but forceful. I hadn't imagined there would be any similarity to the left-handed scribble on Karel Stanislaus Bronski's letter but at least I now had a sample for comparison. And, hopefully, George's fingerprints. I picked up the letters carefully and placed them in the plastic folder. Therese didn't object.

I looked at my watch. It would be 11 a.m. in Washington, not the most auspicious hour to catch Bob Makowski. But I got him on the line almost immediately and quickly put him in the picture.

"Fingerprint job," he mused. "As long as you're at it, why don't you give Clarisse whatever else you have on the rest of your group. She can run them through the computer and find out about everyone in one fell swoop."

"I don't have anyone else's prints," I said but didn't even pause to let Bob answer before I burst out, "Yes, I do, too! You're a genius. I've got the pages from the notebook I carried to Machu Picchu. That's where they wrote down their names and phone numbers because Ivanovich didn't bring the list with him."

"There you go," Bob said. "What's the time at your end now?"

"Just after four in the afternoon . . . ."

"Okay, I'll tell you what. If I catch Clarisse at work you should hear from her within fifteen minutes. If not, find her in the phone book, her last name is Dehors, she lives in Montmartre."

"You wouldn't happen to have it in your little black book?"

"I do, but my little black book is in the bank vault. Now, give me your phone number and address again."

"I'll owe you one . . ."

"It's adding up!" The receiver shook as Bob let out one of his great whoops of laughter. The truth is, I do owe him more than he owes me, but what are friends for.

Then, in his customary fashion of leaving the important news for last he said casually:

"Oh, and about Charles Lupesco . . . ."

"What, what?"

"He's married with three kids. They live in Belgium."

"Belgium? How did you find out?"

"Simple. Payroll. He get's a family allowance for the wife and education subsidy for the kids. There was no address in Belgium but I could get it for you."

"I'm overwhelmed but not that surprised. I don't think you need to take it any further. However, I'll have to alert Vicky without divulging how I know. I'll try to be diplomatic."

We hung up and, amazingly, Clarisse Dehors called in less than fifteen minutes sounding brisk and cool. She said she was just on her way home and could I possibly bring the materials I wanted fingerprinted to her in Montmartre in about two hours. I wrote down the address and assured her I'd be there. I hung up with that feeling I get when the net is about to be pulled in.

I turned to find Therese watching me intently.

"George couldn't have done it. How would he have been able to forge something in Polish? I don't believe it."

"I can understand that," I said, and I truly could. But even if Therese felt a birth certificate couldn't possibly be falsified to look old, I knew better. And a man of George's temperament and experience wouldn't have too much trouble finding an appropriate forger of old documents.

"What are you going to do?" Therese sounded resigned.

"Let's not get ahead of ourselves. Why don't you come with me to Montmartre, we can talk on the way. I really need you to tell me everything from the beginning without leaving anything out."

We went to change and a good half hour later set out for Montmartre.

"I'll drive," I said, "so you can concentrate on talking.

"You will have to cross the Étoile!"

I laughed for what seemed the first time in ages.

"If you can do it, I guess I can do it! Of course, you don't have to talk to me just as I'm crossing."

I swung into traffic and said, "Okay, I'm listening!"

CHAPTER 41

T HERESE pulled out a handkerchief and blew her nose noisily.

"I met George a year after I finished medical school," she said. "I was just beginning in the pediatrics ward at the children's hospital and George—he is ten years older than I— George was on his way up in the Prime Minister's office. He was not then headed for a diplomatic career so, after we married I continued at the hospital for another eight years. By that time, since we had no children, I agreed to go with him to a diplomatic post in Mexico City. His was a political appointment. George discovered he liked being an ambassador and joined the Foreign Office, and I discovered I did not like being an ambassador's wife."

I nodded without interrupting.

"George discovered pre-Columbian art and developed a taste for rich food, glamorous homes, limos, and servants. You should realize that George does not come from either money or an illustrious old family. He gained his power solely through politics. But now he discovered he wanted money as well. I only suspected much later that he began dealing in archeological treasures while we were still in Mexico. Suddenly George had money in France.

That was when he bought the house on the Riviera and our big apartment on Boulevard Haussmann."

Therese stopped talking when we entered the Étoile but, to her credit, refrained from giving me advice. She just hunkered down in her seat and put both hands on the dashboard. I had a couple of close shaves but it was actually easier than I'd feared. When we were safely across, Therese said 'well done' and continued talking.

"George invested in stocks but mostly bought high and had to sell low whenever he needed cash. He then managed to wangle the ambassadorship to Peru. He had met people in Mexico and in Paris who were involved with smuggling from Peru. But that I found out only much later."

Therese blew her nose again.

"George got to know the underground racketeers, among them Pablo Alvarez. I know I said I didn't know him, and I wouldn't normally except George became careless and allowed people to come to the residence. When I found out, he promised he would stop and I would believe him when there were no signs for a while. But then I would discover some deal or other. I know I told you George kept his closet locked, but I actually had an extra key made. I was appalled at the amount of antiquities that were routed through our house. I didn't want any part of this."

I took a right towards Montmartre across the Place Pigalle, a location whose seedy nightclubs and peep-shows defy any romantic notions one may get from popular songs.

"When I learned about Elsa and how rich she had become, I wished George didn't have to know. But, of course, that was impossible once the newspapers got a hold of it. Then Elsa came to visit in Paris just before George's posting to Lima and, although it was clear to me she didn't like George, she agreed to pay us a visit the following spring. She wanted to come because of me. She may have been a difficult woman in many ways but she had never forgotten me, her little sister, and she really loved me. That's why this is all so traumatic. Elsa realized my marriage was in trouble and that I was unhappy. I've already told you how she promised me money once I divorced George, and also that she gave me a large amount before she was killed."

I stopped for a red light and turned to get a look at Therese's face, but she was staring straight ahead, totally absorbed by her own tale of woe.

"Then Elsa returned to Peru for a third visit. She wanted to go to Machu Picchu and I had promised to accompany her. I wanted to, but a few days before the trip I caught a bad cold. I knew it would be folly to travel in the thin mountain air feeling the way I did. Elsa insisted on going anyway and George encouraged her." Therese caught her breath. "Elsa went, and you know the rest."

She stopped talking and when I looked at her at the next traffic light I saw she was crying.

"When did you learn that Pablo Alvarez was on the tour?" I asked.

"Not until you told me."

"And did you confront George?"

"I did. That's when he hit me."

"Ah, yes, the tennis ball incident."

Therese managed to laugh.

"I knew you knew."

"Yes, but I must admit your explanation was imaginative."

"Except, we don't play tennis." Therese made a face. "I know you think George made Alvarez kill Elsa and that George killed Alvarez to silence him. But I just can't believe that."

"You don't think money finally came to mean more to George than human life?"

"I don't feel it in my heart."

I maneuvered the car up a steep hill on bumpy cobble stones, barely squeezing between the rows of cars parked solidly on both sides of the narrow streets. A tiny car pulled out from the curb so suddenly that I stalled and after that it took me three attempts to fit my much larger vehicle into the vacated spot. I could hear car horns beeping all the way down the hill.

"I thought there was a no-beeping rule," I said as I pulled the wheels towards the curb one last time. "Phew, I'm drenched."

We were on the sidewalk heading uphill towards the Place du Tertre and I turned to Therese who was struggling to keep up with me.

"Would you think it very touristy of me if we cut across the plaza?" I asked.

She shook her head and we made our way into the small square. I stood still to take in the old familiar sight of painters' stalls under blue and red awnings, and the tables at the sidewalk cafés where quick-sketch artists were busy drawing quite competent portraits of self-conscious tourists.

The evening shadows had not quite descended, the square was filled with people and the cafés were packed. We managed to find a table, sat down and ordered two café crémes. It was only when a group of five people in front of our table disappeared into a souvenir shop that I saw George.

He was sitting in a dark corner against the wall in the café opposite.

I grabbed Therese's arm and squeezed hard.

"Don't jump now," I said in a low voice, "but George is sitting over there. No, not there, a little to your right. Do you see him?"

Therese nodded and somehow stayed rooted in her chair.

"Go ahead," I said. "You approach him, I'll stay out of the way. He won't make a scene if you're there by yourself."

"And then what do I do?"

"Tell him he won the lottery. Tell him you want him back. Tell him anything you like, but make him return with you to your apartment. I'll be there later."

George was getting up from his chair and I shoved Therese out of her's. She stumbled towards George and I saw his expression change from surprise to defeat. I bent down to tie a non-existent shoe-lace and when I looked up George and Therese were leaving in deep conversation. He steered her by the elbow and I could only hope that their destination was Rue Ranelagh.

I set out to find Clarisse Dehors' house.

The metal sign on the door said 'C. Dehors' and underneath that 'R. Guersant' but there was only one bell. I rang and waited.

When the door was opened I looked into huge almond eyes in a thin dark complexioned face framed by short black hair. The body underneath was equally thin and dressed all in black, a tight ribbed turtleneck over almost non-existent breasts obviously without a bra, and equally skintight jeans. Her feet were bare. This apparition was so far from the Clarisse I had visualized, an image Bob Makowski had fostered in me of this voluptuous floozy whose main purpose in life was to cater to single needy men like Bob. I was completely tongue-tied.

When she smiled, her thin face filled out around a perfect row of teeth. But her eyes remained serious.

"I am Clarisse," she said and stretched out a large, competent hand with which she squeezed mine rather hard. She opened the door wide and I stepped into a small hall. The sign on the first door to the right said 'R. Guersant, Photographe' and Clarisse pushed the door open and shouted inside: "Renée, my guest has arrived." And the male roommate I'd been expecting—and again, I had to attribute my preconceived ideas to Bob's obviously misleading allusions—turned out to be a tall thin young woman also dressed in severe black.

She shook my hand and invited me inside the small gallery. The walls were hung with black and white photographs: Faces of the young, the old, the poor, women, men, and children. And mysterious alleys, dark doorways, and rooftops silhouetted against the moon in its varying phases. A couple of wrought-iron benches and two potted plants constituted the furniture.

After expressing some suitable and entirely sincere compliments to Renée, I followed Clarisse up a narrow staircase which took us to the second floor. The entire space was a large living room. Two low canvas sofas were placed rather conventionally on either side of a small fireplace. The only decoration consisted of black and white photographs of Clarisse in various stages of undress. I was beginning to have some sincere doubts about Bob's sanity.

The kitchen took up most of the space at the back. Copper-clad cookware and bunches of garlic and dried flowers hung from wire baskets. A circular staircase led up to a sleeping loft where I saw just one huge, low bed covered in black canvas, and two red halogen lamps.

Clarisse offered coffee or drinks and I accepted a Kir.

It took me less than fifteen minutes to explain the case to her and she made a couple of notes as I spoke. Then I gave her the documents I'd obtained from Grandjean, the letter signed by George Lecroix, and the notes with names and addresses from the Machu Picchu group members, all of it secured in plastic folders.

"Bob tells me you need this urgently," she said. "I will try to do as much as possible tomorrow. When are you planning to leave Paris?"

I thought of George and had some difficulty envisioning how coming events would unfold, so I shook my head.

"Hard to say but, in any event, Bob is right, it's an emergency. How soon do you think you can have results?"

"As soon as the fingerprints can be scanned into the computer, the identification process won't take that long. I'll do my best."

Clarisse picked up the plastic folders and placed them in a black briefcase.

I stood up and prepared to leave when I remembered Charles Lupesco. I'd already decided the hassle would be too great for me to negotiate with telephone operators about the non-responsive number Charles had given Vicky. I gave Clarisse a brief run-down of the problem and she laughed and promised to solve the mystery.

I picked up the rental car and headed back to Rue Ranelagh. The concierge acknowledged our acquaintance with a brief nod and I ascended, feeling almost like the Parisian I had been long ago.

My pleasant mood was instantly deflated when I opened the door to the apartment. It lay in total darkness. There was no sign of either Therese or George.

CHAPTER 42

I turned on all the lights and looked at my watch. Almost ten. I ate hurriedly at the kitchen table and put the dishes in the dishwasher. I carried the grapes I'd bought earlier to the living room together with a full pot of fresh coffee.

After clearing the large oval dining room table I brought out my notes. There was one for every person I had interviewed, from the Lecroix' to Geraldine Harris.

Three hours later I finished, my eyes smarting and my throat burning from too much coffee, but with twenty pages of summary.

I dragged across to the sofa, settled down in the corner under the reading lamp and read through the summary. On page fifteen I stopped reading and recalled Walter Hughes saying 'remarkable coincidence.' I turned quickly to page eleven and added a paragraph at the top. Then I turned back to page eight and highlighted the first three lines.

I nodded to myself and sat there staring with what I knew was an idiotic half smile thinking that would be almost too easy a solution. I read the last two pages and wrote a couple of additional paragraphs, questions really, at the end. Then I closed my eyes momentarily, but woke up five hours later with a crick in my neck and knowing that Therese had not returned.

It was time to call Topsy. I got her on the first try and listened carefully to the information she had obtained for me.

"You've come through beautifully and it all adds up," I said. "I don't know how to thank you."

"Just come back in one piece," she answered sweetly. "That will be enough gratitude."

There was no time to waste. I knew I must act now.

I showered, had a quick cup of tea with a piece of toast, and was in the rental car before six on my way to Aunt Ludmilla. The A-24 towards Ivry was already jammed but I made good time nevertheless, praying I would remember the way to the house once I got to the Marne. I had no doubt that Aunt Ludmila would be up and about. She had looked like an early riser.

Just as I had imagined, Ludmila was sitting on her bench at the bottom of the garden drinking something hot out of a thermos, with the morning paper in her lap. She leaned forward to look for Therese behind me and manifested her surprise at not finding her by planting her cane firmly on the ground.

"Hello, Aunt Ludmila," I said and sat down next to her. "I know you must be surprised to see me without Therese . . ."

Aunt Ludmila looked so worried that I continued in a hurry.

"Don't be alarmed, I have come only because I need the address of George and Therese's apartment in town and you are the only one I know who would have it."

"Where's Therese? Something has happened, I can feel it. You can tell me. I would rather know everything than imagine the worst. Is she dead? Did George kill her, too?"

"My goodness, no! Therese and I went out last night and happened to meet George in Montmartre. We split up, I returned to Rue Ranelagh and I think perhaps they went to their other apartment."

Aunt Ludmila's head began its familiar shaking and I looked towards the house and the Grand Marnier.

"That George, never any good," she said.

I put my hand over her's.

"If you could tell me the address I'll go find her."

"The apartment is at 2141 Boulevard Haussman, the third floor. A very fine address," Ludmila said somewhat contemptuously.

"I tried to find a telephone number through the directory but there was no listing."

"An unlisted number George wanted. As if I was going to bother calling him!" Ludmila's hands were shaking worse than her head now and I helped her up.

"Why don't we go to the house and get ourselves something calming," I said and led Ludmila up the path, through the kitchen into the dining room. She sat down in her well-worn lounge chair and stretched out her hand for the snifter I filled from the bottle in the sideboard.

Ludmila drank deeply and the cognac had the now familiar effect. Color returned to her cheeks and the shaking stopped.

"How nice to see you again," she said. "I have been thinking a lot about the news you brought, about Eugenia having a son called Karel Stanislaus. It brought back the old times and made me look for the old photographs." She pointed to the sideboard. "Go ahead, open the left door, you'll see a green album on top."

I pulled out the album. The corners of the leather cover had worn thin. The coarse pages were dark gray with photographs affixed with little black corners. I brought the album to Ludmila who pulled it down on her lap and riffled through it quite roughly. When she got to the middle she slapped her hand down on top of a photo and said:

"There you have us! In the foreground, sitting down, my dear sister, Natalya, next to Emanuel." She stabbed at the picture with her bony finger. "And behind them, standing, are Eugenia and Bronislav!" She stabbed again. "And myself next to them!" She cackled. "Handsome, eh?"

"You certainly were!"

"It was taken just after Natalya and Emanuel's wedding. Look at Eugenia's hat, such a lovely creation with those large pink roses. Bronislav liked her to look stylish."

I bent down for a closer look.

The picture had been taken by a professional photographer. The background was imitation forest with the five pictured as if on a stroll in the park. They looked as though they were intimidated by the occasion, and no one smiled. Emanuel spread out like a Pasha. Bronislav loomed protectively over Eugenia even though he was not that tall himself. He was staring straight at the photographer as if giving warning of his exclusive rights. He carried a wide-brimmed hat and wore a tight-fitting jacket with round padded shoulders and wide lapels.

Natalya and Eugenia were in fitted coats, their necks encased in high flounced collars held together with oval brooches. They each wore one white glove and carried the other.

"Here," Ludmila said and rummaged among a stack of newspapers on the pedestal table next to her chair. "Look at them through this magnifying glass. I use it for reading the small print."

I held the glass and studied the inscrutable faces from long ago. Ludmila looked haughty and determined. Natalya had a glimmer of a smile in her eyes. Eugenia had fine features and arched eyebrows and was leaning into Bronislav. I moved the magnifying glass to study his high brow and curly hair. He looked back at me with insolent eyes.

I turned the pages and came upon a photograph of a smiling Therese and a beaming George in swimsuits, their arms around each other, under a beach umbrella. George still had dark hair and no mustache and looked like a completely different person.

When I looked up Ludmila was leaning back in her chair, snoring lightly. She came to with a start when I touched her arm.

"I wonder, would you mind if I borrow this picture? I promise on my honor I will handle it carefully and have it back to you before long."

Ludmila's eyes suddenly looked sharp.

"The CIA will want it," she said. "I understand the proceedings!"

Before I could think of a response Ludmila thumped her cane on the floor and said impatiently:

"You may borrow it. Show it to the whole world. Keep it as long as you like."

"Thank you, Aunt Ludmila. I hope I haven't inconvenienced you too much this early in the morning." I looked at my watch. Seven-thirty. Time to go.

"Nothing ever happens here," Ludmila said matter-of-factly. "You can come any time you like. Give me some more cognac!"

I refilled her glass and left her in her chair with the assurance that I could find my own way out.

The ride back to Rue Ranelagh was uneventful.

As soon as I opened the front door to the apartment, I saw the shoes on the floor and the handbag and Hermes scarf on a chair.

"Therese?"

"Jamie!"

We stared at one another. Therese blushed and I felt ridiculously like the grown-up catching the teenager in the act. She smoothed her hair down, turned her back to me and went into the kitchen where she busied herself with the water kettle.

I remained silent hoping to provoke her into talking, which she did after about two long minutes.

"I lost you last night," she said and opened the refrigerator. When I kept silent she looked around, flustered, and continued:

"We went out for dinner and then back to our apartment . . ."

"You could have called me. I worried about you all night." I laughed inwardly at the sound of my own peevish voice but it had the desired effect. Therese turned to face me.

"You know, I wanted to, but now I must be frank with you. I have engaged you to find Elsa's murderer but I cannot allow you to hunt poor George. You have not said it out loud but it is very clear you suspect him." She looked defiant.

"And where is poor George now?" I directed my gaze at the ceiling. "Let me guess. He's on his way to the airport after spending the night with his estranged wife who has now decided to return to him. I wonder? Is he bound for New York or Lima or, maybe Mexico City?"

Therese looked indignant.

"George could *not* be involved in murder. I know him too well. He is taking the 3 o'clock flight to New York to meet with his broker. Look! I hereby release you from your contract: I do not want you to help me solve the case anymore!"

Therese walked towards her handbag.

"I will pay you now if you will please tell me how much I owe you including, of course, the time it will take you to return to Washington."

"That's fine. It doesn't really make any difference at this point. George will soon have to face the music. In the meantime, I have some loose ends to tie up."

I looked at my watch for the third time in as many minutes.

"I'm going to the Plaza-Athénée for the night," I said. "I'll just get my things together and be on my way. I'll leave the car for you to drop off. And don't worry about my payment right now, I'll send you an itemized bill later."

Therese sat down abruptly on a kitchen chair. She had developed her customary bright patches on both cheeks. I put a hand on her shoulder.

"I'm sorry about George," I said and I really was, if only for *her* sake. I walked quickly to the guest room, packed my bag and was at the front door within a few minutes.

"You don't have to leave in such a hurry," Therese said. "Won't you stay for some breakfast?"

"Normally I'd have loved to but I think I'd better be on my way. Thanks anyway."

"I hope you are not angry with me?"

"No, no, of course not. I'll talk to you soon," I said on my way into the elevator.

As luck would have it, an empty taxi cruised to the curb the minute I raised my hand. I yanked open the door, threw in my bag and followed it into the back seat while giving the driver my destination.

At precisely twenty minutes to ten my cab pulled up in front of Terminal 2 at the Charles de Gaulle International Airport.

I pushed my way through to an empty counter, made a reservation and purchased my ticket. I had just enough time to make one quick phone call and kept my fingers crossed until I got Clarisse on the line. She must have been surprised to hear I was at the airport but kept her voice neutral.

"Someone is working on the fingerprints right now," she said. "I'll be ready to run them through the computer this afternoon."

She wrote down my phone and fax numbers both at the Plaza in New York and at the agency in Bethesda. Then I told her about George and gave her specific instructions as to what she must do.

"I have one more piece of information for you," she said, just as I heard the final boarding call. "The phone number Mr. Lupesco gave does not exist! But the conference he went to is over and he is booked on the 3 p.m. Air France flight to New York tomorrow."

I thanked her for past and future assistance and told her I'd call her later in the afternoon.

Then I headed for the gate and my flight to New York.

CHAPTER 43

BY a combination of luck and persuasive powers I was in my room at the Plaza without having made a reservation. My flight had landed at JFK precisely on schedule and I had wasted no time getting to town.

My bag still unpacked, I dialed Paris and got Clarisse on the line. She had been as good as her word and I listened as she recounted the results of the fingerprinting. Everything I heard turned out to confirm my suspicions.

"And I followed your instructions and went to my superiors about George Lecroix," she said. "I hope it wasn't too late. He was supposed to leave for New York an hour ago. The FBI was informed, as well, so he won't get out of Kennedy Airport if he manages to get that far."

I asked her to fax the fingerprint results to Bethesda and contemplated my next move. I knew I didn't have that much time. But first I called Vicky Anderson.

I let the phone ring a dozen times before giving up. Whether from nerves or hunger, I felt queasy. I unpacked, showered and changed and repeated my call to Vicky without success. Then I went downstairs to eat.

The Oyster Bar was crowded and I took my place in a long line waiting to be seated. I ate the Maine lobster salad combined with tart apples, celery, and fresh tarragon mayonnaise and half-heartedly declined the scrumptious dessert with my coffee. I'd been at it for no more than half an hour but the waiter was quick to bring the check and wipe down my table for the next occupant.

I called from the lobby and this time I got Vicky on the phone.

"Yes?"

"Vicky?"

"Jamie!"

"Listen, I just got into town," I said, relieved to find her in. "I'd like to see you."

"Well, I'm not doing anything fabulous so come on over!"

"Be there in about twenty minutes," I said.

"I'm in 19-G," she said.

"Charles hasn't returned, I take it?"

"He'll be here tomorrow afternoon."

I hurried to my room and changed into walking shoes and jeans. I put on the large denim shirt I carry with me everywhere since it has large roomy breast pockets. Not that sexy looking on, but my main purpose now was to collect the last piece of evidence from Vicky. I placed a tiny tape recorder in the left pocket and looked at myself in the mirror. Unevenly buxom, I decided, and stuffed a wad of Kleenex in the right pocket.

The cab driver griped the entire way from Fifth Avenue to First and 45th, cursing under his breath at every car, every jay-walker, every red light, swerving in and out and braking abruptly at the slightest provocation. From time to time he glared at me in the rear view mirror as if daring me to comment.

A doorman in a brand-new green uniform sprang to the cab, opened the door and saluted smartly before striding past me to set the revolving door in motion. The lobby was empty except for the head of the receptionist floating seemingly disembodied on a tall marble counter. I walked swiftly past two black leather sofa groupings and potted palms surrounding a luscious oriental rug and approached the counter.

"Ma'am?" said the head.

"I'm here for 19-G."

"Name, Ma'am?"

I gave it to him.

"One moment, Ma'am."

Our little ritual completed he looked past me mournfully with large moist eyes. His head fell to the side into the telephone receiver trapping it against his hunched shoulder. He spoke, listened, straightened up, dropped the receiver, caught it in his hand, and pointed.

"Go right up, Ma'am. Left elevator."

The sign above the left elevator said Floors 10 to 23. A young man with pimples and running to fat, dressed in a red gold-braided uniform, punched the button to the 19th floor before I could announce my destination. He looked at me expectantly.

"Telepathy?" I obliged.

He grinned and we sailed silently upward. He held the door open and pointed me to the left. The corridor was well lit by crystal wall lamps and indirect lighting sweeping across the high ceiling.

"All the way to the end, Ma'am," he said and added a bit too familiarly "you have a nice day, now . . ." I felt his eyes at my back as I started down the hall on the thick beige carpeting.

I let the knocker fall twice and was scrutinized through the spy hole before Vicky opened the door. She had her hair in a ponytail and looked sleepy-eyed without make-up. But her greeting was as enthusiastic and breathless as ever.

"Oh, m'God, I'm glad to see you. I've been bored silly here all by myself."

"What about your old friends in the Village?"

"Oh, I don't really have any left."

Vicky closed the door and showed me inside the apartment. There was a guest bathroom immediately to the right. An open door to the left led into a bed-sitting room with a separate bathroom.

The L-shaped living room had a large double glass door leading to a balcony with a view of the UN, the East River, and the Chrysler building. A small Biedermeier dining table stood on an oriental rug in front of the doors surrounded by four cane-seat chairs. The table matched a china cabinet placed against the wall leading into a tiny kitchen.

"Did you ever see such a small kitchen in a two bedroom apartment?" Vicky said. "Two people can't squeeze in there at the same time."

"Maybe Charles eats out?"

"This isn't his apartment, he rents it from a colleague who was posted to Geneva. It's furnished."

Vicky pointed to an upholstered sofa opposite an upright piano. The top of the piano was crammed with newspapers and several metal statuettes on gray marble bases.

Vicky handed me a bowl of salted peanuts.

"Can I get you a drink?"

"Just ice-tea, if you have it, or anything else cold and non-alcoholic."

While Vicky bustled out I turned on the tape recorder in my breast pocket. She returned with two tall ice-teas and looked at me over the rim of her glass as if expecting me to provide the entertainment. I adjusted the shoulders of my shirt which had a tendency to droop, and dispensed with small talk.

"Vicky, I've got some news you won't be very happy to hear."

She stopped sipping at her drink and her eyes bored into mine. When I finished telling her about Charles Lupesco's wife and three children in Belgium she had shrunk down in her chair and her glass clattered down on the coffee table. She bit her lower lip and made a gallant effort to control her voice but it still came out squeaky.

"Oh, no!"

"I'm so sorry," I said, and I was.

"I knew it. Nothing ever goes right for me. I told you, I always fall for the wrong guy, but I thought this was finally right. A wife and three kids! And you're sure he's not divorced?"

I shook my head.

"The bastard." She got up and crossed to the window. When she returned to her chair I could see the anger building up and I felt really lousy about what I had to do next.

"You know, I think it's time for you to come clean and tell me everything."

She looked at me dully.

"What do you mean?"

"You know very well what I mean, and soon the police will know, too."

"The police?"

"Yes, the police. And I understand you've had some previous experience with them."

Now she looked thoroughly deflated and not a little frightened.

"What do you want to know?"

"Exactly what you saw at the torture chamber."

Vicky closed her eyes and took a long pause.

"Well?"

"You seem to know already."

"I need to hear you say it."

"Okay, okay." Her voice was very low.

"Speak up!" I said brusquely.

"OK! I saw Charles come around the corner and walk into the torture chamber. I actually sat with my back to it and just happened to turn my head. He doesn't know I saw him."

"Did you see anyone else?"

Vicky looked surprised.

"Yes, I did, as a matter of fact. That sleazy Peruvian also came by. He stopped to look inside the torture chamber . . . ."

"Pablo Alvarez, you mean?"

"Yes."

"Did he actually go inside?"

"Not really, he just walked far enough to poke his head in the entrance door. Then he scrambled away as if someone had lit a fuse under him."

"And you saw Charles Lupesco come out of the torture chamber after Pablo Alvarez had disappeared?"

Vicky nodded unhappily.

"I repeat: Did you see Charles Lupesco leave the torture chamber after Pablo Alvarez looked inside?"

"Yes! Yes, I did!" Vicky shrieked and burst into tears. "What does it mean?"

"You know very well what it means, my dear Vicky."

The voice came from the hallway. The voice that was not supposed to be heard until the following day.

"Charlie?"

Vicky shot out of her chair and stood in the middle of the room. I jumped up, too, but just a fraction too late to prevent her from rushing to Charles Lupesco's side.

CHAPTER 44

"I've been expecting you," Charles Lupesco hissed. He glared at me and kept a firm grip around Vicky's shoulders.

"Vicky!" My voice cracked and she made a move towards me but it was too late. Lupesco grabbed her arm and twisted it behind her back.

"But Charlie!" Vicky whimpered. "I didn't tell her anything."

"You told her enough," he said viciously, and twisted her arm an extra notch. She stumbled as he maneuvered her past the piano, using her as a shield against me.

His face gleamed translucent, his eyes bright under his high forehead. He was blinking rapidly.

I watched him, still in shock, but realized he didn't have a gun or he would have produced it by now. Where would he have hidden a gun? Not in the bed-sitting room or else he'd have picked it up on his way in. Not in the kitchen or living room where anyone could have found it. More likely locked up in his bedroom. Then why didn't he back in there using Vicky as his protection? Maybe he didn't have a gun at all?

He looked at me and I could practically read his thoughts:

Damn, I thought, he's figured out I don't have a gun, either. He looked triumphant and jerked Vicky closer.

"Stay where you are," he said under his breath when I got up and moved away from the sofa. Vicky moaned piteously and bent over sharply.

I stood still with my back to the window.

"Why don't you let her go," I said, knowing I was speaking rationally to an irrational man.

Lupesco laughed shrilly and kept his grip on Vicky.

I stepped back in an attempt to get off the small carpet and around the coffee table. As I moved closer I said conversationally:

"Vicky, meet Karel Stanislaus Bronski Lupesco!"

"I don't understand!" Vicky fairly shrieked.

"Karel, known to us as Charles," I said, "was born in Warsaw in 1951. His parents Eugenia, nee Lupesco, and Bronislav Bronski were also the parents of Elsa Bronski. The Elsa Bronski who was murdered for her inheritance in the torture chamber at Machu Picchu."

"How do you know that?" Vicky gasped and looked at me with a horrified expression. She kicked violently at Lupesco's shins while I moved towards them sideways. Lupesco lifted Vicky off the floor so that her feet dangled ineffectively in the air.

"Stay where you are," he hissed at me, "or I'll really hurt her."

"*You* murdered her? *You* murdered her?" Vicky screamed and gasped for air as Lupesco tightened his grip.

"No one can prove that." He coughed.

I continued speaking, more than anything, to gain time.

"Karel here watched his sister, Elsa, for, oh, I'd guess about two years. Since she became a rich woman. And at some point he changed Karel to Charles and used his mother's maiden name, Lupesco, as an alias."

Lupesco stared at me as if he, himself, wanted to hear this interesting story.

I moved forward slowly but Lupesco didn't seem to notice. I looked him hard in the eye trying to read what was there, willing him to get into the conversation so I could record him before the tape in my breast pocket ran out.

I spoke directly to him.

"Therese Lecroix has a charming old aunt on the outskirts of Paris. She was the one who told me your parents' story . . ."

I took one more step towards him and studied him closely.

"Did you know you look just like your father, Bronislav, when he was a young man?"

Lupesco shook his head.

"He died, didn't he? When you were just a baby . . . ."

Lupesco nodded.

"And you and your mother were alone . . ."

I had been guessing but Lupesco's eyes grew large and shiny. His face twisted uncontrollably. Abruptly he let Vicky go and she stumbled across the floor to the upholstered chair where she curled up and rubbed her wrist.

Lupesco stayed on his feet.

"My mother was a saint," he said in a monotone so flat he sounded drugged. "They were in Warsaw when I was born but my father sent her to Rumania with me. He tried to evade the Polish army but they caught up with him. He died of typhoid fever on a march."

Vicky gulped audibly.

"When I was five, my mother set out on the road to get to France. I didn't know why she wanted to go there and she never told me. We didn't even get out of Rumania, there was no food, no money, I caught pneumonia, she thought I would die, so she stopped in a small village and that's where I grew up. She made money as a seamstress and sent me to school. By then the Communists had taken over and she never spoke to me about Paris again."

While talking, Lupesco had sidled slowly to the right. I shifted my weight to my left foot. Lupesco took another tiny step which brought him to a position almost opposite me but not quite clear of the coffee table. He watched me with eyes half shut. I felt I was on the receiving end of a snake hunt.

"I was clever in school," he continued, never taking his eyes off of me. "My mother saved every penny so I could go to Warsaw. I received a scholarship to study languages. I finished my degree. Then my mother died in Rumania."

"Poor Charlie," Vicky sniffled.

Lupesco shot her a disdainful look which Vicky didn't seem to catch. He moved another notch to the right and I moved forward as well, but then he stopped and continued his account as if his movements were incidental and his story the most important thing.

"After she died I stayed for a few weeks sorting out her papers. That's when I found the letters written by Emanuel and Natalya Bronski. And I learned I had a sister in Paris. I decided to find her."

Lupesco sent me a brilliant, mad smile and I found myself almost wanting to smile back. But now I knew I must avoid eye contact at all cost to keep him on track. I forced myself to look away at the risk of not being on maximum alert.

"So, instead of returning to Warsaw I went to Paris to look for my sister," he continued, again as if unaware of my presence. "It took me several months. I called five people listed in the phone book with the name of Bronski. All in vain. No one had heard of an Elisaveta Bronski."

Lupesco laughed.

"Then it turned out the information dropped into my lap. I had become a translator at UNESCO in Paris. I read the Herald Tribune every day. That's where I saw the small news item. They called her Elsa but I knew it must be Elisaveta. The paper talked about "the American millionairess from Washington, D.C. who was born and raised in Paris," and explained how she had inherited. I went to the American Embassy in Paris to look up Elsa in the Washington telephone book."

My heart started pumping, his words floated disjointedly through my head. How he had written to her immediately, not begging for money, just to be recognized as her brother. How he could prove it by showing her his birth certificate. Explaining that their mother had never told him about Elsa, said he'd like to visit her. How she never answered. How he found the job in New York, how he'd arrived a year ago.

He conveniently omitted mentioning his sojourn in Belgium and his wife and children there and I was hoping Vicky wouldn't interrupt the flow of his account and get him off track. She didn't, she just sniffled sympathetically as if she'd forgotten what I'd told her.

Lupesco moved and now stood slightly to the right of me. I stood stock still, praying he would keep talking into my recorder. He watched me through half closed eyes. I could feel a cramp develop in my left calf.

He droned on and I shook my leg surreptitiously.

"I took the train to Washington, D.C. I went straight to Elsa's house. It was much larger than I had imagined. And she all alone in it, so why shouldn't she want to share with her only brother? Just as I stood on the other side of the street she drove out of the garage in a black Mercedes-Benz. The car must have been worth sixty thousand dollars. That's when I thought of my mother who often went hungry."

Lupesco's voice sounded almost tearful and he glanced briefly at Vicky.

"I returned the next day to talk to her but just as I got there Elsa left in a taxi with a large suitcase and I understood she must be going on vacation. I returned to New York."

I coughed and Lupesco winced. I knew I needed to hear the rest of his confession and made a desperate attempt to control the tickle in my throat. I could feel the heat in my face and my eyes watered. But, again, Lupesco chose to ignore me.

"I wrote her one more time but she never replied," he continued. "Now I would read the *Washington Post* at the UN library every day. And just about a month ago, there was a notice on the third page of the *Style Section*. Elsa Bronski was going to Lima to visit her sister, Therese Lecroix, at the French embassy. But I knew Elsa did not have a sister. I could not permit this

Therese to get any of my money. I immediately applied for my five weeks of vacation."

Lupesco's eyelids fluttered in that maddening way of his and I saw drops of perspiration form on his pale forehead. I wanted to ask how he found out about the tour to Machu Picchu, but I didn't have to.

"When I first arrived, before moving to the Sheraton, I stayed at a guest house on Dos de Mayo in San Isidro, close to the French Ambassador's residence. I would walk past the house and talk to the guard outside. I brought him a sandwich every day—no one thinks to feed those poor brutes—and he kept his ear to the ground for me. He told me about the tour. You never suspected I knew Spanish, did you?"

Lupesco snickered. He seemed on the verge of hysteria and I held my breath. But he went on.

"At the last moment this so-called sister, Therese, decided to stay home. I was happy. I thought I would get close to Elsa on the tour. But on the plane to Cuzco I didn't sit near her. And on the train to Machu Picchu she was placed with some Americans. Then, at the restaurant, Vicky and I sat together. Once I found Elsa looking at me as if she recognized me. But, of course, she couldn't have."

"What were you planning to do?" I could have bit my tongue, but the words were out. Now Lupesco focused on me with wide open eyes.

"I just wanted to speak to her as her brother. I wanted to be her family. She had more money than she deserved. Why shouldn't she share it with me?"

He looked around wildly.

"Then it happened quite unexpectedly." His voice fell to a whisper. "Vicky and I had been through the torture chamber together. Then Vicky went off by herself. I followed her to make sure she was all right . . ."

"So you weren't just pretending to be in love with me?" Vicky implored. Lupesco ignored her.

"I walked on the ledge and that's when I heard someone in the torture chamber. I went inside and saw Elsa. She was just sitting there, her arms twisted into the holes. Quite the captive audience, you might say."

His face looked pinched and his voice quivered.

"I said hello, and she asked if I would help her out of her seat. I did mean to help her but this was the first chance I'd had to speak to her. So I said, "I am your brother. Your brother, Karel", and I could tell she believed me.

"But suddenly she wasn't smiling anymore. She told me she hated my mother. She hated me. She hated Eugene and Natalya who had pretended to be her parents. She hated an aunt who had lied to her. She hated us all except for Therese. Therese was her real sister, she said, I was a nobody.

"She told me to go away, never to speak to her again. She would call the police. I did not deserve her money. She had sacrificed her life to a tyrant of a woman. Now the money was her's and she was giving it to Therese."

By now Lupesco had gradually inched so close to me that I thought he would soon hear the whirring of the tape recorder. I needed the tape to last for another few minutes.

"She was a nasty old woman, she deserved to die."

"You mean, you killed her?"

"That's right!" Lupesco screamed. "I killed her."

"And then Alvarez blackmailed you because he saw you?"

"He thought he could outsmart me. Me!"

"You didn't return to New York on the night of Vicky's play, did you? You went to town to confront Alvarez . . ."

"He was a fool. He deserved to die. And the Indian woman thought she could blackmail me, too."

"So you killed them both."

"Yes. They were fools. Fools."

My tape recorder turned off with an audible click but the noise drowned in the scuffle which ensued when Lupesco finally lunged at me, arms outstretched.

I was ready for him. I put all my weight on my left leg, my right foot shot out in a front kick. I caught him precisely in the solar plexus.

Lupesco gasped and doubled over but kept coming towards me. His hands, surprisingly large and bony, closed around my throat. I chopped the side of my left hand down on his forearm and brought up the heel of my right hand to his chin.

He lost his grip on my throat with a groan. His head snapped back sharply. I was ready to follow up with a knee to his groin when my foot caught in the Persian rug. I reeled against the piano, struggling desperately to keep my balance.

I saw Lupesco's hand out of the corner of my eye, raised in the air, and I screamed '*No!*' when the heavy metal statue from the piano came bearing down upon me.

CHAPTER 45

I$_T$ felt like cement. When I let my hands glide around in tentative circles the ground resisted with tiny rough protrusions. I willed myself to open my eyes. The ceiling above looked like cement, too.

My jaw felt dislocated and when I tried to open my mouth I tasted blood. A sharp pain shot up the left side of my face. I brought my hand up to my jaw and cried out at the slight touch. I turned my head very, very carefully and saw the thick transparent plastic panels in the balcony railing.

Then I turned the other way. A light breeze blew around my body—laid out on the balcony just outside the living room doors. What I saw inside were the four legs of the Biedermeier table and the sixteen legs of the four cane-back chairs. Beyond that the room was in darkness.

I raised my head and slowly propped myself up on my elbows. A very dead plant, its leaves dry and yellow, stood forlornly in a large flowerpot in the corner. Otherwise I was alone on the balcony. Still leaning on my elbows I waited for my head to clear.

I turned around and got on my knees and then, grasping the rail, to my feet. My legs wobbled under me but I managed to remain upright. My head hurt when I made the slightest turn and

I knew it would be days before I'd feel normal again. But at least I wasn't vomiting. I grabbed at my left breast-pocket and felt for the tape recorder. It was still there. Then I leaned against the glass door peering through my own shadow but there was no movement within. I pulled at the handle just as a reflex but, of course, the door was locked. I pounded on the glass without results.

Now I could just about make out a lumpy shape on the floor between the sofa and the coffee table. I stared as a small shadow became larger and larger and knew it was blood. I looked around for something I could use to break the glass but saw nothing remotely sharp enough. The flowerpot was ceramic. Probably too soft but I had nothing better. When I swung it against the rail, the pot broke into three large and several smaller shards and a bucket full of dry soil spilled over the edge of the balcony. I chose the most jagged looking piece and aimed it at the glass just above the lock. The ceramic crumpled miserably.

I turned around to lean on the railing. The view of the UN, the East River, and the Chrysler Building was of no use now. The flat roof-top across the street was almost at eye height and had one structure with a door which looked as if it hadn't been opened in years. The nearest apartment building with balconies was two blocks away. Two figures stood on approximately the 20th floor.

I took off my shirt and waved it desperately in the air at the two figures. There was no telling if they'd seen me but they made no move to wave back and, instead, disappeared inside.

I walked around the rail to the right and contemplated the neighboring balcony. I picked up a couple of pot shards and aimed them at the glass door. The first fell ineffectively to the balcony floor shattering into even smaller fragments. The second hit the glass with a resounding smack. I waited.

When the third piece hit the glass I saw a shadow inside and I pelted the door and the balcony with large handfuls of shards and dry soil. At long last the shadow inside became the shape of a person peering out. I waved my arms frantically and shouted:

"Hey! Hey!"

But no one opened the door and the shadow disappeared.

I looked at the ledge which ran some eight to ten feet underneath Lupesco's sitting room window all the way to the neighboring balcony. The ledge looked wide enough for me to walk sideways. The window sill would provide support for my hands.

I contemplated the distance and swung my legs over the railing, testing the ledge for strength with my right foot while holding onto the window sill. I looked carefully for signs of cracks. The whole length looked solid.

Without letting go of the railing with my left hand I slid sideways stretching my right foot as far as possible while maintaining a good grip on the sill. I pulled my foot back slightly until I found my balance. Then, slowly, I shifted my weight, let go of the railing and transferred my left foot, then my left hand, to the sill.

I pressed my body hard against the wall. I was now hanging on to the surface like some huge insect. I willed myself not to look at my hands, not at the ledge or the window sill, and certainly not nineteen floors down.

The distance between the ledge and the window sill above was just enough for me to stretch and flatten myself. I slid my right foot along, then my right hand. My left hand followed, then my left foot. I tried to breathe evenly and slowly but could feel sweat forming first in my armpits, then in the palms of both hands.

I repeated the maneuver sliding my right foot along the ledge, then my right hand along the sill. My left foot, then my left hand. My face was pasted flat against the wall, every pore hanging on to the smallest irregularity. I winced when my injured jaw scraped along the rough surface. Fresh blood seeped out through my teeth and dripped down my chin. Out of the corner of my eye I saw the shadow of the neighboring balcony rail.

One more maneuver.

I slid my right foot along and was about to follow with my right hand when my breast-pocket with the tape recorder caught on something in the wall. I couldn't move. Slowly I slid my right foot back. I arched my body while I kept my face pressed into the wall. Then I shook and twisted as hard as I dared. Once. Twice. And, finally, while I swayed tightly from side to side, the pocket snapped free of the wall.

I hung on until my heart stopped pounding. Then I continued, sliding my feet, then my hands. Sweat was now running down my forehead into my eyes, down both sides of my nose into the corners of my mouth, mingling with blood.

I turned my head very slowly and saw the railing close enough to touch. I pressed the length of my body, thigh muscles tightly knotted, even closer to the wall and slowly, slowly let go of the sill with my right hand. I moved it down the side of my leg to wipe off the cold sweat. Then I raised my arm and stretched until my fingers closed firmly around the metal railing.

My face pasted to the wall, I pulled myself towards the balcony. My right foot found a space between the railings. There was a moment when that was the only grip I had. Then I leaped across the empty space until I hung over the railing, head first.

I pulled myself over the top with my last ounce of strength. Then I tumbled down on the cold cement. I stayed there in a heap to catch my breath. When I looked up it was into a pair of frightened eyes under a mass of black hair behind the glass door.

I scrambled to my feet, spread out my arms with an air of submission while I performed a small pantomime designed to show my distress and imploring the woman to open the door.

It worked.

She turned the latch, pushed the door open and quickly stepped aside to let me in. I entered a living room which was the mirror image of Lupesco's. The stout woman, dressed in a long black dress with embroidered panels down the sides and across her ample bosom, retreated to the far wall. Two small children crouched behind her skirt and watched me with large brown eyes, looking more excited than frightened.

There was nothing between us but an enormous oriental rug, almost wall-to-wall, no furniture except a pile of heavy pillows stacked close to a round metal table. Suspended high on the wall was a color wedding photo of the woman and her husband, a man with bushy eyebrows and a generous black mustache.

I managed to shout 'speak English?" and to register the woman shaking her head before I speeded across the silky rug to the front door. I battled briefly with several locks and chains before it flew open with a bang and I was on my way down the hall towards the elevators.

I pounded on the down button and was just about to go for the nineteen flights of stairs when the doors slid open and the pimply operator stuck his head out. I jumped inside and gasped 'lobby'.

Cruising past the tenth floor I heard how my words were slurred by my broken jaw:

"Did you shake Mr. Lupeshhco from 19-G down shust now?"

"Er, yes, Ma'am?"

"How long ago?"

"Not long, Ma'am. I was delayed because of a lady in a wheelchair. I took Mr. Lupesco down just before I came up to get you."

I could imagine his brain cells twisting around the intriguing possibilities, especially when the efforts of speech released a fresh stream of blood from the corner of my mouth. But before we could go into details we reached the lobby and I rushed across to the revolving doors. I was followed by loud exclamations and the mention of emergency and an ambulance from the elevator operator.

Charles Lupesco stood at the curb directing a cab driver to place two large suitcases in the trunk. He pulled out change to tip the doorman and that's when he became aware there was something wrong. He stared at the doorman's face and turned around sharply.

I flew at him like a whirlwind out of a tunnel and the next few moments went by in a blur.

Lupesco gave out a great shout of fright and surprise and stayed rooted to the ground. But it took him less than two seconds to recover. He was in better shape than I'd expected. Before I could reach him he took off down the sidewalk, head tilted back, elbows rotating, jacket flailing in the wind. He had an unobstructed path down the deserted street towards the corner of Second Avenue, except for the piles of black garbage bags at the curb.

The doorman, the pimply elevator operator, and the reception clerk all shouted, whether in support of me or not I couldn't tell. I set off right behind Lupesco, each pounding step on the uneven pavement sending sharp arrows through my jaw to my brain. When Lupesco reached the corner he plunged into traffic against a red light only to jump back as a bus came thundering down.

The delay was enough for me to reach him.

I moved in swiftly, turned sideways, and aimed a bone-shattering kick at his leg. I registered the snapping sound with satisfaction, knowing I'd dislocated his kneecap at the very least. His legs swayed like two blades of grass in the wind. His arms propelled forward and I caught his right wrist in an iron grip.

"Aaa . . . . iiy!" A shrill scream rose from deep within me as I completed the butterfly kick. I drove my right foot under his ribs in a deep, rapid thrust.

Lupesco had time only for a small whimper before he collapsed, deathly white. I twirled him to the sidewalk where he lay unconscious, curled into a fetal position, his face pressed into the ground. My heart was a lump in my chest, black spots swam in front of my eyes. The skin of my palms had been scraped off by the gravel on the sidewalk, and blood dripped from my open mouth.

I fell to my knees and waved to the three musketeers from Lupesco's building who only now reached the corner.

I heard a car screech to the curb just as I fainted dead away.

CHAPTER 46

"I haven't seen you two entire weeks," Topsy complained and settled down on my sofa. She pointed an imperative finger. "Now tell me every single thing that happened after you felled Lupesco!"

I smiled crookedly and winced in pain.

"The cops arrived just as I woke up from a brief swoon. They sent for an ambulance while I told them the short of my long story. They insisted on sending me to the emergency ward to get my jaw fixed. Thank God, it wasn't really broken, but I'm still chewing on all those stitches. One of the cops accompanied us in the ambulance handcuffed to Lupesco. Not that he could have walked away even if he'd wanted to."

"You broke his leg?"

"'fraid so."

"God, you're vicious!"

We were quiet for a moment.

"And Vicky?" Topsy said.

"Yes, Vicky. As it was, she almost didn't make it. The cops found her on the floor next to the piano. Lupesco had caught her in the temple with the same statuette he used on me and left her for dead. Why he dragged me to the balcony and locked the door

I have no idea," I paused. "I should have gotten her out of the apartment sooner. We could just as well have had our conversation at my hotel but I was fooled into believing Lupesco wouldn't be back until the next day."

"Now, don't start that again," Topsy said firmly just as the door bell rang and Bob Makowski's voice boomed outside. She went down to let him in. He bounced up the stairs, settled down next to me and grabbed a handful of pretzels with the drink he served himself.

"You don't look good," he said, surveying my face. "But, then, I've seen you look worse!"

"Gee, thanks!" I lisped, and turned back to Topsy. "I figure Lupesco will be charged in New York on the strength of my testimony. And Vicky's. She's agreed to testify. That'll give him life without parole. I imagine the Peruvians will waive any right they may have to extradition."

"The UN was quick to wave Lupesco's immunity," Bob said. "Dropped him like a hot potato. And neither Rumania nor Belgium want him."

"And what about Ivanovich?" Topsy asked.

"The Peruvians have been told they have the wrong guy," Bob said.

I shook my head.

"They have to do more than tell the Peruvian police to let him go. As a matter of fact, I spoke to your friend James Q. Brown yesterday, as well as to the Ambassador. They don't like to interfere in Peru's internal affairs but we're lucky to have an ambassador with humanitarian inclinations, as it were. He was a Peace Corps volunteer in the early days. He assured me he'd do everything possible."

"And your deportation order?" Bob asked.

"The Minister of the Interior washed his hands of the entire affair. Said he'd never heard of me! Assured the ambassador steps would be taken to investigate the incident. I'll be receiving an official apology."

"And Captain Sosa?"

"Demoted. No longer a captain. The same goes for Bustamante. No longer a police chief. But, believe me, they'll resurface somewhere else soon."

"I'm satisfied you've caused quite a nice shake-up," Bob said.

"Now, let me understand all this thoroughly," Topsy insisted. "What's going to happen to the inheritance?"

"If convicted of murdering Elsa Bronski, Lupesco cannot inherit her money. That's the law. Fortunately, and certainly foolishly, Lupesco made a full confession to the police in addition to the statements I got on tape."

"Will the money go to Therese in that case?"

"I'd think so. Unless some other relative comes out of the woodwork," I said. "I imagine Archibald Brewster will continue to represent her."

Topsy choked on a pretzel, rushed to the kitchen, and washed it down with water. When she returned her face was flushed, her eyes watering.

"Damn pretzels!" She looked at me quizzically, as if considering some option. When she made up her mind she looked at her feet. "Didn't you know?" she said. "Brewster was transferred to his firm's San Francisco office."

I felt a definite twist in the region of my heart.

"And has already left?" I managed to say.

Topsy nodded unhappily but after a moment's vacillation looked me in the eye.

"Well, that was successful," I said.

"I can't foresee things like that!"

"Just do me a favor. Don't try to foresee anything else on my behalf." I tried to smile to take the edge off my words but I could feel the smile twisting into a grimace. I reminded myself that I'd taken the plunge of my own free will and that Topsy's only crime had been to put temptation in my path. She looked relieved when my grimace finally turned into a small smile.

Bob Makowski looked mystified.

"Are you going to explain what the hell you're talking about?"

"No," we both said emphatically.

"Okay, okay, just checking!" Bob held up both hands defensively. "To get back to the subject at hand, then. What did happen to George? I was fooled there for a while. I thought for sure George had done it. I thought he'd arranged for Alvarez to kill Elsa, then had to kill Alvarez to shut him up."

"Me, too, I must confess," I said. "Almost to the end. I had to suspect George when he left Lima only a few hours after Alvarez was killed. He could have forged a birth certificate on the strength of what he knew about Elsa's family."

"But who conked you on the head at Alvarez' shop? Did George?"

"No, it was Lupesco. He'd returned to pick up the unmentionable cretinous ceramic figures and found me lurking about inconveniently."

"When did you begin to suspect Lupesco was the one?" Topsy said.

"When I became aware of the Eastern European connection. Lupesco was from Rumania. And then it turned out that Elsa Bronski's parents were originally from Rumania. Their photograph was what clinched it: Charles Lupesco was the spitting image of Elsa's real father. Same eyes, same high forehead, same lips. I put two and two together and got four: that 'Charles' was the French version of 'Karel,' and that Lupesco was most likely his mother's maiden name.

"The files Bob got from the UN didn't mention Lupesco was born in Warsaw and the year of his birth was different, too," I continued. "Lupesco must have fudged his application to appear ten years younger than he actually was. 1961 instead of 1951! Just as he conveniently dropped half his name and became Charles Lupesco."

Bob Makowski nodded.

"That was why Lupesco didn't show up in the Interpol records. But the moment Clarisse ran a computer search on fingerprints from the Machu Picchu notes, and from the letter sent to Carpentier, Berlioz, Grandjean & Cie., in Paris, red flags went up. Both had prints which matched those of one Karel Stanislaus Bronski. He had served time in Belgium for a bank fraud scheme in the late1980s."

"Why didn't you tell Therese you were going back to New York?" Topsy asked.

"Just instinct. And a good thing, too, because when I called Clarisse from the airport she told me there was an arrest warrant out for George. If he'd been told I was on my way to New York he might have changed his plans."

"Did they get him?"

"Yep. His diplomatic immunity didn't help him in France. He's facing charges of smuggling on a grand scale."

"Probably lost his job?"

"He's on administrative leave without pay, pending the outcome of the trial."

"And Therese?"

"She seems convinced she'll eventually get Elsa's money. I wouldn't be surprised if she spent some on George's defense and took him back afterwards. The balance of power has shifted in her favor."

"And who said money can't bring happiness!" Topsy grinned.

"I certainly didn't," I retorted. "I've always maintained that idea is a fallacy invented by the rich to keep the poor from feeling dissatisfied."

"And what about Dr. Hernandez. Are you going to nail *him* too, as long as you're at it?"

"Nooo, I'll let him get nailed all by himself. The next chief of police won't be related to Hernandez. Or maybe Miami's finest will nab him. Information is leaking to them as we speak. We can only hope!"

"And what about the Inca gold story? Do you think Alvarez invented it?"

"No, I don't. Since we now know that he had nothing to do

with the murder, except for witnessing it, he had no other reason to be on the tour. And Dr. Hernandez had no other reason, either."

Topsy nodded in agreement. Then she said:

"Somehow Elsa Bronski didn't turn out to be such a sweet little old lady, at least not the way Lupesco portrayed her." She hastened to add: "Of course, I don't mean she deserved what she got."

"I should hope not!" I thought for a moment. "But you know, the circumstances that shape people are unfathomable. I've always felt that those sins that, according to the Bible, will be visited on future generations were really early lessons in psychology. When you look at Elsa Bronski she was the product of her family's actions: Elsa shouldn't have been abandoned and, eventually, she should have been told the truth."

"But she didn't have to carry the grudge for the rest of her life. People do have a choice." Topsy looked indignant. "They can decide they don't want to carry the burden anymore and forgive and forget and get on with their lives."

"That's what we'd like to happen," I said. "But she didn't. She took it out on Charles and, foolishly, as it turned out, told him so, not knowing of the deprivations *he* had suffered during his childhood. You know, I can't help wondering who Elsa's 'ghost' was. Do you suppose she had blended the likenesses of the men lost in her life into one romantic fantasy figure. Her real father, Bronislav. Her foster father, Emanuel. Her lost lover, Guillaume. And even, improbably, Walter Hughes, by extension another father figure? She was definitely always looking for that long-lost love."

"I rather imagined she had a lovely shipboard affair coming over on the boat to New York. Tall, dark, and handsome." Topsy smiled wryly at her own romantic notion.

"At least Elsa had no children on whom to visit her grudges." I paused. "Therese has none. That leaves Lupesco, and I can't even begin to imagine how his sins will affect *his* children."

"Philosophy!" Bob exclaimed. "Instead tell me your plans for the rest of the summer."

He stopped and listened. "Isn't that your phone ringing?"

I went to the den and picked up. I accepted the collect call and went to the door to the living room to get Topsy's and Bob's attention.

"Ivanovich?" I lisped.

"Personally!"

"My God, please tell me you've been released from prison?"

I listened to the flood of explanations from the other end while Topsy and Bob gestured to me for information. At last I had to laugh.

"What? Oh, I see! I'll let you know. In the meantime, keep out of trouble, you hear!"

I was still laughing when I hung up.

"Ivanovich was released this morning. Since he hadn't been charged yet, there was nothing to be dropped. He said Jim Brown picked him up outside the jail and took him to his cousin's house, suggesting he call me immediately.

"What's so funny?" Topsy asked.

"He asked me to send him some peanuts so he can visit me in the States!"

"Peanuts?"

"Yeah. He wants me to send him money for a ticket! You haven't met him, but you'd love his malapropisms. He mangles every known idiom."

"With his colorful background I doubt he'll get a tourist visa," Bob said. "Anyway I was asking what you were going to do this summer?"

I looked at Bob suspiciously. He doesn't usually take an interest in our vacation plans.

"I'm off to the Caribbean with husband and kids," Topsy said emphatically. "Jamie will hold down the fort for a change."

"And when Topsy returns," I said, "I'll go to a sunny beach somewhere still to be decided and lie low with a stack of books for at least two weeks . . . ."

Bob cleared his throat and looked at me with a lopsided grin.

"That might fit in nicely. I was going to ask you to make some inquiries for me in Barbados. It'll be sunny for sure . . . ."

"No!" Topsy said.

"It's just an inquiry, nothing dramatic . . ."

"Oh, well," Topsy mumbled.

"When?" I said.

"In two weeks?" Bob said.

"No!" Topsy said.

"In three?" Bob offered.

"Okay, you got it!" I decided.